By Eliana West

EMERALD HEARTS
Four Holly Dates
Summer of Noelle
Falling for Joy
Be the Match

MOCKINGBIRD BRIDGE
The Way Forward
The Way Home
The Way Beyond
The Way to Hope

Dreidel Date
A Homemade Hanukkah
Pavia's Legacy

PAVIA'S *legacy*

ELIANA WEST

Published by

SECOND PRESS

info@secondpress.com

Pavia's Legacy

Cover Art

www.elizabethmackey.com
Cover content is for illustrative purposes only and any person depicted on the cover is a model.

Trade Paperback ISBN: 978-1963011135
Digital ISBN: 978-1963011128
Trade Paperback published January 2024
v. 1.0

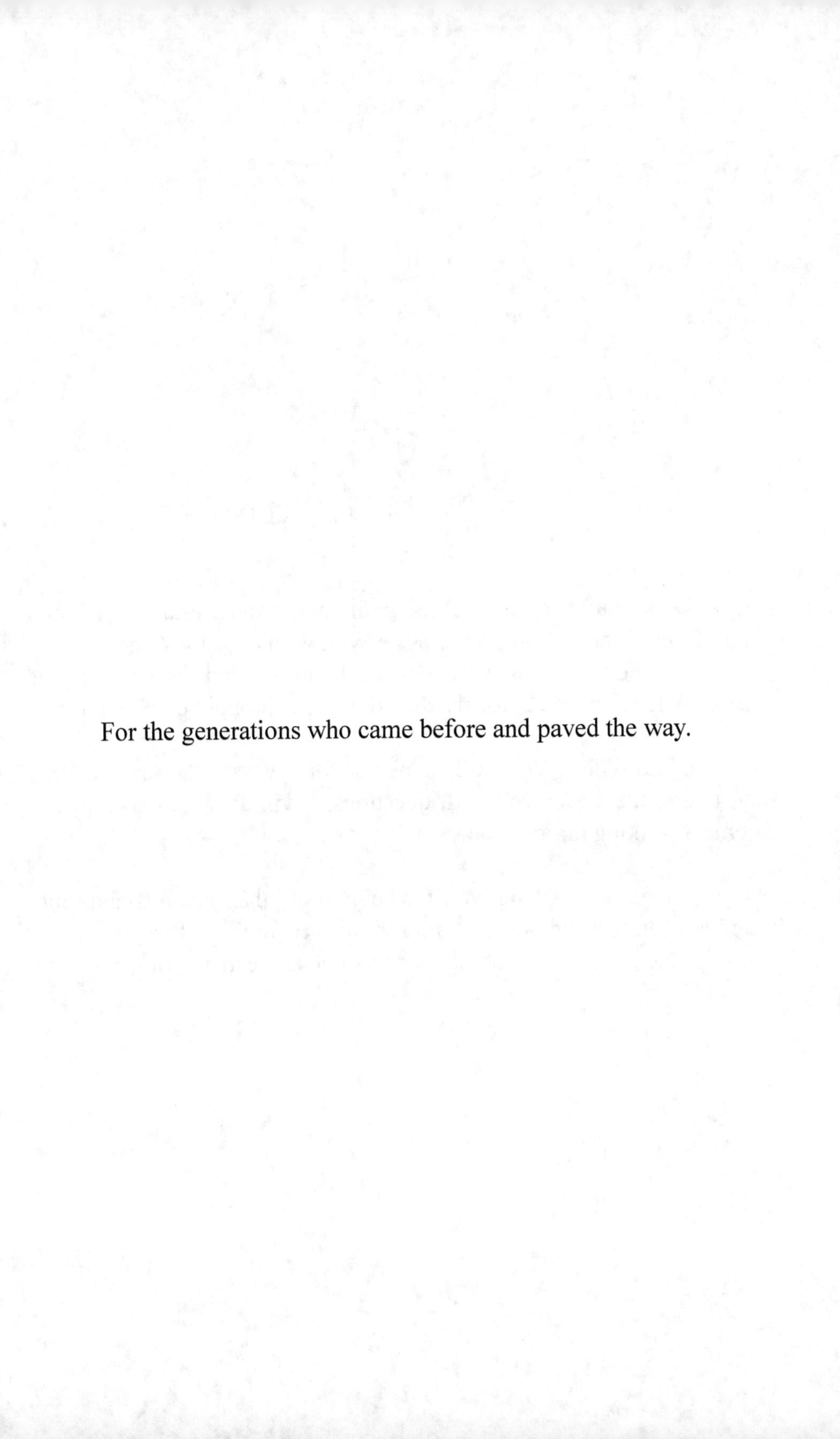

For the generations who came before and paved the way.

Acknowledgments

Thank you to my three wine godfathers, Andy, Frank and Tim at Eight Bells Winery. You let me pester you with questions, included me on trips to the vineyards, let me work the crush, and the bottling line. The knowledge you generously shared with me brought this book to life.

To Red Willow Vineyard, thank you for always being so welcoming and letting me pester you with questions. I will always treasure every moment walking through the vines.

Carmen Cook, thank you for being more than just a friend, but a confidant, and my ride-or-die author bestie. To all the bottles of wine we drank while I was "researching" for this book, cheers to you.

CHAPTER *One*

PAVIA JACKSON stared at the letter in her hand. She rubbed her thumb over the heavy paper with the name of the lawyer's office printed in bold type at the top. She'd never received an official document like this before. Reading it for a third time, she still didn't understand it. Why in the world was she invited to come to the reading of Antonio Conti's will?

When she'd heard the patriarch of the Conti family, one of the founding California wine families, was giving a lecture at her alma mater, Pavia made the three-hour drive to see him speak. Antonio Conti made a point to find her after his presentation "Clones and the Art of Propagation" at Washington State University, making his way through the crowd of admirers to introduce himself to her. Well into his nineties, his blue eyes still sparkled with his love of farming and the craft of winemaking.

"You're Pavia Jackson." His voice held a hint of wonder and his eyes searched her face as he smiled wistfully.

Pavia shook the callused hand he offered. "I am. I'm sorry. I don't mean to be rude, but how do you know me?"

He shook his head, his smile falling. "The Jackson family is one of the finest winemaking families in the country. Your father"—his voice faltered—"and your grandfather are two of the best vintners I've had the honor to know."

Was that a sheen of tears in his eyes?

"I'm so pleased you and your brother are following in their footsteps," he said.

Pavia noticed the other students and faculty watching their exchange with curiosity. She was just as curious as everyone around them. Why had this man sought her out?

"Thank you, sir."

"No, my dear, please call me Antonio."

"Oh, I don't think I can do that. Can we compromise with Mr. Conti?"

He patted her arm. "Yes, of course." Mr. Conti waved off the professors and the president of the program hovering nearby and tucked her arm through his. "I'd appreciate it if you would give me a tour of this facility."

Pavia looked from the shocked staff to Mr. Conti. "I—"

"Please." He cut off her reluctance. "I'm an old man who might not see another harvest. I'd like to spend some time with someone who reminds me of the hopeful days of my youth."

She couldn't say no to such a heartfelt request. Mr. Conti exuded both strength and weakness, and Pavia could see in his eyes a man looking at the arc of his life.

She nodded. "I'd be happy to show you around."

Mr. Conti's eyes brightened. "Now, tell me about your master's degree in molecular plant sciences."

Pavia spent the rest of the afternoon with him touring the viticulture and enology facilities at her alma mater, discussing winemaking methods. The experienced winemaker didn't scoff at her ideas about sustainable and organic production like some of his generation did. He asked probing questions, offering his thoughts and advice.

It had been an amazing experience. She returned home excited to share with her father and brother what had happened. Her older brother, Robert, shared her wonder and enthusiasm for the encounter, while her father sat stone-faced.

The door opened, pulling Pavia from her impressions of that day. A large silhouette of a man was shadowed by the bright snow behind him. Pulling off his heavy work gloves, he rubbed his hands together and stomped the snow off his feet.

"Days like today make me wonder if we'll ever see spring again," he said in his deep, rich baritone.

Pavia held up the letter. "Dad, come look at this. Someone must be playing a joke on me."

Her father moved to her side, peering down at the piece of paper. With a trembling hand, he pulled it out of her grasp. His dark brown skin took on a grayish hue that startled her.

"Throw it away," he finally said.

"Dad?" Pavia grasped his arm. "I don't understand."

Instead of answering, Anthony Jackson wadded up the letter and threw it in the garbage as he stormed out. Pavia stared at his retreating form in shock. He didn't bother to put his hat or gloves back on before going outside into the bone-chilling cold again. She went over to the doorway and watched her dad march through the vines, his breath coming out in tiny puffs, his figure hunched against the cold. He looked small. It was unsettling to see him this way.

Anthony Jackson was a towering figure, both physically and in the wine industry. At just over six feet, years of working the land kept his sixty-year-old body fit. The only hint of his age came from the gray hairs on his close-cropped hair and beard. As a vintner, he was an esteemed figure and a pioneer in the Washington wine industry. Her dad was always encouraging and steady, her rock. She'd never seen him like this before. He'd never said anything bad about the Contis or any vintner. That wasn't in his nature, so to see him react so strongly made her pause.

Should she run after him? Pavia debated what to do, watching her dad's figure grow smaller and smaller. She stepped back inside and closed the door. Whatever had made him upset, he wasn't ready to talk about it yet. One trait everyone in her family shared was a stubborn streak, and Pavia knew from experience her dad wouldn't talk until he was ready. Instead of following him like she wanted to, she closed the door against the cold, went to the garbage can, and pulled out the letter. Placing it on the counter, she smoothed out the wrinkles and read it again.

Her dad's response had puzzled her when she told him about meeting the legendary winemaker a few months ago. He seemed more annoyed than impressed. Now there was no mistaking his anger.

The wine industry was a tight-knit community, and it was rare for there to be any major disagreements. Why would her dad be so angry with Antonio Conti?

With the memory of her day with Mr. Conti fresh in her mind, Pavia folded the document and tucked it in her pocket. Hopefully her dad would be ready to talk by the time they sat down for dinner.

When he didn't appear, Pavia knew exactly where to go. He stood in front of the one stained glass window with a grapevine design in the small stone chapel that overlooked the vineyards spread across the sloping hills below. The chapel had been there when the hills were a sea of wheat farmed by Pavia's great-great-grandfather. It was the place the workers prayed for a good harvest. Others would come to ask for the rain to fall or the sun to shine. The tiny stone chapel was the place where her parents had exchanged their vows. It was also where they'd held her mother's funeral when cancer stole her life. Her family wasn't particularly religious, but the small chapel gave comfort to anyone who sought refuge inside its stone walls. Her dad always came to this spot when he struggled to make sense of whatever burden life had placed upon his broad shoulders.

"Papà?" Pavia stood next to him. "Qual è il problema?" she asked in Italian, the language they used when they spoke from the heart.

Her father released a long sigh. "Your mother said that it is impossible to keep a secret forever, as it will eventually bloom and expose itself to the world."

She rested her head on his shoulder. "What did Antonio Conti do to make you so unhappy?"

Her dad stiffened. "Nothing. He did nothing, and that's the problem."

"I don't understand."

"The only thing you need to know is that there's nothing the Contis can give you. I've worked hard for all these years to make sure of that. I can provide for you and your brother. You don't need anything from him."

Pavia turned to face him. Suddenly, he looked older. Grief when her mother died had aged him, but this was different. She looked down at their hands: his, dark brown, callused, with a few scars here and there from a lifetime of field work; hers, softer, lighter, a golden brown hue, a mix of her father and mother. She'd inherited the faint smattering of freckles across her nose from her mother and shared her dad's warm brown eyes. A lump formed in her throat seeing the pain in them now.

"Dad, I'm not a little girl anymore. You can't just tell me to ignore the letter without giving me an explanation."

His jaw ticked. "I can't… I don't know if I'll ever be ready to talk about the Contis."

"Papà, devo andare. I have to go," she told him.

The same pain Pavia saw in her father's eyes had flashed briefly in Antonio Conti's when she met him. She needed to know what had caused it, and something in her gut told her she'd find the answer at the reading of his will.

"I want to go, Dad. I—I wish I could just let it go, but I can't. There's a part of me that needs to know why Mr. Conti wanted me there."

Her dad's shoulders slumped. "I suppose I knew you would." He reached out and tugged one of her curls with a wistful smile. "You were always my curious child. You'll wonder if you don't go. Just know"—his voice quavered—"you'll find out what this is all about, and we'll go from there."

A WEEK later, Pavia watched the tiny sailboats dancing with the cargo ships on the blue-green waves of San Francisco Bay. She pressed her hand against the large floor-to-ceiling windows in the conference room of the law offices of Hendricks, Jamison, and Steele, craning her neck to take in the breathtaking view. When she squinted, she could just make out someone on a paddleboard bobbing up and down in the bay. Her stomach dipped and rolled along with the waves. Pavia glanced over her shoulder at the other people in the room and sucked in her breath. She'd taken refuge by the window, wishing her father had agreed to come with her.

She should have been with her father and brother. Her brother, Robert, was born to be a farmer and loved being out in the fields, tending the vines and the few acres of wheat and alfalfa that remained along with an apple orchard. All of them helped in the winery, but it was Pavia who spent the most time with their dad, honing her skills as a winemaker. She was at home in the lab, and in the barrel room, looking for just the right balance of acid, sugars, and yeast needed for a perfect bottle of wine. Her interest focused on enology, the craft of turning the fruit into wine. They were a team, and Pavia felt valued but not necessarily needed. It was her father's wine, and his vision. Lately she'd been thinking about her goals, to produce wine using cutting-edge organic production. She wanted to experiment with different methods than what her father used. Pavia loved him, and never took for granted how special it was to work alongside one another, but she was sheltered at home, and she wanted to challenge herself.

Today she missed the security of the familiar feel and smells of the winery back home. Instead of setting up to bottle their Battalion Blend, she was feeling out of place standing in this fancy lawyer's office wearing the only suit she owned that she'd had to dig out of the back of her closet. Pavia ran her hands over her pants, trying to smooth away the wrinkles from sitting on the plane. She eyed the reflection in the window of the people sitting at the conference table. They didn't seem uncomfortable in their expensive suits.

The two Conti brothers, Alex and Nick, looked just like the pictures she'd seen on social media. But instead of smiling as they had in photos with their grandfather, both of their faces became marred with angry glares in her direction as soon as the receptionist introduced her. It was obvious Mr. Conti's family didn't know why she was there either. The digital images hadn't prepared her for the real thing. The Conti brothers were a Brooks Brothers ad brought to life. Tall with dark blond hair, Alex, the older brother, had blue eyes that matched his mother's. The younger brother, Nick, had hair a little darker, and his eyes were deep brown. Alex wore his hair short with a close-cropped beard, while Nick could have just come from the beach with his longer, wavy hairstyle.

Between them sat their mother, Sarah Conti. She didn't have the same social media presence as her sons, so Pavia hadn't been able to find out much of anything about her. Mrs. Conti wasn't glaring at Pavia, but looking at her with an expression that looked almost like longing. When she'd first walked into the room and seen Pavia, her steps faltered, and Alex gently guided her into a seat at the table while Nick poured her a glass of water. She took a sip, eyeing Pavia over the rim of her glass. Even though she'd retreated to the window, she felt the older woman's gaze on her the entire time.

Overwhelmed by the urge to call her dad, Pavia turned away from the window, but before she could escape the stifling confines of the room, the door opened. An older, balding man walked in looking at them over the tops of a pair of tortoise shell reading glasses perched on the end of his nose.

"Ladies and gentlemen, should we begin?"

HE WANTED to hate her. Alex watched Pavia Jackson sitting across the conference table, looking scared. He wanted to paint her as some kind of gold digger who'd conned his grandfather. Alex didn't know what his grandfather had left her, and it didn't matter. He resented having an outsider at the reading of the will. More than anything, he didn't want anyone there to witness their grief… his grief.

He was surprised to find Pavia there alone. Alex assumed that her father or her lawyer would accompany her. Within minutes of their arrival, she'd gotten up and retreated to the large bank of windows overlooking San Francisco Bay. Her back straight and her head held high, the only sign of her nervousness was the way she held her hands clenched tightly in front of her.

The receptionist had introduced her when he led them into the conference room, but an introduction wasn't necessary. Alex knew who Pavia Jackson was. He'd looked her up the minute their family lawyer, Mr. Hendricks, informed them she would also be at the reading of his grandfather's will. There was a vast difference between reading about Pavia and actually meeting her. His research hadn't prepared him for the way her hair fell in light brown curls that rested between her shoulder blades, or how the charcoal gray pantsuit she wore showed off a figure with gently rounded hips and long legs. She wore a silk blouse in a shade somewhere between pink and orange that reminded him of a sunset sky. The color made her light hazel eyes stand out even more. Large and framed with long lashes, those big eyes had been sneaking glances at him since he walked in. His research on the Jackson family revealed that her golden brown skin tone resulted from a union between her Black father and her mother, who was half White and half Native American.

Alex's gut told him that, no matter how much he wanted it to be true, she was not a gold digger. And his body responded with an unexpected attraction that made him feel even more off-kilter than he already did.

His mother's hands trembled as she took another sip of water. Her physical response to seeing Pavia was another surprise. It was almost like she had encountered her before. To Alex's knowledge, they had never met. His mother's gaze seemed to be filled with longing, leaving him more perplexed as to why Pavia was there.

The Jackson family had an excellent reputation in the industry, but they ran in very different social circles. Alex's grandfather had produced one of the first California wines to be honored in the Judgment of Paris wine competition. Everyone knew the Conti vineyard for the quality of its fruit, and Antonio Conti's knowledge of farming and winemaking had made him an icon among his peers. The Jacksons made a quality product, but Brothers in Arms was minuscule compared to the hundreds of thousands of cases his family produced in a year. What was the connection that brought her to the reading of his grandfather's will?

His brother raised a questioning eyebrow at their mother's visceral reaction to Pavia's presence. Alex shrugged with a slight shake of his head.

He reached over and gently grasped his mother's hand. "Are you okay?"

She sucked in her breath and nodded. She kept her head bowed, the silver strands of her chin-length hair hiding her face.

The lawyer walked in, and Alex stiffened, his heart rate going up. He glanced at his brother, trying to gauge his reaction to this moment. Alex knew he and Nick would each inherit equal shares of the family business. Antonio had never kept secret his intentions for its ongoing growth and development. So why hadn't he ever mentioned Pavia Jackson before?

His grandfather's lawyer assumed the position of the head of the table. His gaze shifted to Pavia. "I'm Mr. Hendricks, Mr. Conti's attorney. Thank you for coming today."

Pavia gave a nod of acknowledgment as she clasped her hands together in front of her.

Mr. Hendricks opened a folder and read in a dry, emotionless tone, "I, Antonio Michael Conti, being of sound mind and body...."

Alex closed his eyes, pinching the bridge of his nose while the lawyer read his grandfather's words of love for his family. He'd known this day would come eventually, but he wasn't ready. He would never be ready to lose the man who'd been both a grandfather and a father to him. Without him, he felt lost. There were a million questions he still wanted to ask. He hadn't realized he should have counted the time he had left with his grandfather in minutes instead of years. He died in his sleep just as the vines had gone dormant, ready to rest and recharge for the winter. They would reawaken in the spring, but his grandad would not. Alex swallowed, trying to fight back his tears. He didn't want Pavia Jackson, a stranger, to witness his family's grief. As much as his heart hurt, his mother and brother were hurting as well. Antonio's death had affected them all, and their grief wasn't for public display.

"To Miss Pavia Jackson, I leave the fifteen acres known as the Brothers Block, the cottage and surrounding land, and"—the lawyer cleared his throat—"five million dollars."

"What?" Pavia exclaimed, clutching the edge of the desk.

Everything stopped as the words the lawyer had just read registered in Alex's mind. He jumped up from his seat. "What the hell do you mean she gets the Brothers Block?"

Nick pounded on the table. "He can't do that!"

The lawyer raised his hand. "Please, allow me to finish," he commanded in a stern voice.

The sunlight that streamed through the windows turned cold. He couldn't do this. His grandfather couldn't take away the only thing he'd ever wanted.

"This is ridiculous! Grandad wasn't in his right mind. He never would have done this to me… to us!" he continued to rant, unable to control the hurt and betrayal that swept over him.

His heart thundered in his chest. Alex looked down at his clenched fists, the skin over his knuckles stretched taut and pale. He took a deep breath, trying to regain some equilibrium before he confronted Pavia.

"How much do you want for it?" he asked.

"I…." Pavia's eyes were wide.

Mr. Hendricks jumped up. "Mr. Conti, sit down! I have not finished, and you need to hear this."

Alex was so wrapped up in his thoughts that he hadn't realized he had risen to his feet and was leaning across the table in a way that may have seemed intimidating. He sank down into his seat, glaring at Pavia.

"We're going to fight this," he said in a cold, firm voice.

Mr. Hendricks fixed them with a stern gaze before he resumed his seat and continued. "Any attempt to contest the terms of my bequest to Miss Jackson will cause the entirety of my estate being conferred to Miss Jackson." The lawyer held his hand up in silent warning. "Miss Jackson may not sell the land known as the Brothers Block for five years. If, after that time, she decides to sell, Alex Conti will have the first right of refusal."

"I'll never forgive him for betraying our family like this," Nick spat out.

"Enough… ENOUGH!" Their mother turned to Alex, tears streaming down her cheeks. "Respect your grandfather's wishes," she said in a strangled voice, then directed her attention to Pavia. Alex felt a wave of sorrow emanating from her that left him breathless.

He rested his hand on his mother's arm. "Mom, we can't allow some stranger to—"

The lawyer frowned, shuffling through his paperwork. "The rest of the estate is to be divided between Mrs. Conti and her sons," he said, looking at Alex and Nick. "There are no other bequests."

His mom rose and began heading toward the door, one step in front of another, almost in robotic fashion. Alex rushed after her, with Nick on his heels, but paused in the doorway, staring at Pavia for a moment. Her face was pale, her gaze darting between him and Mr. Hendricks, her mouth turned down. She was just as shocked as he was by his grandfather's bequest, but that didn't stop him from being mad and resenting the hell out of her.

His mother was silent and stone-faced in the elevator down to the parking garage. Alex exchanged a worried look with his brother. He hadn't seen her like this since…. A wave of nausea hit him, his stomach plummeting faster than the elevator. They were all silent until they were in the car and on their way out of the city.

Midway across the Golden Gate Bridge, his mother said in a shaky voice, "He didn't do it to hurt you."

Alex gripped the steering wheel tighter as he glanced at her in the rearview mirror. "But he did."

Nick looked over his shoulder at her. "He didn't have the right to give it away."

"I know you don't understand, but he thought he was…." She shuddered and looked out the window, pressing her fist against her mouth.

"What is it you're not telling us?" Alex frowned, observing his mother's distress in the rearview mirror.

"I'm not ready to talk about this now. But I need you, both of you, to understand what your grandfather did wasn't any kind of punishment or done to cause you pain."

"Did you know?" He asked the question knowing deep down his mother would never keep something like this a secret from him.

"No, of course not. I don't disagree with what your grandfather did, but he shouldn't have let you find out this way. He should have told you… told all of us what he was planning."

What wasn't his mother telling them? What secret was she harboring? "How do you know Pavia, Mom?"

Her forehead wrinkled. "What makes you say that?"

"It seemed like you recognized her when we walked into the conference room."

His mother took a deep, shuddering breath. "I never met Pavia Jackson, but her father was one of the most important people in my life."

Nick shifted in his seat to face her. "What does that mean?"

Her expression became resolute. "It means that we're not going to fight this, Nick. Your grandfather did what he thought he needed to do, and I support his decision."

Even if it means taking away the one thing I've always wanted, Alex thought, flexing his hands on the steering wheel. He glanced at his brother. With the passing of their grandfather, the change they knew was coming, and both dreaded, had arrived. Guilt sat heavy in his gut. He wanted to believe that his brother would finally step up and assume the role of the business partner Alex had desperately wanted and needed him to be. Until now, Nick had been more interested in the perks of a successful business than doing the work to earn them. When they arrived home, they would come together as a family and devise a plan to make sure every inch of the Conti vineyards remained in the family, as it was always meant to be.

CHAPTER *Two*

NUMB, PAVIA flew back to Blue Ridge. She didn't know what she'd been expecting the lawyer to tell her, but it wasn't this. The Brothers Block was legendary. Five million was a generous amount, but to start a winery, she'd have to watch every penny. While her family wasn't poor, they weren't on the same level as the Contis, not even close. She knew what it took to run a vineyard and winery. Equipment alone would cost around $750,000, and that didn't factor in farm equipment. There were labor costs to consider, insurance and taxes. And the time it would take before she poured her first vintage. The money Antonio left her would disappear quickly if she wasn't careful.

In the living room, her dad and brother were situated in the two large leather chairs that stood on either side of the stacked stone fireplace. The scene brought a smile to her face, along with a deep sorrow in her heart at the thought of leaving.

Her dad jumped up when she walked in, setting his glass of whiskey on the coffee table where his feet had been. "Hey sweet pea, I was beginning to worry about you."

His embrace muffled her voice. "The roads are pretty icy tonight."

He pulled away, holding her at arm's length, his gaze searching her face. "How did it go?"

"Did Mr. Conti leave you a watch or something?" her brother asked.

Pavia winced. "*Or something* is one way of putting it."

"Robert, get your sister a glass of whiskey. It looks like she needs it."

"This suit feels like it's strangling me. Let me change, and then I'll tell you…everything."

With a pair of leggings and one of her favorite oversized sweaters on, Pavia shuffled her slippered feet back into the living room, a copy of the will Mr. Hendricks had given her in her hand.

"Have you eaten?" her dad asked.

Her stomach lurched, not with hunger but with nerves for the bombshell she was about to drop on her brother and dad.

"I grabbed lunch before my flight home. I'll have dinner later, after"—she held up the envelope from the lawyer—"we've talked about this."

She snuggled onto the dark green couch facing the fireplace and tucked her mother's quilt around her. The varying hues of green, gold, brown, and blue in an ombre nine patch design represented the rolling hills that surrounded them. Pavia ran her hand over the delicate stitches before she opened the envelope and read Antonio's will.

Her father's face was gray and her brother stared at her with wide eyes when she finished.

"Dad? Do you know why Mr. Conti would have done this?" she asked.

With a shaky hand, her dad downed the rest of his glass of whiskey. "I suppose I should be happy he's tried to make things right, but I can't believe—" He drew in a sharp breath and pressed his hand to his chest.

Both Pavia and Robert jumped up and rushed to his side.

"Sis, call a doctor," Robert said.

"No, no, there's no need for that," Anthony reassured them. "I'm okay. Some memories still hurt, no matter how much time has passed."

Pavia exchanged a worried look with her brother as they both sat back down.

"I've never told you this but I grew up with the Contis. Your grandpa Henry and Antonio were best friends." Her dad squeezed his eyes closed. "Brothers in arms."

The reverence and love in his voice for Henry and Antonio brought tears to her eyes.

"I didn't leave California because I wanted to. I left because I didn't have a choice. Antonio always regretted what he had done. He'd reached out to me over the years trying to…make amends, I guess."

"And you didn't accept any of his offers?" Robert asked.

Anthony pressed his lips together and shook his head. "I try not to be a bitter person, but when it comes to the Contis…." He lifted his eyes to the ceiling. "Your mom took so much of that anger and bitterness away, but I just… like I said, some wounds take time to heal, and some"—his voice broke—"never do."

"*Cosa ti hanno fatto?*" *What did they do to you?* Pavia asked.

"It's okay, Dad, if you don't want to talk about it—"

"It doesn't matter if I want to talk about it or not." Anthony cut her brother off. "Antonio took that choice away from me when he made his will." He took a deep, shuddering breath. "My father and Antonio worked side by side. When my dad passed away, I continued to work with Antonio. But his son, Enzo… Enzo and I were born in the same year. Everyone expected we would have a friendship as close as our fathers had. But he resented my presence for as long as I can remember. When my father died, I looked up to Antonio. I wanted my namesake to be proud of me."

He nodded slowly, and Pavia watched his face crumble as memories washed over him.

"I tried to get along with Enzo, but I couldn't—I can't offer friendship to someone I don't respect. I never wanted to hurt Enzo or anyone. Life doesn't always reveal what gifts it will bring or how cruelly those gifts can be taken away."

Pavia gasped and reached for her father's hand. She could count on one hand the number of times she'd seen him cry. With a solemn expression, her brother got up and went to the kitchen, coming back a moment later with a glass of water and a glass of whiskey.

Robert sat on the edge of the coffee table and held both glasses out. "I wasn't sure which one would help more."

Anthony wiped his eyes and took the glass of whiskey.

"Why this? Why now? Antonio must have known how much pain this would cause you?" Pavia asked.

"Antonio promised my father that I would inherit the Brothers Block. That piece of land was always meant to be passed down to Henry's descendants."

"Then why didn't Antonio leave you the money and land?"

"I've built my legacy. I don't want or need his. When I left, my last words to Antonio were that I didn't want it. I was heartbroken and angry. My world had just been ripped apart. I told him—" He pressed his lips together. "I regret some things I said that day. The day I left, I swore I would never set foot on the Conti vineyard again."

Pavia clutched her stomach, reeling from what her father had just told her.

"Why me and not Robert?"

"I don't want to leave Blue Ridge. This is home. But you, Sis, you've always wanted more. Dad and I know that," Robert said.

Her dad frowned. "He's trying to make up for what happened and give you the opportunity you've always wanted. You don't need this. I can give you and your brother whatever you want."

"*Sì, Papà.* Robert and I know how hard you've worked, and you've given us a wonderful life here. I'm happy here, I really am, but… I want to know I can stand on my own two feet. That I can start with nothing and build my own legacy, just like you did. Please don't be mad at me, *Papà*, but I… there's a part of me that wants to take on this challenge. Five years, *Papà*. If it doesn't work, we'll inherit millions for the land, enough to secure the future of this vineyard for generations." She looked at him and her brother. "I'm not saying I've decided. I just need time to think."

Her dad moved over to the sofa and pulled her into a hug, kissing the top of her head. "You're fearless, like your mother."

Pavia gave him a teary smile. "And stubborn like my dad. I know you want to keep me safe. But I can't fly home if I never leave the nest."

"Now you sound like your mother."

She sighed. "I wish Mom were here."

"Oh, sweetheart." Her dad's voice shook. "There isn't a day that goes by when I don't wish the same thing."

Robert reached for her hand, and they all shared a moment in silent mourning.

The question hovered on her lips for a moment before she took a breath and asked, "Did Mom know what happened?"

"When I came here, I was so… broken. All I wanted to do was work and try to forget. I got turned away from a lot of farms before your mom's family opened their doors to me. Maybe because your mom's parents were a mixed couple, they were willing to take a chance on a young Black man alone without a family of his own. They embraced me and helped me understand this new place that was so different from California. Your mom was the one that encouraged me to plant vines here. Right here, by the chapel. She helped me plant the roses at the end of each row. Rebecca understood they meant more to me than just an early warning system for frost. The roses were a reminder of my father and Antonio. They were a piece of home I didn't know I needed, but she knew it would help me heal. Your mom and her family, they understood love and loss. They pushed when I needed it and gave me space when I needed that too. Maybe it was because of your mother's background that she understood me better. She knew what it was like to have your heart in two places at once."

Pavia nodded. Her mother was half Yakima Indian and half White. When her grandmother married the son of a wealthy White wheat farmer, it caused an uproar with members of both their families. The land that was originally a wheat farm grew into the Brothers in Arms vineyard.

"Dad?" Pavia's voice was just above a whisper. "What would Mom have said about Antonio's will?"

Her dad swallowed, blinking rapidly. He stood up, his body stiff. "I don't want you to go." He shook his head in defeat. "But do what's right in your heart. I know you, and if you don't go, you'll always wonder, what if? I can't put that burden on you. Rebecca would have wanted you to follow your heart."

"*Ti voglio ben, Papà.*"

"I love you too, sweetheart. All I want is for you and your brother to be happy and not live with regret the way I have. I can't give you that if I don't let you go."

Her brother wiped at his eyes.

"I haven't decided yet. I'm scared," she confessed.

"I'd be a lot more worried if you weren't. Change is scary." Anthony took a deep breath. "I want you to promise me, if you decide to do this, that you'll come to me for help if you need it." He turned to Robert. "That goes for you too. If you ever want to try something new or need help, you can always come to me."

Robert nodded. "I will, Dad."

She looked up at her father. "I promise. If I do this, I will make you proud."

"You already do, both of you, every day."

The next morning, Pavia put on a pair of flannel-lined jeans, a thermal T-shirt, and her heavy field coat. Wool socks and her work boots kept her feet warm and dry as she trudged through the snow up to the chapel.

Her dad poked his head in a few minutes later. "I thought I might find you here."

Pavia patted the space next to her on the small wooden pew. She tipped her head toward the small space heater in the corner. "It's warming up in here. Want to sit with me for a while?"

"You've got dark circles under your eyes," he observed as he sat down.

"So do you."

"I guess we were both up last night."

Pavia rested her head on her dad's shoulder. "There's more to the story you told us last night, isn't there?"

He sighed. "Is that what kept you up last night?"

"Your reaction to getting the letter was so… strong. I kept thinking this was more than an argument between you and Antonio's son. You said you didn't want to hurt anyone. What did you mean by that?"

"I can't get nothing past you, can I? The reason Enzo and I fought— we were fighting over… someone."

Pavia pulled away so she could look her dad in the face. "It was a girl, wasn't it?"

"It doesn't matter," he said in a strained voice. "What happened in the past shouldn't affect your decision now."

"What about Enzo? He wasn't at the reading of the will. Will he be angry if I show up?"

"No, sweetheart, he died a long time ago now. I wouldn't have let you go if he were still there."

"You sound… angry."

Anthony clasped his hands tightly in his lap. "He wasn't a good man."

Pavia studied her dad's profile, noting the stern set of his jaw. The Contis had hurt him. His sadness and anger were palpable.

"Is it wrong that I'm relieved he won't be there?" she asked.

Her dad looked at her. "No, it's not wrong. I'm as relieved as you are."

"Is there anything else you want me to know, Dad?"

He shook his head with a heavy sigh. "I don't want to influence your decision. This is your story now, not mine."

"I'm still torn. Part of me wants to go, and part of me is so angry that you had to leave your home. I don't want anything to do with them."

"Don't let anger fuel your decision, sweetheart."

Pavia blew out a shaky breath. "Will you be okay if I say yes?"

"I'll always support you, no matter what." Her dad put his arm around her and kissed her temple. "You've got some thinking to do. Don't worry about work today. Take all the time you need."

She sat in the little chapel for a long time. Her brother brought her a thermos of coffee at one point. Robert wasn't a big talker—the small gesture was his way of showing support.

Winter days were short in their part of the world, and by late afternoon, it was already growing dark. Pavia ventured out of the chapel, heading into the fields. Her breath was visible as tiny white clouds in the frigid air. She climbed to the highest block, making her way through rows of Syrah, the first planted in the state. As she reached the summit, Pavia gazed upon the land her family had held for generations.

Her heart thundered in her chest, not from the climb but from the decision she knew she'd made. Her hands shook as she pulled out the business card from her pocket and dialed the number. She blinked back tears as she told Mr. Hendricks her decision.

"I UNDERSTAND your frustration, Mr. Conti, but there's nothing you can do. Miss Jackson accepted the bequest."

Alex hung up with Mr. Hendricks and threw his phone down. He watched it slide across the smooth mahogany finish of his desk before it clattered to the floor. Only it wasn't his desk. It was his grandfather's. Just because he sat behind it now didn't mean it belonged to him.

Pavia Jackson refused all the counteroffers they had made, she said she wouldn't sell even if she could. Alex dropped his head into his hands. How could his grandfather give away a part of their family legacy? The fifteen acres Antonio left her was land purchased by the first generation to emigrate from California from Italy.

Another wave of grief passed over him. When his grandfather passed away in his sleep several months ago, he'd lost his mentor. The one person he would have gone to for guidance was the person who had caused this mess. Antonio was the guiding light of their family. At ninety-seven, he'd still been a force to be reckoned with. Alex spent all of his time in the fields and winery with his grandfather. Wine ran through his veins. For generations, beginning in the Tuscan hills and now in California, his family crafted fine wine and cultivated some of the best fruit in the state.

Alex shuffled through the papers on his… Antonio's desk. He had been so confident in his ability to run the family business when his grandfather was still alive. Now, without his presence, Alex felt lost and betrayed. His grandfather hadn't just given away the land, he'd also given away a dream, interfering in the plans Alex had made to take the Brothers Block and create his own small winery separate from the behemoth Conti Vineyards had become. His business no longer gave him the joy it once did, and the life he had hoped to live was now shattered.

Memories of working with his grandfather washed over him. He would race to join him out in the fields every morning in the spring, checking the vines for fresh growth. Alex learned every aspect of winemaking, from grafting new vines to bottling the final product, at his grandfather's side. He took hold of the faded picture that was perched on the corner of the desk next to an empty silver vase that was always filled with pink roses when his grandfather was alive. Alex moved his finger over the vines of the grape leaves etched in the antique silver frame. Antonio's face, weathered and smiling, became a blur as a fresh wave of sorrow washed over him. He let the picture fall from his grasp.

"Grandad, why did you do this? What the hell did you think it would accomplish?" He pressed the heels of his hands into his eyes until he saw spots behind the lids. "Why?" he whispered, staring at the smiling face frozen in time.

"Alex, I know you and your brother are upset about the will, but Antonio had his reasons." His mother's soft voice drifted from the doorway. She held out her hand. "Come, take a walk with me."

Alex pulled himself up from the desk and linked his arm with hers. Together, they walked through the french doors that connected the office to the wide veranda surrounding the house. Dew clung to the spiderwebs, creating gossamer threads in the sunlight. He paused and took a deep breath, forcing the fresh air into his lungs. His gaze roamed over the rows of vines that generations of his family had nurtured and tended. He loved this place. The vineyard was a part of his DNA, the good part.

"Have you seen Nick today?" his mother asked with the anxious look she often had where his younger brother was concerned.

"No, I'm sure he's still sleeping off whatever trouble he found last night."

Sarah's mouth turned down, and a flash of annoyance clouded her expression. Alex knew without being told that she shared his frustration. They were five years apart in age, but a thousand years separated their attitudes about the family business. Alex was methodical in his approach to managing the vineyard and winery, spending hours on spreadsheets and analysis, weighing the impact of every decision. Nick would follow whatever idea he'd woken up with that day without considering the long-term consequences. Alex and their grandfather often rejected his ideas, and he knew it frustrated his brother having the reins pulled so tight, but Nick's impulsiveness often cost the company both time and money.

He anxiously watched his mother. Ever since the reading of Grandad's will, she had been quiet and guarded. He looked over the vines his family planted over two hundred years ago.

"I just thought I'd have more time," he confessed. "I thought Grandad would always be here. Who is going to hold us together?"

"Alex, I wish…." Sarah turned to look toward the little cottage nestled in the valley below. "It shouldn't have happened this way. It never should have come to this." Her voice dropped to a whisper.

Alex swept his hand over the fields below. "How could he give away land that's been in our family for generations?" *And not tell me.*

"Because your grandfather didn't see it that way," she said.

His brows drew together, and his forehead wrinkled in confusion. His mother wasn't making any sense.

"In his own way, Antonio did keep it in the family. Henry Jackson was like a brother to him, and the Brothers Block was always supposed to go to his descendants," she said.

"What are you talking about?" Alex had heard nothing about the Brothers Block going to Pavia's father.

"Anthony was more of a son to Antonio than his flesh and blood. He loved his namesake." She looked over the field wistfully. "I wish you could have seen them together. Anthony would walk the fields every morning with Antonio the same way you did."

Alex stared at her while she reminisced about Pavia's father. It was rare for her to talk about the past. He knew that his grandfather and Henry Jackson served together in World War II. The two men worked together for many years. When Henry died suddenly, Anthony stayed in the cottage alone. He was barely a grown man forced to live on his own. He was going to ask why Grandad didn't have Anthony move into the villa and realized he already knew the answer. Enzo. Grandad was probably trying to protect Anthony from his son.

"Why didn't Grandad give the inheritance to Anthony instead of his daughter if that was the promise he made?"

"Anthony has built one of the top wineries in Washington State. He doesn't need fifteen acres here, or the painful memories that come with them."

"What happened, Mom? What happened with the Jacksons?"

The color drained from his mother's face. "Alex, some things are better left unsaid."

A sick feeling unfurled in the pit of his stomach. "It has something to do with Dad, doesn't it?"

Enzo Conti wasn't a good father, husband, or human being. His abuse escalated until Antonio threw him off the estate. Enzo continued to live a life filled with violence until he finally encountered a bully bigger than him who killed him in a bar fight three years after he left. Alex didn't miss his father. He was old enough to remember the abuse. Nick was too young when their father left and had made up a fantasy of a perfect father instead of facing the truth.

Sarah grasped his arm, looking up at him. "It's important to me that you and your brother welcome Pavia if she accepts the bequest."

"I just spoke to the lawyer. She has."

Alex exhaled, looking down at the cottage and the vines that surrounded it. He should have shared his plans with Grandad. Maybe if he had known, he wouldn't have given away the Brothers Block.

"Does Nick know?"

"No, not yet. We both know that he won't take the news well."

Nick had changed since the reading of their grandfather's will. He'd become sullen and belligerent in a way he'd never seen before.

"I'm worried about what Nick will do. Please keep an eye on him, Alex."

"That's what I've always do."

"I know you will," she said, wiping away her tears.

Keeping Nick safe was the burden he'd carried every day since his brother was born. When Antonio discovered Enzo's abuse, his grandfather never forgave himself for refusing to see what a monster his son had become and tried to make up for, taking on the role of father to his grandsons.

A few weeks from now, Pavia Jackson would move in. The little house that had sat alone and empty for all these years would come back to life. Nobody could live in the cottage while his grandfather lived. Antonio kept it sealed, almost as if it was a sacred site.

Alex wandered back into his office and slumped into his chair, staring at the supply orders waiting for his signature. Corks and bottles could wait. At the moment, he didn't give a damn if the cellar master thought the Cabernet needed another two weeks in the barrel before it would be ready to bottle. He pushed the papers away and reached for his phone instead.

"What?" his best friend's gruff voice barked.

"One of these days, you're going to learn to say hello like a normal person." Alex chuckled.

"Why should I when I know it's you?"

"Just because I'm your friend and business partner doesn't mean you get to be rude."

"I'm busy. What do you want?"

The clanging and clattering of pots and pans, as well as the voices of the kitchen staff in the background, indicated The Vyne was preparing for a hectic evening. Alex happily played the role of silent partner in his friend Brandon McCall's culinary vision. He'd only be in the way if he tried to interfere, and he didn't want to. Brandon found fulfillment in the kitchen. Alex sought his in the vines.

"It's nothing important. I can call you later."

His friend's voice softened. "What's going on?"

The noise faded as he spoke. A second later, he heard the click of Brandon's office door closing.

"Everything is turned upside down since Grandad died, and I don't feel like I can get a handle on it," he confessed.

"She's coming, isn't she?" Brandon asked.

"She's coming."

"I still can't believe Antonio gave that block away. I know you were looking forward to taking it over."

Alex accepted his friend's condolences. "I wanted something that wasn't part of the Conti vineyard. Something that wasn't so big, where I could be hands-on from start to finish. It was a ridiculous idea. I wouldn't have had the time to have my own winery and run the family business."

"It's not about the time, and you know it. You were completely caught off guard by your grandfather's will. I'm sure he didn't do it to hurt you, Alex, but I know it did." Brandon repeated what his mother had been telling him.

"Yeah, logically I know that." He glanced toward the cottage again. "Grandad and I didn't have any secrets between us, or at least that's what I thought, and then I find out about the Jacksons."

"Your mom never said anything?"

"No, never."

"So, how are you going to handle this?"

"There's nothing to handle. She's coming, and that's it."

There was a shout and a clattering of metal in the background, and the line went dead. Alex shook his head with a smile. Brandon ran his kitchen with the precision he'd learned in the military. He was a demanding boss, but a fair one, and it was all in the cause of providing the best for his customers.

Alex looked down at his phone. He paused a moment, then clicked on the Brothers in Arms website. A breathtaking photo of a glass-and-wood structure with a lengthy porch running along one side and a view of the vineyard below filled the screen. He clicked on the About Us tab and viewed the photo he'd looked at many times over the past few weeks, more times than he wanted to admit.

Pavia stood with her father on one side and her brother, Robert, on the other, all wearing jeans and Brothers in Arms T-shirts under their field coats. Smiling at the camera, they stood arm in arm, the complete opposite of the stiff formal portrait on his family's website. Pavia's eyes sparkled, and her cheeks were pink from the sun. A jolt of need made him jerk his hand back and shove the phone back in his pocket. *Make up your mind. You can't hate her and wonder what it would be like to kiss her too.*

Not long after, Nick walked in sporting a pair of plaid pajama pants and a T-shirt. Yawning, he ran his fingers through his already disheveled bed head.

"So nice of you to join us."

"It's still morning." Nick yawned again.

"You're right. It's a quarter to twelve. You should probably go back to bed. It's way too early for you," Alex deadpanned.

Nick ambled over and dropped into the chair in front of the desk. "It's not like I have anything to do. It looks like you have everything under control."

Alex tried his best not to roll his eyes. This was a conflict they'd been having since their grandfather died. Nick always asserted that Alex had taken care of everything, so there was no need for him to lend a hand. There was a kernel of truth in the accusation. Alex took his role as big brother and protector to heart. He did it out of both love and necessity. He was keenly aware, from a very early age, that he was much better equipped than his little brother to absorb their father's abuse. Habits formed early in life were hard to break, and even after their father left, Alex stayed in his role as protector.

"There's plenty that you can do."

Nick waved his hand dismissively. "Who cares about this stuff? What are we going to do about that girl?"

Alex dropped his hands into his lap, clenching them into fists, dreading his brother's reaction to the news he was about to deliver.

"Mr. Hendricks called this morning. She's accepted the bequest. She'll be here in two weeks."

His brother scowled. "We have to figure out a way to get rid of her."

"Nick, it's done. Mom asked that we make her feel welcome, and that's what we're going to do."

Nick drummed his fingers on his knee, his eyes narrowed.

Alex knew that look well. It meant trouble. He leaned forward and clasped his hands in front of him on the desk the same way his grandad used to. He hoped it would have the same effect.

"Whatever you're thinking, don't."

"I'm not thinking anything." Nick got up and gave Alex a mock salute before walking out.

Alex collected the papers lying in front of him and attempted to concentrate on his work again. He carelessly threw them back onto his desk a few moments later. He rested back in his chair and looked at the barren vines through the window. The first signs of budbreak would happen just about the same time Pavia arrived. This year's harvest would not be like any other.

PAVIA GLANCED in the rearview mirror one more time. Her entire life was packed into the back of her truck. She'd cried in her dad's arms after he and his brother helped her load everything she owned into it.

"*Ho paura.* I'm scared, *Papà*," she whispered.

He rocked her gently, patting her back. "If you weren't scared, I would be even more worried. No risk ever comes without fear." He sighed. "You're afraid to go, and I'm afraid to let you go. You're taking a risk starting your own winery. I'm taking a risk with my heart letting you go. We're both resilient, like the vines we've tended. The more the vines struggle, the stronger they become, and we do the same thing. I'm proud of you, sweetheart," he said, his voice breaking.

When Pavia left for an internship with a winery in Italy, she'd thought it was hard to say goodbye. Standing in the circle of her dad's arms, she understood what it really meant to say goodbye when you didn't know when you were coming home again. She cried for the first hundred miles after she drove away.

Even now, as the miles took her farther away from home and closer to an uncertain future, she wrestled with her decision. Robert had moved into a small one-bedroom house closer to town a couple of years ago, while Pavia had been content to stay at home. The house was designed with two separate wings, one with her parents' bedroom and the other for the kids. With Robert out of the house, she had plenty of privacy. Other than a year of studying abroad, this would be the first time she truly lived on her own. The first time she was on her own for everything, managing fifteen acres and a winery. Believing she could handle all the challenges she would face and actually doing it were two different things. She chewed on her lip and focused on the road ahead.

A day and a half after leaving her home in Blue Ridge, her stomach dipped with the potholes as she turned onto the road that would lead her to her new home. She scanned the scenery, looking for anything that looked familiar from the pictures her dad had shown her. The night before she left, he brought a handful of old pictures to the kitchen table to share with Pavia and Robert, photos of the vineyard he played in as a young boy and the little cottage he'd grown up in. The skin over her knuckles stretched taut as she gripped the steering wheel tighter. Her eyes traced the graceful curves of the grand metal archway and the Conti logo emblazoned in gold as she passed by the entrance to the estate. She'd passed smaller signs along the road for the past few miles, labeling the rows of vines in their vineyard. The Contis owned a vast estate, much larger than the land her family farmed, bigger than any vineyard she'd ever visited.

It was clear they weren't happy when she turned down not just their first counteroffer but also the two others that followed. Each one was more generous than the last. Pavia could have bought the land she now owned three times over if she'd accepted their last offer. Now that her dad had started sharing his history, she'd learned why the Contis would fight so hard for such a small piece of land when they owned so much. Now she understood. These weren't just fifteen acres. These were the first fifteen acres that the Conti family bought from a group of Franciscan monks in 1800. When Antonio returned to California with Pavia's grandfather after World War II, his father gave the two young men those acres, and the Brothers Block was born. Of course Alex Conti and his brother were going to put up a fight to keep part of their family legacy. Now Pavia understood it was part of her legacy too. It was strange to feel a connection to a place she'd never been to.

There was a part of her—which her dad would have said was the stubborn streak she'd inherited from her mother—that wanted to make the best wine she could. Pavia was determined to craft beautiful wine from the same vines her dad had been forced to abandon. She wanted to show the Contis that she was as worthy of the land as they were.

She slowed down, checking the map one more time, before she turned onto the smaller dirt road that would lead her to her new home. The cottage came into view, and her heart raced as she pulled up to the front. She jumped out of the truck and stood in front of the house her father grew up in, taking it in for the first time. The little white cottage sat nestled between two oak trees, with a small barn behind it. Despite the faded paint, crumbling stucco, and a yard that was more than a little overgrown, it looked just like the pictures her dad had shared with her. Pavia instantly fell in love with her new home.

The leaves rustled in the trees when a slight wind blew. With the next gust of wind, she heard a creaking sound as she made her way up the stone walkway. The arched front door, covered in faded and peeling robin's-egg blue paint, was slightly ajar. She frowned and slowly pushed it open. Her heart slammed into her rib cage.

"Oh my God!" Her voice shook, along with the rest of her body.

The cottage looked like a tornado had blown through it. Splintered and broken furniture was scattered throughout the living room. Carefully stepping over the remnants of what had been a table, she moved through the debris toward the arched opening to the kitchen. Broken dishes littered the floor, and her feet crunched against broken bits of pottery. She dropped to her knees and picked up a shard of an old plate. The delicate morning glory vine that circled the rim blurred as she fought to hold back her tears. One escaped and splashed onto the faded floral pattern.

The paperwork from the lawyer stated the cottage had sat unused since they forced her father to leave but that everything should be intact. She picked up another broken piece of pottery and clutched the pieces to her chest as she stood up and continued through the house. Every single room was in shambles. Her anger grew with each broken chair and shattered piece of pottery.

"No!" she shouted, throwing the broken shards she carried to the ground. "You may have forced my father to leave, but you won't do the same to me!"

There was a sharp gasp from the doorway. Pavia turned and found Sarah Conti staring at the chaos with wide eyes.

"I saw your truck heading down the road, and I wanted to welcome you. I brought"—she stared down at the basket in her hand—"well, it doesn't matter what I brought now." Her lips pressed into a thin line as she set the basket at her feet.

"Mrs. Conti, I…." Pavia cleared her throat, blinking back tears. She couldn't make polite conversation right now, when she was trying to comprehend what had just happened.

Mrs. Conti reached for her cell phone and punched in the numbers while her gaze darted around the room to take in the damage.

"Melinda, I'm going to need you to bring some things to the cottage." She fired off a list of cleaning supplies and hung up, then took a deep breath before turning back to Pavia. She rested her hands on her hips and frowned. "Well, let's get this cleaned up. You can't sleep here tonight, or for a while, with all the work that needs to be done."

Pavia stared at her, openmouthed. "You don't have to do that, Mrs. Conti. I can—"

She held up her hand. "Please, call me Sarah. I'm sure I'm the last person you want to have helping you, but I'm here, and you can't deal with this mess by yourself." She blew out a shaky breath, her eyes darting around the room. "You should have had a better welcome than this."

Sarah moved farther into the house, wincing at the crunching under her feet.

"I am not leaving here until I know you're safe and comfortable. Our housekeeper, Melinda, will be here in a few minutes to help. I think we should start by making a pile of the larger broken pieces out in the yard." She picked up a piece of a chair and carried it out the front door.

This wasn't the same shattered woman she'd seen in the lawyer's office. Pavia's first impression of Sarah Conti was of a frail, sad woman, not this person with fire in her eyes and a determined slant to her mouth. Sarah marched back in and grabbed a small table, then took it outside and set it down next to the chair with force. Pavia followed her out to protest, but before she could, Sarah whirled around to face her.

"You know why your father had to leave, don't you?"

Pavia nodded, and Sarah closed her eyes and took a deep, shuddering breath. When she opened her eyes, they were bright with unshed tears.

"It never should have happened." Her voice sank to a whisper. "I was a coward. The night they forced me to leave Anthony was the worst night of my life." Her voice broke.

"It was you!" Pavia exclaimed.

Sarah blanched. Her lips trembled. "I thought you said you knew."

"My dad said he got into an argument with Enzo. I asked him if it was over a girl. He didn't say who."

"I never thought that night would be the last time I saw your father. It won't change anything or make up for what happened, but please let me help you now."

Pavia swallowed and nodded. "Thank you for offering, Sarah, but I think… this is an awkward situation for all of us, and…." She sighed, unsure of what to say.

Sarah winced. "I'm so ashamed. I should tell you, Alex and Nick don't know about this. Please don't say anything," she pleaded, twisting her hands. "I was such a coward. I'll never forgive myself. Antonio leaving you this gift was his way of trying to make up for the past. If you'd let me help you now… it would be a small way of… it's the least I can do."

There was a knock on the door, and a woman about the same age as Sarah poked her head in.

"What in the world happened here?" she asked, looking around the room.

"Melinda, this is Pavia Jackson. Pavia, this is our housekeeper, Melinda Garza."

The petite woman with a heart-shaped face and kind eyes held out her hand to Pavia. She wore jeans and a pink oxford shirt similar to what Sarah had on. Her dark hair was shot through with gray and woven into a braid that fell to the middle of her back. She shook Pavia's hand with a friendly smile.

After the introductions, Melinda made a slow circle, surveying the damage and muttering to herself about the state of the cottage before springing into action.

"We should get started," Sarah said with a pleading look at Pavia.

Pavia couldn't say no, and as soon as she gave a slight nod, the two women became a whirlwind of activity. She could barely keep up with them as they hauled the larger pieces into a pile outside and filled garbage bags with the smaller debris. More than once, Pavia caught Sarah wiping away a tear as she worked.

Pavia's own emotions were a mix of sadness and confusion. She wasn't expecting to interact with any of the Contis right away. Sarah was the woman her dad and Enzo had fought over. It never occurred to her that Mrs. Conti was a part of her dad's story. Sarah asked about her drive down and made small talk while they cleaned, but never once did she mention Pavia's father.

After the damage was swept clean from the cottage, Pavia could finally take a look around her new home. The front door opened into a small living room with a fireplace on one side and a dining room and kitchen on the other. A short hallway led to two bedrooms with a bathroom in between. The house had good bones, but the years of neglect had taken their toll, and Pavia's heart sank as the reality of the situation hit her.

"You can't stay here," Melinda said with a disapproving look.

"She's right. You need a new furnace and water heater. The plumbing barely works." Sarah ticked off each item on her fingers, looking at the damage. "Not to mention the floors need refinishing, and everything needs a fresh coat of paint."

Pavia looked around. It would be a challenge, but she could make it work. She had her sleeping bag with her, and dorm life had taught her how to cook with just a hot plate and an electric teakettle.

"I'll have to find a contractor right away, but I can rough it for a while."

"Absolutely not. You'll move into the guesthouse until we get the cottage ready for you," Sarah said with a note of steely determination.

"I can't possibly do that," Pavia protested.

Sarah gently grasped her forearms. "This isn't easy for any of us. I know you don't want to stay with us. I understand it is an incredibly uncomfortable situation, but this way you'll be close to the cottage and the Brothers Block. I don't know what your plans are, but you can work in the field and supervise the repairs on the cottage." She gave her a wistful smile. "You're Anthony Jackson's daughter, so I suspect you're here to make wine. You have an enormous challenge ahead. Throwing in home repairs isn't part of the plan. At least stay in the guesthouse until you've had the electrical and plumbing checked. I can't bear the thought of you taking cold showers and dealing with blown fuses."

Pavia hated to admit it, but Sarah was right. "Okay," she said in a shaky voice. "I'd like to walk the field before I come up, and… I need to call my dad." She noted the flash of pain in Sarah's eyes. She wasn't going to avoid talking about her family or her dad in front of the Contis. Her father and her brother meant everything to her, and she wouldn't pretend like they didn't exist because it made Sarah sad.

Sarah backed toward the door. "Of course. Melinda and I will head back and make sure the guesthouse is in order." She patted Pavia's arm. "Come up whenever you're ready."

When Pavia was alone, she immediately left the cottage and went to the field. The first row of vines was less than 150 feet from her front door. She peeked into the barn on her way. It wasn't large, but there was enough room for a small production facility, an office, and a tasting room. It needed almost as much repair as the house, but it could wait. Having a place to live was her first priority. She fought back a wave of panic and continued out to the vineyard.

Scanning the vines in front of her, the value of what Antonio had given her hit Pavia. He hadn't just given her land and money; he'd entrusted her with a legacy. Was she up to the task? Five million dollars was a lot of money, but running both a vineyard and a winery was an expensive undertaking. She would have to manage her finances carefully, she thought, as the list of necessary updates in her head grew longer and longer. All of the equipment and the minimum number of workers to hire would cost a lot of money in the first year. A crusher, de-stemmer, and stainless steel vats, it all added up. Then there were bottles, tables, and corks. The list seemed endless.

The land she'd inherited had Malbec, Petit Verdot, and Cabernet Sauvignon vines, a classic Bordeaux blend. Pavia moved through the rows, assessing the condition of the block. She didn't have to trudge through the snow in the California climate. The vines looked healthy, and the trellises were in good condition. While she waited for budbreak, she could put most of her energy into getting the house habitable. It wasn't what she'd planned on, but if she got the house done quickly, and the barn remodeled, when the time came, she could focus all of her energy on the vineyard.

Turning in a circle, Pavia took in her new surroundings one more time before pulling her phone out. Her dad answered before the first ring finished, bringing a smile to her lips. He must have been hovering by the phone, waiting for her call.

"Hi, baby girl. I was wondering when I'd hear from you. Did you make it okay? How"—he cleared his throat, trying to cover the tremor in his voice—"how does everything look?"

"The house looks exactly the way it looks in the pictures. It's going to be great. I can't wait to get unpacked and moved in," she lied, unable to bring herself to tell him the truth.

"What about the land? Are the vines in good condition?" he asked.

"From what I can see so far, everything is okay. The trellises and irrigation lines are all intact." They talked about the conditions and the differences in terroir from Blue Ridge to Seneca and her plans to move to organic production.

Finally, Anthony cleared his throat. Pavia closed her eyes, bracing for the question she knew was coming.

"Have you seen any of the Contis yet?"

"No, not yet." She winced. "I just got here. I'm sure I'll see them eventually. Don't worry, everything will be okay, and I'll let you know when I do. Unless"—she closed her eyes, choosing her next words carefully—"it makes you uncomfortable. We don't have to talk about it."

There was a beat of silence. "I'm only interested in what you're doing."

Pavia nodded, blinking back tears. *"Ti voglio tanto bene, Papà."*

"I love you too, my darling daughter."

Pavia held the phone in her hands, staring at the screen after her dad hung up. She wanted to call him back and tell him about the cottage and about Sarah. Her heart hammered in her chest as she stood frozen in the field, picturing herself jumping back into her truck and driving back to Blue Ridge. Squeezing her eyes shut, she took a few deep breaths. She opened her eyes and knelt down, taking a handful of dirt warmed by the sun. The color of the soil had a similar gray-tan hue as back home, with small chunks of rock and clumps of clay. Pavia scanned the surrounding land, familiar rows of vines with an unfamiliar landscape in the distance. The seas of gold from the low rolling wheat fields back home were replaced with willow and pine trees in the foothills.

Pavia headed back to the house and unloaded her truck, stacking the boxes in the middle of the dining room. She pulled out her laptop and started a list of repairs, prioritizing what she needed to do to get moved in as soon as possible.

When she'd put it off for as long as possible, Pavia got back in her truck, drove down her road, and turned onto the road leading to the Contis' estate, going under the large, imposing archway. She tapped nervously on the steering wheel as she turned onto the road leading to the main house. She looked at the sleek silver BMW and black Mercedes in the driveway with derision when she pulled up next to them. No one in her family would ever own cars like these; they weren't practical on a proper farm. She patted the hood of her truck with a certain amount of smugness before she headed up to the front door.

The main house sat at the top of a hill with the vineyard spread out like a ruffled skirt in shades of brown and green around it. Her cottage sat at the bottom of the hill, nestled in a little valley below. The Tuscan-style stucco walls, terra-cotta tile roof, and dark green shutters blended in elegantly with the surroundings. Orange nasturtiums and white geraniums spilled from planter boxes beneath large arched windows. Olive trees in giant pots framed each side of the walkway leading to the front door. It was an elegant estate built to impress.

She straightened her shoulders and pressed the doorbell. Rapid footsteps echoed, and the door was flung open.

"Pavia, welcome." Sarah gave her a warm smile and led her through the large, elegant foyer and straight into the kitchen. "I realized you must be starving. I made something to eat for you."

"Thank you, Mrs.—Sarah," Pavia corrected herself as she was ushered toward a row of leather barstools on one side of a large marble-topped island.

While the kitchen could have been in any home and garden magazine, it was nice to see it wasn't just for show. There were pots bubbling on the stove and various jars of spices on the counter. Despite the high-end finishes, the room had a warm and cozy feel.

Sarah went over to the huge commercial stove and ladled two bowls of soup, then placed them on the island along with a salad and some bread.

"This looks wonderful, thank you."

Sarah gave her a small smile. "It's the least I could do." She picked up her spoon and then set it down again, turning to her with a pained expression. "I know I've already apologized, but I am so sorry, Pavia."

"Sorry for what?" Alex Conti walked into the room.

ALEX STOPPED short at the unexpected sight of Pavia Jackson sitting in his kitchen—and the grim expressions on both women's faces.

His mom's shoulders were rigid. She stared at him with a hard expression. "Alex, someone broke into the cottage and ransacked it."

"What?"

She continued in a steely voice. "Pavia will stay in the guesthouse until the damage is fixed."

Alex took a step backward. What the hell happened? Last night, he visited the cottage to take a last look before Pavia showed up. The place was worn down from years of neglect, but that was all. Nick. His brother was the only one who would do something so reckless. He mumbled a curse under his breath.

"When did it happen?"

"Oh please, like you don't know," Pavia muttered.

"What's that supposed to mean?" Alex shot back.

"I know you're upset that I didn't accept your offer, but tearing apart the cottage was a little immature, don't you think?"

His jaw ticked. "You think I would do something like that?"

She narrowed her eyes. "It's pretty obvious you don't want me here. I'm on a first-name basis with your lawyer after all the offers you made to buy me out."

Sarah gasped. "Alex, you didn't."

Alex turned to his mother. "Of course I did, Mom. You can't expect me to let the Brothers Block go without a fight. But"—he turned back to Pavia—"I wouldn't destroy someone else's property even if it shouldn't have been theirs to begin with."

Anger simmered in his gut, not directed at Pavia, but toward the suspected culprit.

"Ms. Jackson, I'm sorry about what happened at the cottage, but I guarantee you, I had nothing to do with it."

She eyed him warily. This close, he could see the flecks of deep gold and brown in her eyes. Her full lips pressed into a thin line.

Pavia turned to Sarah and blew out a shaky breath. "I need to apologize. I'm a guest, and I let my anger get the best of me." She looked at Alex. "I'm sorry."

"I would be upset too if I drove a long way to find someone had vandalized my new home," he conceded.

His mom patted Pavia's hand. "It's okay. You must be exhausted after today."

"I can't stay here, Sarah. I appreciate the offer and all of your help today, but I'll make do at the cottage."

"Pavia, please, you can't stay there. The plumbing is ancient, and there's no heat," she pleaded.

"I'll be fine. The cottage isn't in the condition I was expecting"— her eyes darted toward Alex—"but this won't work."

Pavia rose from the kitchen island and made her way out of the room, leaving Sarah with a look of distress upon her face and Alex angry and frustrated.

"Alex, it is not possible to live in the cottage in its current condition. Pavia should stay at the guesthouse until all the repairs that need to be done are taken care of. There's not a single window that hasn't been broken. She can't stay there like that."

He sat next to his mom. "Tell me what happened."

Alex was seething by the time she finished describing the damage to the cottage.

"Have you seen Nick?" he asked between clenched teeth.

Sarah's voice quivered. "You don't think he had anything to do with this, do you?"

"Knowing Nick, he thought of it as one of his fraternity pranks."

"Go to the cottage and try to convince her to come back to the guesthouse, please, Alex."

Despite his doubts that he could convince Pavia Jackson, he couldn't brush aside his mother's plea. With a nod, he got up and went to find her.

Alex jumped into one of the four-by-four utility vehicles from the garage. It would be faster driving it through the vine rows to the cottage than driving a car. In a short amount of time, he was standing at the weathered wooden door of the cottage, knocking on it.

The door opened, and Pavia sighed. "What are you doing here?"

"Ms. Jackson, I—"

She put her hand up. "For better or worse, we're going to be neighbors, and I'm not going to call you Mr. Conti. Just call me Pavia, okay?"

Alex couldn't fight the urge to smile. "Thanks, Pavia."

The spark that had been in her eyes earlier had faded away, replaced instead by a look of weariness.

"Can I come in?"

She stepped back, and for the first time, Alex walked into the cottage he'd dreamed of moving into. It had sat locked for as long as he could remember. He knew his grandfather would visit sometimes. One day when he was in high school, he followed him there. Late at night, he crouched in the vines and watched his grandfather turn on the lamp in the living room and sit in front of the unlit fireplace. He'd crept closer to the window and saw his grandfather sitting with a book in his lap. He wasn't reading, but staring off into the distance. When he saw the tear roll down his grandfather's cheek, he crept away. He knew Antonio had returned to the little cottage from time to time over the years, but Alex never went inside.

"I'd offer you a place to sit, but as you can see, there's nothing left."

A few candles on the mantel provided a dim light. Alex glanced toward the sleeping bag in the corner before noting the rest of the room, empty except for a stack of boxes. The candles flickered from the air coming through the broken windows.

Pavia was looking at him with a curious gaze. "You're looking around as if you've never been here before."

"That's because I haven't. I've always wondered what it was like in here."

"There's not much to see, but you can take a look if you'd like."

He tried to compare the empty rooms with what he remembered from the few times he'd looked through the windows. Pavia followed him down the hall while he poked his head into the two bedrooms and small bathroom. He leaned into the last room, resting his hands on the doorframe.

"My mom said there was nothing left, but I didn't expect it to be so…empty."

Pavia let out a small huff. "It won't be the first time a Jackson had to start over with nothing. I guess it runs in our family."

He pushed away from the doorframe and looked at Pavia. There was a determined glint in her eyes that was like steel, radiating a strong will.

"You have the Brothers Block and a lot of money. I wouldn't call that nothing," he said.

Anger radiated from her. "This house is a part of my history. My dad was forced to leave this place, and now someone"—she paused with a raised eyebrow, leaving no doubt she still thought Alex might be that someone—"is trying to keep me from being here."

He started to object, and then her words sank in. "What do you mean your dad was forced to leave? Your dad moved away."

"Who told you that?"

"No one, I just assumed… It never…." He frowned. "My grandfather never said anything about your dad being forced to leave here."

He could hear the doubt in his own voice. First the will and now this. He began to realize that his grandfather had been keeping more than one secret from him.

"You shouldn't make assumptions," Pavia said with a hint of sadness in her voice.

"I could say the same about you. I know you still think I'm responsible for this." He swept his arm around the empty space.

Alex watched her bristle for a moment before her shoulders sagged. "I know it wasn't you."

"Okay, can we agree not to make assumptions about each other going forward?"

Pavia's lips curled into a small smile. "I suppose we can try."

Alex met her smile with one of his own. "I don't want you to make any assumptions about why I'm here, so I want you to know my mom asked me to come down here and convince you to stay in the guesthouse."

Pavia's smile faded. "I think we both know that's not a good idea."

"Why not?" he challenged.

"Because there's too much history between our families." She threw up her hands. "Because it would be awkward as hell."

Alex ran his hand through his hair. "Yeah, you're right, this is… uncomfortable. But that doesn't mean you have to suffer and sleep on the floor in a cold house with"—he glanced around—"no electricity and broken windows. Come on, Pavia, this isn't safe, and you know it."

"There was electricity until I turned the lights on. Apparently, the knob-and-tube wiring decided it was finally done."

"You can't stay here. You probably don't have water either. It's not safe. You can stay in the guesthouse for as long as you need to." He held his hand up and stepped back. "I promise I won't bite."

Pavia's eyes grew wide for a second before her lips quirked. "Okay, you win," she sighed.

"Can I help you bring anything?"

"No." Pavia picked up a duffel bag that had backpack straps and slung it over her shoulder. She went to the fireplace and blew out the candles, cloaking the room in darkness.

Alex heard her footsteps coming near right before she walked into him. He reached out to steady her, his hand grasping the curve of her waist. Her scent washed over him, earthy and natural. People who worked with wine didn't wear perfumes and often avoided scented body products altogether. What he smelled was all Pavia, and it was the sweetest scent he'd ever encountered.

"Sorry," she muttered.

His eyes adjusted to the darkness enough that he could make out her face in the moonlight. He let go of her waist and took her hand, guiding her out of the house. Her hand wasn't soft and dainty in his. He could feel the strength in her grip and the calluses on her palm. This was a woman who worked hard, and that made her even more attractive.

"Can I give you a ride back to the house?"

Pavia shook her head. "I can drive."

"It's late, and the Gator is quicker. You can use it tomorrow when you come back to the house, and for as long as you need to."

She hesitated before she said, "I'm tired of being stubborn. To be honest, I'm just tired, so I accept your offer."

Alex grinned. "Hop in."

The wind whipped her curls around and she smiled at him as they rode through the vines. She laughed when they hit a large bump and caught air. The sound went straight to his groin. He was in big trouble. He didn't want to be attracted to Pavia. He shouldn't be thinking about wanting to touch her again or wondering what the strip of skin between the hem of her T-shirt and the top of her jeans would have felt like if he'd lowered his hand a fraction when he grasped her waist.

They were at the house within minutes, and Alex was already trying to think of an excuse to spend more time with Pavia.

"The guesthouse is over here," he said, guiding her toward the pool.

"Swanky," she said under her breath.

They reached the guesthouse, and he held out his hand. "Give me your phone."

Pavia wrinkled her forehead at him.

"I'm just going to put in the door code."

She pulled her phone out of her back pocket and handed it to him. Alex quickly added the code, along with his number, in her notes.

He handed her phone back and opened the door, then stood aside to let her pass through. With a flick of the switch just inside the entrance, the lights came on, illuminating the room in a warm glow.

Pavia looked over her shoulder at him with a raised eyebrow. "This is pretty nice for a guesthouse."

Alex took a moment to survey the space, seeing it from her point of view. The pool house was a much smaller version of the main house, with wide pine flooring and cream walls. A fireplace with a Spanish tile surround in shades of blue, rust, and pale green sat between two large windows that faced the pool. The furniture was the same style as the main house's, upholstered in shades of cream and tan with blue and green accent pillows.

"It looks like a spread in *House Beautiful*, doesn't it?" he admitted. Alex walked toward the refrigerator in the open kitchen and checked the contents. "Knowing my mom and Melinda, the kitchen is fully stocked, but if there's anything you need, I put my number in your phone just in case."

Pavia raised an eyebrow. "That was a bold assumption. I can always ask your mom or Melinda if I need anything."

"Ah, there I go again," he said in a teasing voice. "I've already broken our agreement. I'll try to do better."

There was that hint of a smile again. He'd never become addicted to anything so quickly as to seeing Pavia's smile. Alex wanted to know more about the vibrant woman standing in front of him. What would it take to get her to share her father's story with him? Was she aware of any other secrets his grandfather had kept?

ALEX FOUND his mom in the kitchen after he left the pool house. She was sitting at the large farm-style table with cookbooks scattered around her, taking notes on a notepad. Whenever his mom was upset, she turned to cooking or her garden for comfort.

"I saw the lights come on in the guesthouse. Were you able to convince Pavia to stay?"

Alex nodded and sat down at the table. He fanned the pages of one of the cookbooks. "She's settling in and said she'd let you or Melinda know if there's anything she needed."

Sarah sighed. "Good, I'm glad. I couldn't stand the thought of her staying in a cold, dark house. I've been planning some meals I can take over. She's going to have a lot of long days ahead of her getting settled, and I want to make sure she doesn't go hungry."

"That's nice of you, but don't do too much."

"There's no such thing as too much. It's the least I can do after—" She pushed away the pile of cookbooks and rested her elbows on the table, looking at Alex with a pensive gaze. "We both know your brother was behind this."

Alex wanted to object, he'd just been talking about making assumptions with Pavia, but this was one time when he knew his mother's hunch wasn't wrong.

Nick walked in, and Sarah sat up straight, glaring at her youngest son. "I went to the cottage to welcome Pavia this morning."

Alex flinched at the coldness in her voice.

"It was a harmless joke, Mom," Nick said, dropping a kiss on her cheek. "I don't see what the big deal is. She can't just expect to come here and take our land. I don't know how you can sit by and let her move in." He straightened up and crossed his arms. "I have no intention of making this easy for her."

"Nick, you've pulled a lot of stupid stunts, but this isn't one of your fraternity pranks. Pavia has every right to file a police report for vandalism, breaking and entering, or whatever."

"Maybe I just have the guts to stand up for my family while you don't."

"Seriously, Nick, this makes all of us look bad. What happens when the news spreads in town about what you did? And trust me"—Alex cut his brother off when he started to object—"they will find out."

Nick's confident expression faltered. "I didn't think about that."

"We're all dealing with the reality of Grandad's last wishes the best we can. But you can't just act without thinking about the consequences, Nick." Sarah paused. "It's time to grow up. Antonio's gone. You've had plenty of time to play around, but it's time for you to take more responsibility."

His brother's jaw ticked. "I'd take more responsibility if you"—he pointed at Alex—"and Grandad let me instead of lecturing me all the time. I'm the one being loyal here." Nick's expression morphed into one of contempt. "If the two of you want to welcome a con artist who swindled our grandad, that's your problem. I'm not going to be the one who's disloyal to our family."

Alex glared at his brother. "Trashing the cottage doesn't show any kind of loyalty. It was disrespectful to Grandad's memory and hurtful to Mom. As for Grandad and me, there's a big difference between lecturing and working together, having a discussion, and working as a team. But you won't do that. Over and over again you take action without consulting with anyone. I want you to be a part of the business, Nick. I need the help. But I also need you to be a partner and not my reckless little brother."

His mother's voice was low and tight. "You will apologize to Pavia for what you did, and pay for the repairs."

Nick glared at both of them. "The hell I will."

"I'll take it out of your paycheck, the one you haven't been earning anyway," Alex shot back.

"You can't do that. We're all equal owners of this company now," Nick seethed.

"Then it's two against one." Sarah stood up. Crossing her arms in front of her, she stared Nick down.

Sarah's whole body shook even though she was standing firm. Alex felt sick at the sight of her willing herself to be brave. He jumped up, moved to her side, and put his arm around her shoulder.

"I'm right here," he whispered.

She relaxed a little, but he knew her heart was beating just as fast as his.

"The two of you are always a team, ganging up on me," Nick declared.

"That's not true," Sarah said in a shaky voice. "I'm only asking you to take responsibility for your actions. I've stood by and watched you play while your brother worked."

"I'm twenty-six, Mom! I'm not playing."

"Whatever you want to call it then. Playing, partying, running around. It all adds up to you receiving all the benefits that come with having money without you actually doing anything to earn it."

Nick's face turned bright red. Alex felt his mom stiffen when his brother's hands balled into fists at his sides.

"You need to leave," Alex said in a deadly calm voice that masked the fury he felt inside. "Leave now, Nick, before you do something that we'll all regret."

His brother stared at him for a moment before he walked out. As soon as he left, Sarah let out a small sob, pressing the back of her hand against her lips. Alex hugged her.

"You're okay, Mom. I was really proud of you for standing up to Nick just now."

"It doesn't change anything, though, does it?" she sniffed into his shoulder.

"What's the definition of insanity doing the same thing over and over again and expecting a different result? We need to stop expecting him to apologize when he messes up."

"It was like watching history repeat itself," she whispered, pulling out of his embrace.

She voiced exactly what he was thinking. The anger in Nick's eyes, the balled fists at his sides. His brother's demeanor brought back unwelcome memories of his father. Except Enzo wouldn't have walked away the way Nick just did. No, he would have used his fists and taken out his anger on them. They had to find a way to make Nick understand. He couldn't keep acting on impulse without considering the consequences. The thought that he'd end up hating his brother the way he hated his father terrified Alex.

Pavia's comment about her father being forced to leave came back to him. "What happened with the Jackson family? Why did they leave Seneca?"

Sarah took a deep, shuddering breath and sat back down at the table. "It doesn't matter, and it can't be undone. If Nick won't take responsibility for the damage he caused, then I'm going to do what I can to make it right."

They both jumped when the front door slammed and the sound of Nick's car peeling out of the driveway reached their ears.

Alex breathed a heavy sigh. "I've been asking you about the Jacksons since Grandad died, and you keep brushing me off. I don't like feeling like I'm stumbling around in the dark. You're telling me it doesn't matter why the Jacksons left, but it does. Whatever happened all those years ago is why we're here today and why Pavia's sleeping in the guesthouse."

There was a pang of guilt that came when he saw his mom flinch. He wasn't trying to cause harm. He only wanted to know the truth. He realized there wasn't going to be a way of doing that without inflicting some pain.

Alex went over to the stove and went through the motions of making a cup of tea. Soon the fragrance of chamomile wafted through the air, and he carried two mugs to the table and slid one in front of his mother. He noted the slight tremble of her hand as she took a sip. After setting the mug down, she clasped her hands tightly and looked at Alex with a sheen of tears in her eyes.

"Pavia's father was trying to help. Enzo and I—" Her voice broke.

His heart seized. Anthony must have intervened during one of Enzo's fits of rage. "You don't have to finish."

"It's my fault Anthony was forced to leave his home."

"It's Enzo's fault. Everything bad that's ever happened is because of him. I hate—no, that word isn't strong enough. I despise him, loathe him," he spat out.

"I'm sorry, Alex," Sarah said in a strangled voice. "I should have fought harder."

"And what, wound up dead? You are a good mom. You've sacrificed so much to give Nick and me a good life."

They'd had this conversation many times over the years. To a certain degree, his brother was right. Alex and his mom did share a special closeness that Nick wasn't a part of. They were bonded through trauma. Nick was too young to remember what their father was like. He was only three when Enzo left. Alex and his mom did their best to keep Nick from suffering the bruises and scars they lived with.

Sarah exhaled. "I thought I was doing the right thing keeping the truth about Enzo away from Nick. Your grandfather agreed. We didn't want him to have to live with the memories you and I share, but I can see now that was wrong."

"We've both tried to talk to him about what Dad was really like. He doesn't want to listen."

She glanced toward the guesthouse. "There can't be another incident with your brother. I won't let another member of the Jackson family be hurt here."

The way she spoke, the tone of her voice, there was something more. The story she'd shared wasn't that simple, leaving Alex with an uneasy feeling in his gut. There was more to her story, but seeing the lines of tension across her forehead, he wasn't going to demand any more from her that night.

Sarah pushed herself up from the table. "I'm going to bed. Today was…."

"Not what any of us expected."

"Not even close. I'd hoped—I don't know what I was hoping for, but I couldn't have imagined this would happen. All I can do is start over tomorrow."

"Try to get some sleep."

She gave him a weary smile. "You too."

Alex swapped out his tea for a glass of whiskey after his mom left. He wandered out onto the patio hoping the cool night air might help soothe his mind.

Pavia told him her dad was forced to leave, and now he knew it was because of his dad. Anthony wasn't the first person who'd been run off the estate for trying to interfere. Too many workers quit until his grandfather demanded Enzo leave. That wasn't the reason, though. The last straw was when Enzo's rage almost killed Sarah and left Alex with broken bones for trying to defend his mother.

He closed his eyes trying to block out the memory of his grandfather weeping at his bedside at the hospital. Antonio was a proud, confident man, but that day he withered under the disapproving glare of the hospital staff. His grandfather had been sure he could rein in his son's behavior, and he'd paid the price for his certainty.

Alex took another swig from his glass, letting the smoky liquid settle in his stomach. A shadow in the guesthouse caught his eye, and he turned his mind away from his troubled memory. A fresh wave of frustration with his brother washed over him. He'd pictured a much different welcome for Pavia Jackson. Alex hoped being a good neighbor would open the door to perhaps convincing her to sell the Brothers Block to him before the five-year limit. He wasn't sure how he was going to stand watching someone else farm the land he'd coveted for so long. Nick had made his task much harder. If he were in Pavia's shoes, he wouldn't want to have anything to do with his family. Hell, after what just happened, even in his own shoes he resented his family after tonight. No matter how hard he tried, he couldn't seem to escape his father's legacy, and now Nick was doing his best to keep Enzo's memory alive, completely ignoring how much pain it caused them.

The lights went out in the guesthouse, and Alex sighed. Tomorrow he'd figure out how to make amends. He hoped he could get Pavia to look at him with those big brown eyes with something other than disdain.

CHAPTER *Three*

RUNNING HER hand over the silky soft sheets on the king-sized bed, Pavia had to admit it was much nicer waking up in the Contis' guesthouse than on the floor in the cottage. She wandered into the small kitchen that was still twice the size of the one in the cottage and made herself a cup of coffee. As tempting as it was to climb back under the covers, there was too much that needed to get done, starting with finding a contractor.

She sipped her coffee, staring at the cobalt blue water in the large rectangular swimming pool through the living room window. Pavia eyed the rolling hills that surrounded her. There were no snowcapped mountains in the distance to admire. In fact, there was no snow at all. A shiver of excitement ran through her. Budbreak would come weeks earlier in this warmer climate.

Her phone rang, and Pavia smiled at the familiar face on the caller ID.

"I've been waiting, but I couldn't stand it anymore, so I called," her brother said.

"Sorry I didn't call yesterday. Things were a little… intense when I got here."

"What happened?" Robert could always tell when something was wrong, no matter how chipper Pavia tried to sound.

"It's complicated. Don't say anything to Dad. I don't want him to get upset. He's already worried enough that I decided to move here." She told Robert about the cottage being ransacked and her first encounters with Sarah, Alex, and Nick.

"What the hell?"

Pavia held the phone away from her ear while he let out a stream of expletives.

"You know if you need me, I'll come down and help," he said when he finished his rant.

She sighed. "You've got your own farm to run. It's going to be fine. I'm just feeling overwhelmed right now and wanted to hear your voice."

"Seriously, Pavi, are you okay? This is a lot to handle."

"I'll admit I'm fighting feeling overwhelmed and… confused. But I just got here, and once I've had some time to get settled—"

"What do you mean, confused?"

"The Contis weren't what I expected, and I'm learning more of Dad's story."

"I still can't believe what happened. I wish I could have been there when you found out about the will and everything else."

"Remember how I told you Dad had to leave because there was a fight? The fight was about Mrs. Conti."

Robert let out a low whistle. "Wow, that's a pretty important detail Dad left out."

"There's more. Mrs. Conti's sons don't know."

"And now you're supposed to keep the secret?"

"She asked me not to tell. I don't—" She exhaled. "There's a lot of history to untangle here."

"You need to sage the cottage before you move in."

Pavia laughed. "You might be right."

Once she ended her call with her brother, she jumped in the shower and dressed quickly, eager to get a start on the day.

Alex waved to her from the french doors off the kitchen as she approached. "Good morning, you're just in time. Coffee's ready."

"Thanks, I already had some. I want to get down to the cottage. I have a lot to do today."

"Melinda just pulled out a batch of her lemon blueberry muffins," he said. "Wait a minute, and I'll grab some for you to take with you."

Alex was wearing a pair of dark chinos and a blue button-down shirt with the sleeves rolled up to his elbows. It was a casual outfit, and yet he still looked more like a polished business owner than a farmer. A handsome executive, Pavia noted, following Alex into the kitchen.

"It's early. I wasn't sure if anyone would be up," she said.

"Early mornings are the only way I can get anything done. Once the tasting rooms open, there's usually something that comes up. That or a million other little fires I have to put out that wreak havoc on my schedule for the rest of the day."

"You have two tasting rooms, is that right?"

"Three, one here on the estate, one in Seneca, and one in Napa."

Pavia shook her head. "I'm glad we've never had to manage anything on that scale."

"You just have a tasting room at the winery?"

"We do. It's not open very often. We usually sell out with the wine club, so we rarely have it open for anything other than private tasting events. That's one thing I'm looking forward to, being able to pour for customers and see their expression when they try what I've created. I'll finally have the chance to use my own techniques and methods."

Alex set his cup down and leaned his elbows on the countertop. "What techniques and methods?"

"I'm planning to introduce biodynamic methods."

He groaned. "Great, so you're going to pray to some goddess or moon deity for a good harvest?"

Pavia scowled. "That's a really dismissive and uneducated attitude."

"Burying cow horns won't make better wine, and astrology isn't going to make better wine."

"Using cow horns along with other natural elements to create an herbal pesticide and following the stars like farmers have done for centuries to know when to plant, prune, and harvest is a naturopathic approach that respects our planet."

"Yeah, okay, sure."

She bristled. "I have a lot I need to do today, and it doesn't include arguing with you, so I'd better get going."

Alex finished putting the muffins into a bag and held it out to her. "I didn't mean to upset you. I just don't think what you're doing is practical."

"Maybe not on the scale of Conti Vineyards, or my father's, but fifteen acres is the perfect size to try."

A strange look passed over his face before he said quietly, "You're right. The Brothers Block is just the right size to try something new."

Alex got up and poured her another coffee in a to-go cup. "Here, I know you said you already had a cup, but…." He shrugged.

She took the cup from his hand and backed toward the door. "Thanks."

One minute Alex was friendly, the next defensive. Right now, she wanted to focus on getting her house in order. She could deal with getting the emotions he stirred in her sorted later.

Instead of using the Gator to get back to the cottage, Pavia walked down the access road through the vines Alex had driven her up the night before. The dew was quickly evaporating as the sun rose higher. She took in the ground under her feet, noting the dryness of the soil and the wild clover growing between the rows. Pavia knew she'd reached her property when she saw the first dark pink rosebush at the end of the row. The bushes were bare now, but small, swollen buds on the stems showed signs that the flowers had had enough of their winter rest and were getting ready to bloom again. She swallowed the lump that formed in her throat, picturing her dad planting them for the mother he never knew. Pavia's grandmother died giving birth to her son, leaving Henry to raise Anthony on his own. Her dad left Seneca an orphan to make his way alone in an unfamiliar place.

Leaning against the hood of her truck, she nibbled at a muffin and sipped coffee while staring at the cottage. Its neglected state renewed her anger. Squinting at the roof, she began to plan. It seemed that the terra-cotta tiles were holding up well, but she had a feeling that there were bound to be issues lurking beneath the surface. Thinking about her father's mistreatment brought on a wave of determination. She'd make sure she restored the house to the condition it was in when he'd left. When he showed Pavia the pictures of the house he grew up in, there was so much pride in his voice. She wanted to ensure he'd have that same pride if he ever saw it again. She envisioned pink pansies and geraniums in the planter boxes, contrasting nicely with the blue-gray trim. Pavia tilted her head, narrowing her eyes to study the paint on the trim and planter boxes. It was the same shade of blue as Alex's eyes.

"Stop it," she muttered. She had come to Seneca to chase her dreams, and Alex Conti was not one of them.

A faded green vintage truck with a Matsui Construction logo on the side pulled up alongside hers. An older man with salt-and-pepper hair got out from the driver's side, and a taller, younger version of him emerged from the passenger seat. The older man, whom she guessed was of Japanese descent, walked up to Pavia with a broad smile, offering a handshake.

"I'd know you anywhere. You look like your father," he said, pumping her hand.

The younger version of the man smiled sheepishly behind him. "Introduce yourself, Dad. She has no idea who you are."

The man threw his head back and laughed. "My son is right. I've forgotten my manners. I'm George Matsui, and this is my son, Sam."

"It's nice to meet you." The laugh lines around his eyes spoke to a life well lived, and his smile was infectious. She looked from father to son. "Um, how can I help you?"

"We're here to help you," Mr. Matsui said. "Sarah Conti called last night. Let me tell you, that's a call I never thought I would get, and to be honest, one I wouldn't be interested in taking. But when she told me Anthony's daughter needed help, I said of course I would come." He put his hands on his hips and shook his head. "It took a lot of guts for Sarah to call. I'll give you that."

Pavia had a lot of questions, but she started with the easiest one first. "You knew my father?"

Mr. Matsui's smile grew. "Anthony and I were best friends growing up. We worked in the field together, played on the same baseball team. We were thick as thieves." Then his smile fell, and his eyes clouded over. "It was a sad day when he left," he said, his voice breaking.

Sam patted his father's shoulder.

Mr. Matsui smiled at her again. "Let's look at the house, and we'll figure out where we want to start."

Pavia couldn't decide if she should be grateful for or irritated by Sarah's interference. She decided to be thankful for now and work on boundaries with her later.

After a tour of the house and the barn with Mr. Matsui and his son, Pavia's head was spinning with the list of repairs that were needed. Plumbing, electrical, hot water heater, and furnace—the scope of work was more than she'd originally thought and meant she'd be staying in the Contis' guesthouse longer than she wanted. While Mr. Matsui made phone calls to schedule an electrician and order a new furnace, Sam approached Pavia.

"Were you planning on keeping the kitchen cabinets?" he asked.

"I don't know. I haven't thought about it."

"I think my grandfather made them." Sam ran his hands over one door. "I'll ask my dad if he remembers. They're in excellent condition. You just need to refinish them."

The Shaker-style cabinets were clearly made by a master artisan. "If your grandfather made the cabinets, I definitely want to keep them."

"Thank you. That means a lot to me. My family was here for a generation before the war and internment. When my grandfather came back, most folks in the valley wouldn't hire him. The Contis were one of the first families to give him any work. If I remember the story right, working on the cottage was the first job he got when he came back."

"Wow." Pavia looked at the cottage with a new appreciation. "I thought my family were the only outcasts."

"Japanese families farmed some of the first vineyards in the valley. Many didn't come back after the war, and it certainly wasn't easy for the ones that did. Antonio and his father did a lot for the community. But my dad was telling me on the way over here that Sarah's husband didn't have the same attitude as his father and grandfather."

"What he said about being surprised that Sarah called him. Do you know why they haven't spoken all these years?" Pavia asked, even though she could guess the answer.

Sam shared his father's smile. Taller with broad shoulders and muscled arms, he reflected the handsome young man his father must have been in his youth.

"My dad just said he couldn't forgive any of the Contis for what happened to your father. Both my mom and dad said that they couldn't understand how Sarah could have married Enzo."

Poor Sarah, Pavia wanted to say something, to set the record straight, but Sarah had asked her not to tell.

"There are a lot of terrible memories in this valley."

"It's good that you're here to make some new ones," Sam said.

Mr. Matsui approached them, rubbing his hands together. "The electrician will be here tomorrow. Sam, let's head back into town and pick up a new hot water heater, and we can get started on the plumbing today."

"Thank you so much, Mr. Matsui—"

"Please call me George," he said.

"George, I can't thank you enough."

"Like I said, anything for Anthony's daughter. How is your dad?"

"He's wonderful, and I know he would love to hear from you, but"—her eyes darted toward the cottage—"I would appreciate it if you didn't say anything about the damage to the house. I don't want to have him worry."

George squinted up at the Conti villa and turned to Pavia, his lips pressed into a thin line. "I understand."

"Thank you."

Pavia pulled out her phone and called her dad, handing the phone to George. She stood by, watching with Sam while his father reconnected with hers.

"This means a lot to my dad, thank you," he said.

"Please, I'm the one who is grateful. I thought I was going to have to spend my day calling around trying to find a contractor, and you guys show up on my doorstep. I'm overwhelmed with how much work there is, but I am relieved now that you're here."

Sam grinned at her. "Don't worry, we've got your back."

GEORGE AND Sam left to get supplies and would be back in a few hours to get started on the work. They'd have to tear out some walls to replace the wiring under the original lathe and plaster and add outlets to bring the house up to code. New drywall was another repair Pavia hadn't expected. She stripped off her sweater on her way back into the cottage. Her new home was considerably warmer than Blue Ridge, and the sunlight streaming through the windows felt good against her skin. She entered the additional repairs George had reviewed with her into a spreadsheet she'd created the night before. She realized her savings would take a hit after the repairs and updates. Yes, she had millions thanks to Antonio, but he'd specified that money to go toward the vineyard and creating a winery. She could use it for the work on the barn, not the house.

Wandering into the kitchen, Pavia took another look at the cabinets. Now that she knew the story about Sam's grandfather, she had a deeper appreciation for his work. She traced the delicate light grapevine inlay against the darker walnut. The cabinets needed a good cleaning. Otherwise they showed little signs of wear. The faded yellow linoleum countertops needed to be replaced, and a tile backsplash would be a nice touch. Pavia could picture pale green walls against the dark wood cabinets with white countertops and white subway tiles for the backsplash.

Inspired to bring her vision to life, Pavia found a soft rag and some wood polish in the cleaning supplies Melinda had left behind and wiped away the dust and grime on the upper cupboards. She scrubbed from the top shelf to the bottom of each cabinet, making sure it was spotless before moving on to the lower ones. It felt good being productive. She'd had enough of having her home torn apart. It was time to take care of what was left.

The physical work helped ease some of her restlessness and gave her time to think about everything that had happened since she'd arrived. No one and nothing were what she'd expected. Pavia felt sick at the thought of someone coming into her home and causing so much destruction. She'd ordered a wireless alarm system for the cottage first thing when she woke up that morning. The rag stilled in her hand. She'd come away from the reading of Antonio's will thinking Alex would be the one she'd butt heads with, and his attitude that morning about her approach to farming irritated the hell out of her, but not once did she feel unsafe around him. Yes, she'd accused him of damaging the cottage. But when she looked into those stormy blue eyes, ones that stared directly into hers without flinching, she knew this wasn't a man who was reckless. She continued wiping down the shelves, trying to push her conflicted feelings about Alex aside.

When Pavia reached the final cabinet, the last drawer resisted her efforts and wouldn't open. She grunted in frustration, grasped the handle with both hands, and pulled with a quick jerk. The drawer flew from the cabinet, the force sending both it and Pavia to the floor. She shook her head and laughed at her antics. Then she looked down to see a small package in the drawer wrapped in brown paper and tied with twine. All the air left her lungs when she saw her name written on the top. She looked over her shoulder, but there was no one there. Was this some kind of prank? Had whoever caused the damage to the house left it here?

Pavia sat up, cradling the drawer in her lap. Her hands were shaking so badly she almost dropped the package when she pulled it out. She turned it over, looking at the neatly tied twine and taped edges before turning it over again to study the handwriting on the wrapping. Slowly, she pulled the string, and the paper fell away. There was another layer of waxed paper underneath to unwrap that revealed a small book with a worn leather cover.

She held it between her palms for a moment, breathing deeply, as if that might slow her racing pulse, before she turned it over in her hands. Bringing it to her nose, Pavia took in the scent of leather, old paper, and wine. The faint scent of grapes brought a smile to her lips. Fanning through the pages, she stopped at one marked with a faded circle dotted with splotches. She stopped to caress the pale purple wine stains before she continued to thumb through the book. As she flipped through the pages of old, worn handwriting, a black-and-white photograph peeked out from between them.

"Oh!" she whispered as she gently pulled it out.

For the first time, she saw a picture of her grandfather and Antonio Conti together. It was an image of the two young men squinting against the sunlight, their arms around each other, and huge grins on their faces. The image became blurred, and Pavia wiped at her eyes, careful not to let any wetness touch the image. Henry's dark skin and Antonio's pale face were covered in dirt and sweat. They had their rifles slung over their shoulders and their helmets sitting haphazardly on their heads. St. Peter's Basilica stood in the background. She stared at the picture, seeing her grandfather as a young man. She'd never thought of him that way. He'd been this larger-than-life figure that she always imagined as being the same age as her dad was now. Not a young man who'd faced death and destruction and was still smiling in the sun. Having met Antonio, she recognized the younger version of him. Alex had the same build and shared his grandfather's smile. What had happened that day to make them so happy and carefree? She took a deep breath and turned the book back to the first page.

July 7, 1943

I can barely contain my excitement that I will soon see my homeland. Today, the sergeant briefed us. We will be part of the first assault on Italy, Operation Husky. We sail from Tunisia and land in Sicily in two days.

My friend Henry managed to find a camera, film, and this journal. Henry has become a master of procurement for our unit. While many of the men don't appreciate any of Henry's talents, I'm grateful to have such a friend. He gave me the camera and journal tonight, explaining that he thought I might like to record my first visit to Italy to share with my family when I return. Henry is determined that we will return home.

I've learned that family is very important to him. An orphan from Mississippi, he always asks about my family. I share every letter I get from home, and I think Henry cherishes them as much as I do.

She closed the book and held it to her chest. A small sob escaped her. Her dad never said much about his father's time in the military. Henry's life was always a mystery to her. Until that moment, having met Antonio only once, he was still an enigma. Now she was reading his words. She shook her head and blew out a shaky breath, running her hand over the cover. Why would he leave his journal behind wrapped up with her name on it? How could Antonio betray his best friend, someone he'd faced death with, and send Henry's son away? She frowned at the book. Did he leave this for her, trying to explain? Was this his way of making amends or trying to say that he regretted what happened with her dad?

Blinking back tears of frustration, Pavia rewrapped the book, tracing her name with the tip of her finger. She didn't see herself as a vengeful person, but she struggled to find it in her heart to forgive what had happened to her father. Maybe with time, but not today. The weight of her questions and uncertainty made it difficult to pull herself to her feet. After setting the journal on the counter, she carefully put the drawer back in its slot.

George and Sam returned just as she was carefully tucking the journal into her bag. The rest of the day flew by while she worked with the Matsui men, and her discovery was at the back of her mind the entire time. Together, they started on demolition. They quickly filled the dumpster that had been dropped off with debris that Sarah and Melinda helped her clear out the day before, along with what they had demolished that day.

"You know, I think I can repair this," Sam said, crouched down in front of a badly damaged Craftsman-style rocking chair.

"Really?" Pavia brightened. "That would be amazing if you could."

"Construction is the family business, but I have a small custom furniture business on the side." He picked up the chair and set it carefully in the back of the Matsui Construction truck, then pulled off his work gloves and tucked them into his back pocket. "What's your plan with this place? Are you going to keep what's planted or start over with something new?"

"Oh no, I'd never tear out those vines unless I had to." She pointed toward the vineyard. "That's legendary rootstock. The only thing I'm going to change is the fertilization methods. And the wine production."

George came out of the house with a notepad under one arm and a pencil behind his ear. "The electrician will be here the day after tomorrow and the roofer next week. There's no insulation in the attic, so we'll have to take care of that too."

Pavia groaned, reaching into her back pocket for the check she'd already written. "Hopefully, this is enough to get started. I realized I haven't asked you about your rates or how much—"

George held his hand up. "You're getting the family discount, and the Contis have already taken care of paying for all the major repairs." He took the check out of her hand. "This is plenty to cover the rest of what's needed in the house. I'll work up a budget for the work you want done on the barn tonight, and we can talk about it when Sam and I come back tomorrow."

"I—" Alex had said he wasn't responsible for the damage to the cottage, so it didn't feel right to have them pay for the repairs. Plus, she didn't like the idea of being beholden to the Contis.

George put his hand on her shoulder, his gaze filled with understanding. "You've had an eventful twenty-four hours filled with a lot of unexpected"—his mouth turned down—"events. We'll take it one day at a time, okay?"

Pavia exhaled. "Thank you."

He nodded, his smile returning. "We're happy you're here. Hopefully, we can convince your dad to return for a visit one day."

"Thank you, both of you. I would have been lost without your help today."

She waved at the Matsuis' retreating truck, feeling tired and overwhelmed but happy. She'd begun her new life in Seneca today. All day, Pavia had expected Sarah to make an appearance, but it wasn't until a few minutes after George and Sam left for the day that she showed up on the Gator.

"I just wanted to check and see how the day went," she said with a worried look at the dumpster.

"George and Sam are amazing. But you didn't have to do this—pay for the repairs, I mean. You didn't do the damage."

A shadow passed over Sarah's expression. "No, but I know who did. I'm sorry, Pavia, but my son Nick is the one responsible."

"Nick, he's the one who did this?"

"I'm afraid so."

"Then he should be the one who apologizes, not you," she said with a slight tremor of anger in her voice.

So it was one of the Contis after all. Pavia hadn't thought about Nick, maybe because she hadn't seen him since she arrived in Seneca.

She thought back to the day in the lawyer's office and the superior look on his face. She was upset at hearing Nick was responsible, but the pinched and drawn look on Sarah's face showed she was more disturbed by her son's actions than Pavia was.

"Thank you for telling me."

Sarah reached for Pavia's hand. "I promise, nothing else like this will happen. I'll make sure Nick behaves."

Pavia gave Sarah's hand a squeeze. "Nick is a grown man. You're not responsible for his actions."

"I'll understand if you want to press charges."

"No, I don't want to do that. We're going to be neighbors. We need to learn how to get along with each other."

A sheen of tears covered Sarah's eyes. "You're a lot like your father. You have a generous heart, Pavia, thank you."

Pavia blew out a shaky breath. Every interaction with the Contis had been so… heavy since she first arrived. She glanced toward her truck, where Antonio's diary was in her bag on the front seat. Should she tell them what she'd found? What about Sarah? Maybe she should tell her? Everything was too new and in too much upheaval. She'd decide about what to do after she had some time to read the journal and get settled in. Tracing Antonio's words with her finger, she had sensed the history of the place. Could she create a future when the past was still present?

CHAPTER *Four*

ALEX CAUGHT the shadow of movement at the guesthouse. He'd been distracted all day thinking about Pavia and fighting the urge to go to the cottage for… for what? He wasn't needed there. It was just his own desire to spend more time with Pavia that had distracted him all day. Over the past few days, she'd barely spoken to him. Alex shoved the keyboard on his desk away with a disgusted grunt. He'd been an ass when she told him about her plan to use biodynamic farming. The truth was, he'd been looking to incorporate some elements of biodynamics into his plan to convert the Brothers Block to organic production. He'd responded like a child throwing a tantrum because Pavia had the toy he wanted. Instead of working in the Brothers Block, he was at his desk, his days filled with endless spreadsheets and meetings. There were new releases to juggle and contracts to negotiate with distributors. Since his grandfather died, the family had received several very impressive offers to sell, but that was out of the question. The Conti vineyard would stay in the family for at least one more generation.

Alex steepled his fingers, his gaze straying toward the cottage. With the Matsuis' help, progress was happening quickly. His mom told him that morning Pavia planned on moving in by next week.

"It can't be ready yet," he blurted out when his mother gave him the news.

"Of course not, but Pavia thinks it will be livable."

Sarah told him the key systems were in place, so she'd at least have hot water and could plug something in without blowing a fuse. Considering her reluctance to stay at the guesthouse at all, he was thankful that she'd stayed long enough that she wouldn't be taking cold showers.

Before he could second-guess himself, Alex walked out of his office and stopped in the kitchen to grab a bottle of wine and two glasses before heading over to the guesthouse.

Pavia's eyes grew wide when she opened the door.

He held up the bottle. "I heard you're making good progress on the house. I thought after all the hard work you've put in, you might like to take a break."

She stepped back, eyeing him cautiously. "I was just about to eat. I think there's enough to share, if you want."

He walked in, and the scent of garlic and white wine filled his nose.

"I'm just reheating the pasta your mom brought over," she said, heading toward the kitchen.

Alex sat down at the bar, frowning at the bottle he'd grabbed. The Merlot would be too heavy. He got up and started looking through the wine rack built in next to the pantry cabinet.

"I already put a bottle of white in the wine fridge," Pavia said, dividing the pasta onto two plates.

Alex nodded and took out the Conti Monastery White Blend. "Have you had this before?" he asked, opening the bottle.

"No, I haven't. I was wondering about the name."

He swapped out the glasses he'd brought for two suitable for white wine. "We made this from the grapes that were planted in part of the vineyard that was a monastery. It was the first parcel of land my family purchased from the monks."

Pavia placed the plates on the island and sat down next to the seat Alex had returned to. Resting her chin on her palm, she watched him open the bottle. "It's always interesting what inspires a name, don't you think?"

"I never considered the meaning behind Brothers in Arms until we learned you were going to be at the reading of Grandad's will. Battlefield Red, Campaign Syrah—your dad was paying tribute to his father's service." He pushed a glass toward her. "Let me know what you think."

Pavia sniffed and swirled, and Alex felt his body react. He'd seen hundreds of people perform the same act, men and women, and he'd never responded the way he did watching her. She lifted her glass, inhaling deeply, her eyes flickering to him, her lips curving into a slight smile before she took a sip.

"Sémillion, Sauv Blanc." She wrinkled her nose. "But not Muscadelle?"

"Colombard."

Pavia took another sip. "Nice, I didn't know you grew Colombard here."

"We don't. It didn't do as well as we'd hoped, so we replanted with more Muscadelle last year. You're drinking the last of a failed experiment."

She shook her head. "I would hardly call this a failed experiment. This is a good blend, Alex. The one thing you can't control is terroir. The dirt, the weather, Mother Nature is an independent woman. You can't tell her what to do."

Alex twisted the stem of his glass between his fingers. He nodded in agreement.

"I don't mean to be rude, but I'm starving," Pavia said, digging into her pasta.

Alex hadn't eaten either. He'd been too busy trying to fill his grandfather's shoes and not wonder what Pavia was doing at the cottage and in the Brothers Block to remember to eat. He inhaled, and his mouth watered. For a few minutes, the only sound in the room was forks scraping on plates. When he finished, he pushed his plate away with a satisfied sigh.

"I guess you were hungrier than you thought."

He laughed. "Yeah, I guess so." Realizing she'd split her portion with him, he asked, "Did you get enough?"

"Yeah, this was perfect."

"My mom said you're making good progress at the cottage," he said while refilling their glasses.

"The Matsuis are amazing. I'm sure I'd still be interviewing contractors instead of getting ready to move back in if it weren't for them."

"They're good people."

"Sam mentioned you went to school together."

Alex took a sip of wine, allowing himself to take Pavia's words to heart and appreciate the suitable notes of melon, apple, and sage. She was right. It wasn't a failed experiment.

"We've known each other since kindergarten, but by the time we were in high school, we didn't really hang out much."

Pavia was looking at him with a curiosity that made him want to squirm in his seat. How could he explain that for all their wealth and philanthropy, he and his family were seen as pariahs in Seneca? That they still lived with the damage his father had caused? People didn't want their children to hang out with the Conti brothers. Who knew? They could be just as volatile as their father.

"It's… our family has a complicated history here. My grandfather was well respected here, but not my father. There are some people who…." He sighed heavily. "I guess you could say we're guilty by association."

"I'm sorry, Alex."

"So am I."

Their eyes locked. Alex saw the understanding there and realized it was the first time he'd ever felt… seen. Her apology wasn't from pity, but understanding.

"What about you?" he asked to take the focus away from him. "Did you have a lot of friends in high school?"

"Blue Ridge is a small town. Everyone knows everybody. We all got along out of necessity, for the most part, because there weren't that many of us."

"Your family farm is pretty isolated, isn't it?" Alex asked.

Pavia nodded. "It's the easternmost vineyard in the state. In the top region of the Yakima Reservation."

"Can I ask, how was it possible that your family owns land within tribal lands?"

Her eyes brightened. "That's a great question. It's part of my family history. In 1887, my grandfather's family purchased land when the Dawes Act was enacted. They were Swedish immigrants, the Olssons, wheat farmers. It was quite the scandal when my grandpa fell in love with my grandmother. She was Yakima. There wasn't a lot of intermarriage then, and they ran away and eloped. When my mom married my dad, the land passed to them, and someday it will pass on to Robert."

"Does that bother you?"

Pavia wrinkled her nose. "No, not at all. If I wanted to stay in Blue Ridge, Robert would split the farm with me. But I've always wanted to build something of my own. I'd shared that with your grandfather when he came to speak at my alma mater just a few months before he passed away."

Alex jerked back in surprise. "You met my grandfather?"

"I thought you knew. I went to hear him speak when he gave a lecture at Washington State University. He approached me afterwards and said he'd recognize Anthony Jackson's daughter anywhere. He asked me to give him a tour of the viticulture school. We spent the afternoon together."

How could he? How could Antonio spend one afternoon with Pavia and decide to give away his future? His eyes narrowed, and he glared at her.

"It's pretty convenient. After you spent time with my grandfather, you come into a very nice inheritance. Exactly what did you say to him?"

Pavia's eyes widened as she jumped up from the stool. He could see her breath quicken. "How dare you? How dare you suggest—get out!"

The minute he said it, Alex knew he'd made a mistake. "Pavia, I—"

"Don't you dare say you didn't mean it. You wouldn't have said it if there wasn't some part of you that believed I'd conned your grandfather." She pointed a shaking finger at the door. "I mean it, get out."

Alex stood up slowly, his mind racing, trying to figure out how he could make amends. Looking at Pavia, he knew she was in no mood to listen to him.

He felt numb walking out of the guesthouse. His steps were heavy with self-loathing. He stopped in the house just long enough to grab his wallet and keys, and fifteen minutes later, he pulled up in front of The Vyne. He avoided the restaurant, entering through the back. The kitchen was winding down for the evening. It was relatively quiet, with sous chefs putting food away while the dishwashers worked in rhythm, spraying dishes and filling the racks before pushing them through the industrial dishwasher. Brandon came through the swinging doors between the kitchen and the dining room. His eyebrows lifted when he spotted Alex, and he gestured him to his office. Alex nodded to the staff as he walked past.

As soon as he was in the office, Brandon closed the door and leaned his six-foot-plus frame against the door, folding his arms in front of him. "What's wrong?"

Alex ran his hand through his hair and blew out a shaky breath. "I fucked up."

Brandon was his best friend. They'd shared their biggest fears and their secret goals with each other. Alex was embarrassed as hell to admit what he'd just done. When he did, the scowl on Brandon's face made the band around his chest grow even tighter.

"Yeah, you're right, you totally fucked up. What were you thinking, Alex?"

"I wasn't. I just… reacted. It feels like every day I find out about another lie, another secret Grandad kept from me. Mom too. I found out that Anthony Jackson left Seneca because he got into a fight with my dad trying to defend my mom."

Brandon opened the door and informed his staff that he was available if they needed him. They responded with a chorus of "Yes, Chef." Before sitting down behind his desk, he unbuttoned the top buttons on his chef's jacket. He scratched his full beard, his dark green eyes studying Alex. This wasn't a surprise. Brandon was a thinker. He could make a quick call when he needed to, but if he had the time, he'd turn the problem over in his head.

Alex clasped his hands, waiting.

"Let's start with: you know your grandad and your mom never wanted to cause you pain. Secrets are… they're secrets for a reason. I wonder if some people keep secrets as a way to protect the people they love and themselves. I read this book once that talked about how people think they're keeping secrets, but all the time they're unconsciously giving clues, hints. It comes out." Brandon sighed. "About Pavia, I don't know what to tell you. You're going to have to figure this out yourself."

Nothing Brandon was telling him wasn't true, just hard to swallow. He pushed himself up. "Thanks, I should get back."

"Naw, there's nothing you can do tonight. Why don't you stay? We'll play some pool, and one of my distributors just left a very nice bottle of scotch."

Alex dropped back down into his seat. "That sounds like a better plan than not sleeping and kicking myself for being such an ass."

"I gotta say, Alex. She's not going away, so you'd better figure this shit out."

No, Pavia wasn't going away, and now that he'd met her, Alex didn't want her to. He'd sought her out tonight to get to know her better. He learned more than he wanted to.

Sprawled out on Brandon's couch with a slight buzz from what turned out to be an excellent bottle of scotch from the supplier, Alex could finally let go of the tension from the day. He pictured his grandad with Pavia. Antonio was a charmer. Alex grinned in the dark, imagining him doing his full courtly gentleman act. He realized he was happy Pavia had gotten to see him that way. If only he could have had that chance with Henry or Anthony. He was jealous. In some ways, Pavia knew his family better than he did, or at least their family history. When his eyes finally drifted closed, Alex knew what he wanted to share with Pavia to make amends.

"JERK," PAVIA muttered under her breath, shoving her clothes into her backpack. Under no circumstances was she willing to spend another night in the Contis' guesthouse. It didn't matter what condition the cottage was in, she'd make do. She double-checked and then checked again to make sure the guesthouse was spotless before she loaded her stuff into her truck. She wasn't about to give Alex any excuse to accuse her of stealing anything.

She hesitated, her hand on the handle on the door of her truck, eyeing the main house. She shouldn't leave without saying goodbye to Sarah. With a sigh, she pushed herself away from the cold metal and trudged toward the front door like a petulant child.

"Get a grip, girl. It's not Sarah's fault her son is a jerk," she said to herself.

The doorbell rang. Even the tone sounded snooty, her hearing tinged with her anger.

Sarah looked at her in surprise when she opened the door. "Pavia, why are you at the front door?" She glanced over her shoulder with a frown, then back to her. "Why didn't you come through the back?"

What should she say? *I got into a fight with your son, and now I'm leaving?*

"I just wanted to let you know I'm moving into the cottage. The repairs are far enough along... I don't want to intrude on your hospitality any longer."

Sarah's face fell. "Are you sure? You're welcome to stay. You can't leave before the Matsuis can complete the repairs."

"They're far enough along that I can move back in now."

"I was looking forward to... hoping... would you come back for dinner on Friday?"

"I—" Pavia sighed. "Sure, I can do that."

She didn't have the heart to say no. She could put up with Alex for one evening if she had to, and Nick still hadn't made an appearance, so he probably wouldn't be there. If she were lucky, it would be just her and Sarah sitting at the kitchen counter. Maybe she could get her to open up more about her past, not just with her father, but Pavia wanted to know more about her life with Enzo.

On impulse, she leaned forward and pressed a quick kiss on Sarah's cheek. "Thank you for everything, giving me a place to stay and for trying to help. I appreciate it, I really do, but…it's time for me to go."

Sarah stood in the doorway, her hand raised in farewell, when Pavia drove away.

Yes, a lot of progress had been made at the cottage, but when she walked in and flipped the light switch, she faced a bare room lit with a single light bulb and a house with no heat. It wasn't cold enough to make it uncomfortable. If she had any firewood, Pavia would have been able to make a fire. Standing in front of the fireplace, though, she realized she wasn't even sure if it was in working condition.

At least the stove worked. But she didn't have any tea.

"Fine," she spat out before she realized she didn't have a teakettle, dishes, or silverware either.

Uttering a stream of curses, she grabbed her handbag and keys before heading back out to her truck. It was a thirty-minute drive to the nearest town that was large enough that it had a big-box store. Three hours later, she came back to the cottage, the cab of her truck piled with bags. She sent a silent note of thanks to whoever figured out how to put mattresses in boxes and that the store had a decent selection to choose from. They also had a grocery section, so with one stop she had enough to take her time while she furnished the rest of the house and could visit some of the antique stores in the area to find the vintage pieces that she preferred.

Finally, with a warm cup of chamomile tea in her hands, she wandered around the cottage, admiring the work George and Sam had completed. The original floors were refinished and satiny smooth beneath her sock-covered feet. New drywall replaced the damaged plaster and was ready for paint. White subway tiles in the bathroom had been grouted, and a new toilet installed. The only thing missing was the vanity and sink. Having the kitchen sink play double duty was a small price to pay for being in her own space.

Unpacking her purchases, Pavia realized, for the first time since she'd arrived, she could relax. This was her home. She didn't have to tread lightly, worrying about putting something away in the wrong place or breaking a glass. She took a sip from the new mug she'd bought. She'd been excited to have the vintage china that she'd hoped to find when she arrived instead of shards. Instead, she settled for a box of basic white china until she could find something that suited her taste. With a scowl, she took another sip, replaying her fight with Alex. She scoffed at his audacity, suggesting she would steal from him. There was nothing she wanted from the Contis. They were the takers, not her.

The night had slipped into the morning. Glancing at her phone, Pavia realized it was past 1:00 am. She added making her miss a good night of sleep to her list of grievances with Alex, and wandered into the larger of the two rooms, her new bedroom. Her frustration eased seeing her mother's quilt spread on the mattress.

She got ready for bed and climbed under the covers. Her fingers traced the pattern of the stitches on the quilt. It was the last one her mother made before she passed away. Maybe it was the move or spending time with Sarah, but her mom was in her thoughts more than usual. The pain of missing her seemed more acute now than it did when she died. Pavia lost her just when she needed her the most. Navigating the perils of middle school and mean girls without her mother to provide guidance and wisdom still hurt. She ran her hand over the squares of batik fabric. They had picked it out together. Vibrant purple, blue, and green material flowed together perfectly in a traditional nine patch design. Her mother had lovingly embroidered grapevines and appliquéd clusters of grapes and leaves throughout, giving the traditional design a modern twist. When she pulled it around her shoulders, Pavia could pretend she was wrapped in her mother's embrace. Her mother's smell had faded long ago, but the memory remained. She took a deep breath, taking comfort in the scent of memory.

Her father did everything he could to fill the void she left behind, and most days, it was enough. On a night like tonight, nothing could fill that hole in her heart. She moved her hand from the uneven textures of the stitches on the quilt to the smooth, worn leather of the book in her lap. Leaving her own memories behind, she read Antonio's.

July 8, 1943
The first unit shipped from North Africa to Italy yesterday. Henry and I ship out early tomorrow. The reports are the fighting will be fierce, and there will be many casualties.

Despite my fear and dread for the battle ahead, I'm eager to set foot in Italy for the first time. I asked Henry how he felt when we arrived in North Africa. His answer humbled me. He explained that coming to Africa was bittersweet. While my family left Italy, his ancestors were taken by force. I will never forget the haunted look in his eyes as he explained this to me. I will cherish the freedoms we are fighting for.

During our briefing today, one of the men whispered to me, "I hope you remember whose side you're on, greaseball."

Henry was so angry. He wouldn't stop glaring at him. We both know better than to pick a fight. Once again, I'm thankful to have Henry by my side. An immigrant and a black man—we're both outcasts. The battles that we can choose to fight, we have to pick carefully. Some, no matter how brave you are, no matter how much you struggle, even if you're in the right, you can't win.

July 9, 1943

We made land at 10:00 am. It's late now, my watch has stopped, I don't know what time it is, and I don't know if I want to. The death and destruction we saw today! I'm laying on my bedroll too exhausted to climb in. My heart is still beating hard in my chest, not just from dodging bullets. Here I am in a land that was a stranger to me, and yet I feel like I've come home, but home to what? Fascism and carnage. This is my homeland, this isn't home.

Pavia closed the diary. Lying on her back, she held it against her chest, staring up at the ceiling. Her little cottage felt like home, but something was still missing. Lying on her mattress on the floor in her empty bedroom, loneliness engulfed her.

George was furious when he and Sam arrived at the cottage the next morning. An angry scowl replaced his usual easygoing smile the minute he saw the mattress on the floor in her room.

"What happened? What did the Contis do?" he questioned her, his fists clenched at his sides.

"I just… don't want to stay at the guesthouse anymore. Enough work has been done here. I can move in. You said so yourself the other day," she pointed out.

"You still don't have heat."

"I'm from Blue Ridge, remember? We can get snow in April."

"That doesn't mean you have to freeze your ass off in the middle of the night," Sam said.

"I called a chimney sweep this morning to come look at the fireplace. He'll be out later today. If the fireplace is in working condition, I can make do with that. I also picked up a space heater last night in case it gets too cold."

George shook his head, stomping away with a thunderous expression on his face.

"Sorry about Dad." Sam dropped his voice to a whisper. "But between you and me, what really happened?"

"I got into a fight with Alex," Pavia admitted. "I can't stay there when they think I've conned their grandfather."

Sam reared back. "Is that what he said?"

"No, but it's what he implied."

Sam pressed his lips into a thin line.

"Look, it's not like I expected to be welcomed with open arms."

"No, but you shouldn't have to put up with this shit either."

"And that's why I'm home." She swept her arm over the room. "And here to stay."

"I know my dad. He won't leave until you have heat tonight."

"Both of you have been so great. I feel guilty. You must have other projects you should work on."

Sam shook his head. "This means a lot to my dad. He's been slowing down the last couple of years anyway, thinking about retiring. Although between you and me, I don't think he'll ever really retire."

"What about you? Are you taking over the family business?"

Sam looked over his shoulder. Even though it was just the two of them, he still leaned over, speaking in a hushed voice. "I don't want to follow in my father's footsteps. I want to follow in my grandfather's and make custom furniture."

"And your dad doesn't want you to do that?"

"Dad is a practical businessman. I inherited my grandfather's woodworking skills and my mother's artistic heart. It's a combination he has a hard time accepting."

Pavia nodded with understanding. "You're like me. You'd rather forge your own path than follow someone else's."

"Exactly." He grinned at her.

"Sam!" His dad's shout made both of them jump.

"Come on, let's get this cottage together so you don't have to deal with the Contis any more than you have to."

ALEX HADN'T crossed paths with Pavia since he'd run her off. It was strange to miss someone you barely knew, but he did. Before he messed up, he'd been enjoying their conversations. In those few moments where talking with her was easy, he realized it had been a long time since he'd enjoyed being with a woman the way he did with Pavia.

He wasn't a monk. He'd had dates but no long-term girlfriends, no one who lasted more than a few months at a time, a year at most. His relationships never ended in dramatic breakups, but more like a Pét-Nat, starting out with a bright, bubbly fizz and quickly fading into a flat wine. Half the time, the relationships were over before Alex noticed. He'd gotten the "you're too caught up in your work" or "you're so distant" breakup lecture more times than a normal person should. Sure, a few of his dates were only interested in the Conti name or money, but most were women he should have been able to open his heart to, but for some reason he held back.

So how was it that the one woman who'd taken away what he'd always wanted was the person he wanted to share more of himself with? If he could get her to talk to him, he wanted to tell her about the Brothers Block and what he'd been planning, hoping for, with the land his grandfather had given away.

Alex had been locked away in his office all day with orders to review, supply vendors to deal with, and… it was all a lie. He was hiding in his office, avoiding doing what he should have done the night Pavia left—apologize. He forced his gaze away from the cottage and got up from his desk with a sigh.

I'm lonely.

Pavia's presence made the truth as glaringly bright as the morning sun. He had friends and dated occasionally, but he didn't have a life beyond his responsibilities with the family business. Other than his best friend, Brandon, he kept the people he considered friends at arm's length. He'd entered his thirties last year feeling restless and wanting to find the spark, the passion for what he'd always wanted to do—work in the vineyard—again. He thought working in the Brothers Block would help reenergize him.

Working alongside Pavia would. Having someone in my life who shares my passion, my dreams, is the spark I'm looking for.

A piece of land wasn't going to bring back his passion for wine. It wasn't Pavia's fault he didn't have the Brothers Block. He'd directed his anger and frustration with his grandfather toward her, and that wasn't fair.

"Get your shit together," he muttered, leaving his office. He wandered into the kitchen and found his mom piping frosting on a cake that could have been the winning entry on *The Great British Baking Show*. The scent of saffron chicken, freshly baked bread, and white chocolate blueberry cake mingled together to make his mouth water.

"Wow, you're really going all out."

His mother stuck the tip of her tongue out, concentrating on piping delicate curls on the top of the cake. "I want everything to be nice for Pavia," she said without taking her eyes off her task.

Alex leaned against the counter. "I'm sure whatever you do will be fine. You've been bending over backwards to help her. Don't you think you might be going a little overboard?"

Sarah jerked her head up. "I'm trying to make things right, and I like Pavia. I… I owe it to her father to make sure she's okay here."

"She's a grown woman. I'm pretty sure she can take care of herself."

"Of course she can." Sarah frowned. "It's not that. I just—it's hard to explain. When Pavia's father lived here, I wasn't a good"— she shuttered her eyes for a moment—"I wasn't a good friend. Having Anthony's daughter here is giving me a second chance."

"What do you mean you weren't a good friend?"

The color drained from his mother's face. She looked away, blinking rapidly. "I didn't stand by Anthony when I should have."

"Mom, Enzo probably would have beaten you to death if you'd tried," he said in a low, soothing voice.

She drew in a shaky breath and nodded.

Nick sauntered in and frowned as he saw all the food. "I can't believe you're going through with this. I don't know why you had to invite her."

"Because it's the polite thing to do. You've avoided her since she arrived, but Pavia is our neighbor, and I want you to meet her. Maybe that will help you realize that she's a lovely woman, and you'll finally show some remorse for what you did. You will be on your best behavior, Nick," Sarah said, wagging her finger at him.

"Come on, Nick. I'm sure you can behave for one night," Alex added.

"You never give me any credit for anything."

When their father was around, Alex never resented his role as Nick's protector and defender. They were little, and they were a team. Over the years, Nick's assumption that he would always take his side in any argument was wearing on Alex. The pride he used to feel that came from keeping him safe had faded into fearing that his protection may have done more damage than good.

But it wasn't always Alex being the protector. After their father left, there was a time when they could just be boys playing hide-and-seek in the vines and splashing in the swimming pool. Their relationship became strained as they got older. The more responsibility Alex took on, the less interest Nick took in the winery. His brother chose partying over working with their grandfather, which led to Antonio spending more time with Alex and further alienating Nick. It became an unbreakable cycle. Every time Antonio tried to engage with Nick, his brother would point out how Alex was Antonio's favorite. Nick's rejection meant that Alex would spend even more time with his grandfather.

Alex offered an olive branch. "I've been thinking about making some changes at the vineyard, and I could use your help, Nick."

His brother cocked his head with a skeptical look. When had his brother become so distrusting of everyone? Before Nick could respond, the doorbell rang. His mother wiped her hands on her apron, tugging it off, before practically sprinting toward the front hall and returning with Pavia a few moments later.

"I am so happy you're here," she said, ushering her into the kitchen.

Pavia's smile waned when she saw Alex and Nick. She set the two bottles of wine she cradled in her arms on the counter.

"I wasn't sure what you were serving, but I didn't want to come empty-handed," she said to Sarah.

Her voice was soft, but firm and clear. She wore a floral skirt, its shiny material in shades of purple skimming over her hips and matching her purple sweater that looked soft and made her hazel eyes sparkle. Her hair fell past her shoulders in perfect ringlets that Alex had spent way too much time thinking about over the last week.

"We haven't had a chance to introduce ourselves yet," she said, holding out her hand to Nick.

His brother looked down at her outstretched hand and reluctantly shook it. "Welcome to Seneca, Miss Jackson."

His patronizing tone immediately set Alex on alert. He moved closer, glaring at his brother. Pavia's eyes darted between the two of them as she stepped back.

"Thank you," she replied coolly.

Alex watched the scene play out with a sense of dread and the urge to strangle his brother. He wouldn't enjoy dinner without worrying about Nick making some kind of scene. Bracing for the worst, he kept himself positioned as a buffer between Pavia and his brother.

"Thank you for the wine," Alex said, gesturing toward the bottles she'd left on the counter.

He looked admiringly at the two bottles of Brothers in Arms Syrah. It was the vintage that had made her father a legendary figure in the Washington wine industry. Anthony Jackson was one of less than a handful of Black vineyard owners from the over four hundred growers in the state. You couldn't get a bottle at any grocery store the way you could with Conti wines. The wait list for the Brothers in Arms wine club was extensive, and you were lucky if you could get in after ten years. Even with his industry connections and his own family influence, Alex had a hard time procuring a bottle.

Pavia watched him as he opened it, making him as nervous as the first time his grandfather handed him a corkscrew. Grandad had scrutinized his every movement. Alex carefully centered the pin into the pliant cork, and it slipped from its constraints with a soft pop, the bottom shaded a rich purple. He passed it under his nose, catching the first hint of spice and ripe fruit. Pouring the wine into the decanter, he admired the deep plum color as the liquid slid down the sides of the glass. He already knew he was about to experience something special.

Bringing the decanter over to the table, he ignored his brother's insolent glare. Alex set the wine down and hurried to place himself behind Pavia's chair. She hesitated for just a moment, glancing at him over her shoulder, before she slid into her seat. Her hair brushed against the back of his hands, and his gut tightened with a jolt of lust. He longed to reach out and wrap one of the silky spirals around his finger.

Nick's smirk caught his eye. Alex jerked his hands away from the back of the chair and stepped aside. Instead of taking his usual seat next to his brother, he pulled out the chair next to Pavia. Nick raised an eyebrow, his drink hovering at his lips while he watched. Alex was playing with fire, and he didn't care. He wanted to be close to her.

She leaned forward to grasp the stem of her glass and pull it toward her.

"It's wine, in case you were wondering." Nick's smile was malicious, as if he was proud of his pathetic dig at her.

"Sarah, can I do anything to help?" Pavia asked, ignoring Nick while their mother bustled around the kitchen, bringing the food to the table.

"No, thank you, sweetie," Sarah said, placing a large platter of chicken surrounded by rice in front of them. She patted Pavia on the shoulder and took her seat, beaming at them.

It had been a long time since Alex had seen his mother so happy, too long. *This is the first time we've sat at the table as a family since Grandad died.* Why was that, he wondered. Why did they all pretend to be the perfect picture on the postcard when that wasn't what they really were? The image of Pavia with her father and brother on the Brothers in Arms website played through his mind. They probably ate as a family every night. Envy cast a cloud over his heart.

Pavia picked up her wine, and a slight smile played over her lips as the glass hovered for just a second before she took a sip. Fixated on seeing the ritual she practiced, Alex stared, watching her hold the liquid in her mouth for a second and inhale before swallowing. He reached for his own glass and lifted it. The liquid glowed garnet in the light from the windows. He sniffed and sniffed again. Plum, tobacco, and sage— the aromas filled his senses. He closed his eyes and tipped the glass to his lips. Sometimes, you taste a wine that you know the experience of drinking it will become a part of your sense memory. This was one of those wines.

When he opened his eyes, Pavia was watching him, along with everyone else at the table. He held the glass up to the light again, pretending to study the contents, while in reality, he was trying to get his emotions under control. Sometimes tasting wine was less analytical and more about the memory or mood it evoked. This wine reminded him of late summer afternoons walking through the vines with his grandfather, the smell of the woody stems on his hands after he'd spent a day pruning, and the Italian plum trees at one corner of the vineyard heavy with overripe fruit, with him as a little boy hiding in its branches.

Alex cleared his throat, but his voice still held the slight tremor of emotion. "This is excellent. I can see why your family's wine is so sought-after."

His mother nodded approvingly. Taking a sip, she closed her eyes, and he could see the moment her memories mingled with taste as her expression transformed.

"Incandescent," she murmured under her breath.

Pavia smiled. "Thank you."

Nick scoffed and downed the contents, without taking any time to savor it, before forcefully setting his glass on the table and pushing it away. He cocked his head, and Alex recognized the look. He was calculating his next dig.

"Pavia is an unusual name." Nick picked up the decanter and swirled the contents. "Is it some sort of ethnic thing?"

Alex clenched his fists under the table. Arrogance and alcohol weren't going to do his brother any good, but Nick didn't remember that lesson the way he did.

Before Alex could say anything, Pavia's expression changed from friendly to annoyed. She leaned across the table, pointing at Nick while speaking in rapid Italian.

Alex tried to follow, while Nick just blinked at her. His mother turned to Pavia and replied in Italian, her voice quiet and firm. She answered with a hint of pride in her eyes while she spoke. With his own limited knowledge, he understood the apology, and that she explained her sons weren't fluent in Italian.

Pavia nodded and turned to Nick. "I said that I am named for the town in Italy where our grandfathers were fighting when the war ended." She straightened her shoulders and put her hand over her heart. "You may not care, but history is important to my family." She then reached out and put her hand over Sarah's. "I shouldn't have come."

Nick sat stone-faced, anger rolling off him in waves. Alex winced. Grandad had always tried to teach them Italian. His brother wasn't interested in learning, and other than picking up a few phrases and terms used in the wine industry, Alex never learned more, always using that he didn't have time as an excuse.

"Please don't leave. I think it's lovely that your father carried on the tradition, Pavia," Sarah said with just a slight tremor in her voice. She turned to Nick with a steely gaze. "If you can't be polite, you will leave the table."

Alex looked at his mother with surprise. It was rare to hear her speak so forcefully.

Nick slumped in his chair, glowering. A heavy silence descended around them while they all toyed with the food on their plates. When their glasses were empty, Nick got up and retrieved a bottle and a fresh glass from the bar. He wrapped a towel around the label and filled Pavia's glass with a smirk.

"Let's see how much you really know about wine, Miss Jackson," he said.

Alex leaned forward. "I'm sure Pavia doesn't—"

Pavia held her hand up, interrupting his attempt to defend her. "It's fine, really."

She held the glass under her nose before she took a sip. Then she held it up to the light, twisting and turning it. She smiled and set the glass down, rested her hands on either side of it, and looked at Nick with narrowed eyes.

"Château Ausone. Fifty-five percent Cabernet Franc and forty-five percent Merlot, I believe, for this vintage. New oak, aged ten years. I'm surprised you could get your hands on it, since they only produce about two thousand cases a year."

Alex sat up straighter in his seat, staring at Pavia in surprise, while his mother beamed with pride.

Pavia sat back with her arms crossed. "Perhaps now would be a good time to mention I have a stage-three Master of Wine certification." She picked up her glass and took another sip, her lips curling around the rim while her eyes sparkled with amusement. And it was sexy as hell.

"Your father must be very proud," Sarah said.

"The institute made a special exception, and they assigned my father as my mentor."

Sarah nodded with approval.

Nick slammed his hand on the table and shoved his chair back. "I don't give a shit what you are. You and your family are scum," he said before turning on his heel and stalking out of the kitchen. A minute later, the front door slammed.

Alex sighed and shook his head. "Pavia, I'm sor—"

"No," she interrupted, "it's my fault. I was showing off and taunting him. I shouldn't have done that."

"Maybe this is too much to ask of you children," Sarah said, looking across the table at the two of them. "Nick's behavior is… there's no excuse."

"Nick is a pompous asshole," Alex muttered. "I know he's my brother, and I love him, but he's spoiled and acts like a jerk. I'm worried that we may never undo the damage."

"I should go." Pavia stood up. "This is a family discussion, and I don't want to intrude."

Alex jumped up and grabbed her hand. "Don't go. Don't let Nick ruin dinner. I promise he won't cause any more trouble."

She shook her head sadly. "Your brother is a grown-up. He's not your responsibility."

How many times had he wanted to have someone say that to him, to recognize the burden he carried?

Sarah stood up and braced her hands on the table. "We can't force her to stay, Alex, and I don't blame her for wanting to leave."

He squeezed Pavia's hand, looking at her with a silent plea.

Her gaze flickered over the beautiful meal his mom had prepared, and she reached for her chair. "This is a beautiful meal, and we shouldn't let it go to waste."

He pushed in her chair again, took his seat, and refilled their glasses.

"You must miss family dinners at home," Sarah said.

"Depending on the time of year, we eat most of our meals in the winery," she said with a soft chuckle. "None of us can cook like this, though. Your chicken is amazing."

"I can teach you how to make it," Sarah offered.

"I'm afraid that would be a waste. I understand the chemistry of wine, but for the life of me, I don't seem to be able to follow a recipe."

Sarah shook her head with a smile. "You sound like Alex. So far he's only been able to master boiling water."

"Hey, that's not true. I can also make toast."

Pavia looked at him, her eyes bright with amusement. "We'll have to exchange recipes."

Alex laughed, and for the first time that night, he relaxed and enjoyed the company.

"WE HAVE some furniture stored in the garage that I thought you might look at," Sarah said while she packed up leftovers for Pavia after dinner. "You told me you like antiques. Alex, take her to the storage room, and she can see if there's anything she'd like to have at the cottage before she goes."

Pavia got up and carefully set down the empty dinner plates on the counter. She glanced at Alex, trying to gauge his reaction.

"Mom's right. The furniture isn't doing anyone any good stored away. I'm sure there are some pieces that you might like," he said with an encouraging smile.

Pavia finally gave Sarah a tentative smile. "Okay."

As soon as they were outside, she told Alex, "I only said yes because I didn't want to hurt your mother's feelings."

"I know, and I appreciate it. I also know you've been avoiding me, and I haven't had a chance to apologize for the way I behaved. I shouldn't have lashed out at you. I'm sorry, Pavia."

"You were hurt and frustrated. I'm not excusing what you said, but I understand. Thank you for saying you're sorry."

She wasn't expecting an apology. It was just one more unexpected moment in an evening that had her off-kilter. After Nick's outburst, she didn't think she'd be able to relax and appreciate the amazing meal Sarah had prepared. But, once he left, the mood lifted, and Pavia enjoyed listening to her share stories about her attempts to teach her sons to cook. The food was delicious, and she had to admit she enjoyed being around Alex when he was at ease.

He led her toward a side entrance at the back of the garage. Opening the door, he stood back and let her climb the staircase to an upper floor. In the dim light she could see the cavernous space was filled with large, shadowy, unidentifiable shapes.

He flipped the light switch, and Pavia let out a gasp when she saw antique furniture scattered around the room. She drifted toward a dark cherry dresser and reached out her fingers to trace the delicate swirls and curves carved into the woodwork. Antiques were her kryptonite. She preferred a more midcentury style, but this dresser would fit the cottage perfectly.

Alex moved to her side. "Mom hates to throw anything away. She doesn't realize that not everyone likes antiques."

"I do," she whispered. "My mom and I used to stop at every garage and estate sale in the county. My mom, my cousin Sophie, and me, the three of us, would drive into Pendleton and go to our favorite antique mall once a month." She exhaled a shaky breath. "Mom would have loved this."

"You must miss your family."

She turned to him with a wistful smile. "I do. I miss walking the fields with my father and brother every morning and hanging out with my cousins and my brother."

"It's nice that you're all so close."

It was hard to miss the envy she saw in Alex's expression. But then it darkened.

"It didn't help that you didn't have a home to move into when you got here."

"It's going to take more than that for your brother to get rid of me. I'm committed to the five years I need to be here, and if I can achieve my goals, I plan on staying."

Alex put his hand on top of the dresser where her hand rested, their fingertips almost touching. "I was angry when I found out what Grandad did. I had no idea. What hurts more is that he didn't talk to me about his plans. But—" He put his hand on hers when she started to back away. "I'm not like my brother. I don't want to run you off. That's not who I am."

Her eyes searched his, and the surrounding air stilled for a moment before she pulled her hand away and wrapped her arms around her middle, fighting the sudden urge to comfort him with a hug.

"I believe you, but your brother definitely doesn't feel the same way," she said, reminding herself that it didn't matter if she found herself drawn to this man. His family had hurt her father, and getting involved would make a complicated situation even worse.

He frowned. "No, he doesn't. His impulsiveness is going to get him into more trouble than I can get him out of one day."

"You keep talking about your brother like he's your responsibility."

Alex shrugged. "He is."

The way he said it, so matter-of-factly, made her pause.

"There's a difference between caring and enabling." She softened her tone seeing the flash of pain in his eyes. "It's not my place to lecture you about Nick. It's none of my business." Her lips curled into a wry smile. "When I came here, I had every intention not to like any of you and keep my distance. That hasn't exactly gone to plan."

"For my mom's sake, I'm glad you didn't. She's been different since you came here."

"How? I keep thinking my being here makes her sad. She seems so… wistful when I'm around."

"She's always been that way. I thought after my father left she would be happy, but there's always been… sadness around her."

"The way your brother behaved tonight didn't help."

"No, it didn't."

It looked like he wanted to say more, but he pressed his lips closed, his expression shuttered.

Pavia's gaze returned to the furniture. She thought about the conversation she had with Alex the last night she stayed at the guesthouse, and his brother's behavior at dinner. With a resigned sigh, she said, "Thank you for the offer, but I don't want to be accused of taking something that isn't mine."

"I apologized for what I said," Alex said with a flash of frustration in his eyes.

"And I accepted it. But… can't you see?" She shook her head, trying to come up with the right way to explain. "You might be okay with this, but your brother won't be, and if it's not the furniture, it's going to be something else. I have enough challenges ahead managing my vineyard and winery for the first time. I can't fight the past too."

Alex pinched the bridge of this nose, drawing in a deep breath. "I was going to ask Grandad to let me take over the Brothers Block. But I didn't get the chance. I wanted everything you have. Not the house and the land, but the independence."

The pain and anguish in his voice at his confession broke down Pavia's defenses. She reached for his hand.

"What a mess Antonio made."

Their eyes met. "He has no idea."

Alex let go of her hand, trailing his fingers up her arm until they reached her shoulder. He hesitated for a moment before he gently wound one of her curls around his finger, letting his thumb brush against the strands before he let his hand drop to capture hers again.

Her breath caught. "You don't—you don't like me."

He drew her closer until his face hovered over hers. "I think you know that's not true."

It wasn't true. She was attracted to Alex, feeling a connection with him she'd never felt with anyone else before. It was physical, emotional and… something she couldn't define.

She lifted her face when his lips ghosted over hers. The moment was so brief she'd wonder for the rest of the night if it had really happened. Before she could give in to the kiss like she so badly wanted to, he pulled away.

"I shouldn't have done that." There was a slight tremor in his voice that showed he was just as affected by the moment as she was.

"Why?"

"Because I can't hurt you."

He was gone before she could respond.

Pavia looked around the room one more time before she made her way back to the staircase. She turned off the light, turning the beautiful antiques back into shapeless shadows again, and carefully made her way back down the dark staircase.

Moonlight bathed everything in a silvery glow. Pavia shivered. The cool night air wasn't what made her quiver, though. Looking around, there was no sign of Alex. She started toward the house, when she heard a faint shout. She stopped in her tracks, realizing what she was hearing was an argument. Three distinct voices—Sarah's, Alex's, and Nick's— raised in anger.

She turned and walked away. This wasn't her argument. She wasn't here to play peacemaker. That didn't mean guilt didn't weigh her down knowing she was probably the reason for the fight.

Pavia hadn't been sure what to expect at dinner, but it certainly wasn't the disaster that it turned into. She'd been wrong to blame Alex for what happened at the cottage. It was obvious now who she needed to keep her eye on. Alex didn't have malice simmering just beneath the surface the way his brother did. No, Pavia saw only sadness in the depths of Alex's blue eyes.

Antonio's diary sat on top of a stack of viticulture books and articles untouched that night. There was nothing he could say, no words of wisdom hidden in his diary, that would ease her troubled thoughts. Pavia wanted Alex to kiss her. She wanted to run her hands over his shoulders, to know what it would feel like when her body pressed against his. She'd never known what wanting someone, truly wanting with your entire being, felt like until now. The spark was there, but the fire that she knew would burn bright between them could engulf them and leave nothing but ashes.

Drawing her mother's quilt around her, she sat up against the wall, pulling her knees up to her chest as if somehow curling herself into a ball would block out her need.

"Because I can't hurt you."

He wouldn't hurt her. Instinctively, Pavia knew Alex wouldn't harm her, not physically, but she also understood he might have the power to break her heart. She also realized she had the power to do the same. Antonio, her dad, and Sarah, they'd all, in their own way, put her in an impossible position, keeping secrets and taking away dreams. She allowed herself a few tears of frustration. It wasn't her fault. She hadn't known what Alex wanted when she took what Antonio offered. Was she supposed to give up her dream so he could achieve his? No, Antonio wouldn't have given her the vineyard for her to give it up.

She sniffed and burrowed deeper under the covers with his journal.

September 4, 1943

We have reached the mainland! I was six months old when my parents left for America. Now I am back in the land of my birth. I don't know how Henry has put up with me. I can't sit still I am so excited, like a child at Christmas. The minute I saw the look on Henry's face when I said those words, I realized he had never felt that joy. Is it wrong to wish I could make up for all the happiness missing from his childhood?

They promoted Henry and I from digging latrines to being the unofficial translators for our unit. I didn't realize that Henry never went to school, working in the cotton fields instead. He explained that this was common for Negro children in the South. Through sheer will and determination, he taught himself to read and write. He is eager to learn everything he can, so I am teaching him Italian. The bonus is that we can curse out our sergeant without him ever knowing!

The other men in our unit will put up with us now, especially when they see a pretty girl they want to talk to. Henry and I talk to them as well.

Henry is very popular with his warm smile and dark skin. But we enjoy the conversations we have between us more. I don't think I've ever felt a connection with someone the way I do with Henry. We are so different and yet....

The reaction of the Italians to Henry is fascinating. Many have never seen a Negro before. I don't know how he can be so patient. Children climb all over him like a toy. If he sits for just a moment, they want to touch his skin and hair. Sometimes, the adults are just as curious as the children. They squeal with delight when he speaks their language. Somehow, he always finds a chocolate bar in his pocket to break up and dole out the pieces. If the Americans were smart, they would make him an ambassador!

I know this will be one of the last days of peace and calm. I can hear the gunfire in the distance. Every hour it gets louder. I'm not afraid to fight, but I am scared of losing what I've come to treasure. What will I do if they kill Henry? I'm willing to risk my life for my country, but I'm determined to fight for my friend. I know this doesn't make sense, war doesn't make sense. The world is on fire, and nothing makes sense, especially what I know is true in my heart.

Pavia closed the journal, clutching it close to her chest. How many regrets would she have if she didn't take a risk with Alex? She thought about the look of remorse she saw in her father's eyes and the look of longing in Sarah's. Years and decades of longing, wouldn't it be better to take the chance?

Alex heard the raised voices when he reached the front door. Heart thundering in his ears, he raced back into the house. The sound of his brother arguing with their mother flooded him with memories. As a child, if he heard raised voices, it meant Alex would find his father towering over his mother with his fists raised. Now, he found his mother and brother standing toe-to-toe in the kitchen.

"Nick, how could you? Your behavior at dinner was unforgivable." Her voice shook with anger.

Nick stood with his arms crossed, glaring at her. "I'm only saying what needs to be said. Why are you doing so much to help her?"

"Because I'm doing what's right," Sarah shot back.

"There's nothing right about her taking our land. The Brothers Block is part of the Conti legacy."

"It's a part of the Jackson legacy too," Alex said when he entered the room.

He exchanged a look of understanding with their mom. Nick wasn't going to listen. He never did. He was stubborn, a trait he got from their father.

Nick looked at them with a scowl. With a heavy sigh, Alex went over to the glass-front cabinet holding various spirits and poured himself a glass of whiskey. He held it up to his mom.

"Do you want one?"

She shook her head, folding her arms in front of her, continuing to glare at her younger son.

"What, nothing for me?" Nick asked.

"I'm not in the mood to do you any favors, Nick. Mom's right. You were out of line with Pavia. Way out of line. Like it or not, she's here now, and she's going to be our neighbor."

"Not if I can help it," Nick said, glaring out the window toward the cottage with a look of disdain on his face.

"Leave Pavia alone, Nick." Sarah poked him in the chest. "This family has caused enough hurt to the Jacksons for a lifetime." Her voice was raw with emotion. "I won't allow you to do anything to hurt her."

Alex did a double take. It was rare for his mother to speak so forcefully. Although she didn't have to fear retribution, and she hadn't for many years, she often acted like she did. Sarah always kept her anger in check, presenting a calm façade. For a long time, she did it as a way to survive. Now she was standing up to Nick the way Alex had always wished she would stand up to their father. There was a small pang of anger that took him by surprise. Why Pavia? Why couldn't she have stood up for her own children the way she was for someone who wasn't her child?

"The reckless younger brother act is getting old, Nick," he added. "I'm tired of cleaning up your messes."

"No one ever asked you to."

That wasn't true, but Alex would not try to argue that point.

"How many times do I have to remind you that your behavior reflects on the whole family? Our standing in the community and in the industry is affected when you act so recklessly. Speeding tickets, loud parties, and you and your friends' drunken escapades make all of us look bad."

They glared at each other, locked in a silent battle of wills. Alex was fighting against his rising anger at his brother's willful, belligerent attitude.

Sarah looked up at Nick. "Like it or not, Pavia is going to be our neighbor, and you're going to have to interact with her, and when you do, you will behave. I won't have you walking around acting like—"

She stopped and clamped her mouth shut. Alex winced. *Like your father* was what she was going to say.

"I can't believe the two of you." Nick pointed at Alex. "I didn't expect you to come down with a raging case of jungle fever so fast," he shouted with a bitter edge to his voice.

The glass left his hand. The sound of it shattering against the wall made Alex realize what he'd done. The pounding of his heart muffled the sound. Nick looked at him, his eyes bulging wide, his hand lifted to the spot on his head that the glass had just missed.

He was on his brother in an instant, grabbing the front of Nick's shirt in his fist. "Never. Say. That. Again. Ever," he choked out between clenched teeth.

Someone was tugging at his arm. Alex glanced down to see his mother looking up at him with tears in her eyes. "Don't do this, Alex, please," she whispered.

He released Nick and stepped back, drawing in a ragged breath.

His brother opened his mouth and snapped it shut again. The color drained from his face. "Why do you always try to turn Dad into a monster?"

"Because that's what he was," Alex said in a flat, emotionless voice.

Nick turned on his heel and stormed out of the room.

A heavy silence descended. Alex grabbed the counter with one hand and pressed the other to his chest. The room blurred around him. He blindly reached for a chair and dropped into it, fighting to get enough air into his lungs.

"Alex...." His mother's voice sounded far away, barely a whisper that he had to strain to hear.

It hurt to breathe. Alex forced air into his lungs until he could speak.

"I can't believe I lost control like that." He looked at his mother. "I acted just like Dad."

"Alex, what Nick said was wrong… so wrong." His mom knelt down in front of him, taking his hands in hers. "But you are not your father, and you never will be."

He wanted to believe her. He did everything he could to be a better man than his father was.

He jerked his head up, looking his mother in the eye. "What about Nick? Can you say the same thing about him?"

Sarah's eyes clouded. She shook her head.

They embraced, silently sharing the pain that still haunted them after so many years.

"Even if we told him everything he was too young to remember, I think it's too late," she said, pulling away, wiping her eyes.

"Sometimes, I'm glad he doesn't remember Dad and what he was like when he got angry." He swallowed and shook his head. "But when Nick acts like this, I think it would have been better if he had been old enough to remember. This is why we should have talked about Enzo more, what he was like. When Grandad kicked him out, we all just… shut down. The abuse stopped, and we healed on the outside, but we never really dealt with what he did. Grandad's guilt, thinking he could get his son to change, ate at him for the rest of his life."

Sarah sighed. "I know."

Alex got up and headed toward the french doors leading out to the veranda. They stood side by side, looking out over the rows of vines bathed in moonlight.

"Budbreak will happen anytime now. It's hard to imagine having a harvest without Antonio," she said wistfully.

"Why didn't he ever say anything about the Jacksons?" he blurted.

Sarah shifted and set her wineglass down. "I think"—she paused, clasping her hands in her lap—"no, I know he missed his friend every day."

"Pavia's father?" he asked, trying to make sense of a relationship that he never knew about.

"Him too. But I'm talking about Henry, Anthony's father, Pavia's grandfather." She pointed a shaking finger toward the south slope of the vineyard. "Henry Jackson died right over there. It was a massive heart attack." She took a deep, shuddering breath and continued. "I'll never forget Antonio cradling Henry in his arms, weeping."

A gust of wind sent the trees' leaves rustling, their branches creaking, sounding like a low moaning of grief. Did the trees remember that day?

"When Henry died, your grandfather became Anthony's father figure. The two of them were more like father and son than—" Her face crumpled.

"His actual son," he finished for her.

"If Grandad loved Anthony so much, why did he let him leave?"

Sarah leaned forward. "That was my fault"—her voice dropped to a whisper—"all my fault."

"Are you ever going to tell me what really happened?"

"I need to, and I will. I'm just waiting for…." She shook her head, her silver hair falling in a curtain that hid her face.

"There's never going to be a good time, Mom."

"I know that." She sighed. "I know that," she repeated as if she was trying to convince herself.

"Because I can't hurt you."

He was right to walk away from Pavia, but he wasn't sure how he could live with the regret. Could he spend the rest of his life walking around with the same cloak of heartache he saw in his mother's eyes?

"I see the way you look at her," Sarah said quietly, staring into the dark.

Alex jerked his head up. "I…." He snapped his mouth shut. He didn't want to have this conversation, not when he was still sorting through his feelings. "I want to get to know her better, that's all."

"You can't play with her heart, Alex. If you feel something for Pavia, make sure you know what you want before you act. If it doesn't work out, you can't walk away. She lives next door. You'll still have to see her."

"Marriage, kids, family life aren't for me. I never want to end up hurting someone. I don't want… what you went through with Dad. I'm not a monster like he was. I would never hurt her. I would never hit a woman or"—Alex shuddered—"say the things Dad said to you. But there's a part of me that worries I'll turn out like him. It's not rational, I know, but that's why I've decided it's better to stay single. Then Pavia came here, and… there's something I—" He dropped his head into his hands. "I don't know what I'm doing."

Sarah pulled him into a fierce hug before she stepped back and grasped his shoulders, giving him a little shake. "You will never be like Enzo. Do you hear me? Never. Don't let him take away your chance for happiness." Tilting her head, she looked him in the eye. "Don't give up on the idea of marriage, Alex," she said softly. "Don't let Enzo hurt you anymore."

He tried to take a deep breath to loosen the tightness in his chest.

"Did Pavia find any furniture that she liked?"

"She liked the furniture, but she didn't pick anything out. She… she didn't want to do anything that would cause more trouble."

Sarah's smile fell. She wrapped her arms around herself.

"I'd hoped…." she sniffed and looked down at the floor, blinking back tears.

"I need to tell you something, something I told Pavia tonight. I was going to ask Grandad to give me the Brothers Block after this year's harvest. I wanted something of my own. I was going to do exactly what Pavia's doing, but he… just gave it away without talking to me."

Sarah's eyes widened with understanding. "That's why she said she didn't want to cause more trouble. Oh sweetheart, I… if I had known…." She sighed. "I can't undo what your grandfather did, but I can help. This is your vineyard." She swept her arm over the fields surrounding them. "Take the land you want and make it your own."

"I appreciate that, but running the business without Grandad, I just don't have the time. I thought Nick might finally step up and take some responsibility, but that's not going to happen."

Sarah took a deep breath. "I was brought up at a different time. My parents were very traditional and raised me to believe that girls were supposed to be obedient. Business was for the men. Enzo agreed and drilled it into me that my only job was to be a mother. I know how hard you're working, and I haven't stepped in to help because… I'm scared." She drew herself up and looked Alex in the eye. "Starting tomorrow, I'm going to work with you in the office. You'll have to teach me a few things and be patient with me while I learn. I want to help. I need to stop listening to my doubts. It's been easier not to try than to face my fear that I'll make a mess of anything I try to do. We can hire someone too. You need an executive assistant."

"I wish I'd known that's what you were thinking. Did Grandad keep you from working?"

"No, Antonio was always encouraging me to come out of my shell. You might not remember, but I took some college classes after Enzo left. Your grandad pushed me to do it. I just didn't have the courage to keep it up. For a long time, I had your father's voice in my head telling me how worthless I was." She reached up and stroked the hair at his temple. "That and my own voice telling me I wasn't worthy of doing anything for myself or that would make me happy because I didn't protect the people I loved."

"Mom, you can't blame yourself for what Dad did."

"No." She straightened her shoulders and looked Alex in the eye. "But I can do better now and help you."

"I was frustrated when I said that stuff about Nick not helping. I didn't mean to make you feel bad."

Sarah held up her hand. "It's not because you said anything. I need to do this, and I want to help. We both know that Nick will not step up and take responsibility. He's never shown the same interest in the vineyard that you have, and he probably never will."

It was the first time she had ever admitted that Nick might not be a part of the family business. Saying it out loud was the sad validation of what Alex had been thinking for so long.

"Alex, it's going to be okay," she said, looking at him with a determination he'd rarely seen from her before.

"I want to believe that."

"Don't wait for life to happen to you. It will pass you by. Don't do what I did. Don't hide away because you're scared. Do what's in your heart, Alex."

He replayed his mother's advice over and over again while he lingered on the veranda long after she left. By morning, he'd made up his mind. He was going to follow his heart, right to Pavia's doorstep.

CHAPTER *Five*

A loud knocking on her door woke Pavia from a restless night spent tossing and turning, replaying again and again the moment Alex almost kissed her. With a groan, she rolled out of bed and padded toward the door.

"I thought you weren't coming today—" She gripped the doorframe tightly seeing Alex on her doorstep instead of George or Sam.

"And yet here I am," he said with a wide smile, spreading his arms open.

She looked over Alex's shoulder at the large truck with the Conti Vineyards logo emblazoned on the side, the back of it filled with furniture and a few boxes.

"Alex…." She said his name with an exasperated sigh. "I told you last night I'm not going to take—"

He held his hand up. "You're not taking. This is a gift from Mom."

"You're playing dirty using your mom like that," she grumbled.

His lips quirked. "I'm not playing any games, Pavia." He rested his hands on his hips, clad in a pair of worn jeans. His gaze roved over the cottage before turning to her. "It's looking good. I like how you kept the original trim color."

The faded robin's-egg blue trim had a fresh coat of paint, which made it look bright and cheery again. But Pavia wasn't interested in making small talk about the repainted trim.

She gestured to the furniture piled in the truck. "Changing the subject won't work either."

Alex looked at the back of the truck, then back at her. "Look, all this stuff"—he waved his hand toward the furniture—"is just going to sit in a dark attic collecting dust, or it can come here where it will be loved and cared for."

The way he looked at her when he talked about the furniture being loved and cared for set butterflies loose in her stomach. She blinked at him, her common sense and want battling in her head. Neither side was going to win without some coffee.

"Let me get some clothes on, and some coffee, and then I'll decide."

Pavia closed the door and shuffled into the kitchen before he could answer. Twenty minutes later, she clipped the buckle on her favorite Carhartt overalls over a faded pink T-shirt and shoved her feet into her work boots. After pouring a second cup of coffee, she stepped outside and squinted at the sun before her gaze settled on Alex sitting on the bed of the truck and grinning at her.

She was as annoyed that he looked so hot this early in the morning as she was that the caffeine hadn't kicked in yet. She looked down at her mug and remembered her manners.

"Do you want some?"

"I'm good, thanks."

She tilted her head. "You're one of *those* morning people, aren't you?"

"Exactly what kind of morning person are you accusing me of being?" he said, his voice dripping into a flirty tone.

Good lord, it was too early for flirty banter. Pavia took a sip of her morning elixir, squinting at him over the rim of her cup. She swallowed and licked her lips.

"The kind who can make intelligent conversation first thing in the morning without caffeine."

He held up his hand. "Guilty."

"Fine," she grumbled. After gulping down the rest of her coffee, she set her mug on the step and walked toward him. "Let's get this stuff unloaded."

Alex jumped up and started unhooking the straps holding the load down. He pulled out a chair and handed it down to her.

As soon as her hands wrapped around the reddish-brown wood and she saw the delicate yellow flowers on the needlepoint cushion, her grumpiness dissipated, replaced with an eagerness to see how the chair would look in the corner of her bedroom.

Other than Alex asking where she wanted to put things, there wasn't much conversation between them until they were at each end of a library table that would fit perfectly behind a sofa, if she had one.

"I was wondering, your Italian, how—"

"Antonio taught Henry, and he taught my dad. They spoke it at home when he was growing up, and he kept up the tradition with my brother and me." She laughed. "Most folks didn't know what to make of the Jacksons, who ran around the vineyard yelling at each other in a mix of English and Italian with a few words of Yakima thrown in. Kids used to tease me that I called my parents *Papà* and Mama, but it was just what we did. We blended our Italian, Native American, and Black cultures into something that worked for us."

Neither one of them moved when they set the table down.

"Yakima?" Alex asked with a quizzical look.

"Yup, the Yakima have their own language. You can even find a dictionary online. I only know a few words, not enough to make any kind of claim that I'm fluent."

"Based on what I heard, I'd say you're definitely fluent in Italian."

"I spent a year living in Italy. I… I was surprised you and your bother don't speak it."

Alex looked away, clearly embarrassed.

"I shouldn't have said anything. It's none of my business."

He shook his head. "No, it's fair. I just… honestly, I think I took it for granted. I just assumed I'd learn someday, but I didn't make the time. It's one regret I have about Grandad. I should have listened, put more effort into learning when he tried to teach me."

"Both my parents always said that language was an important way to connect us to our past."

They walked back to the truck side by side, their hands almost brushing. She took stock of the remaining contents.

"This is too much. I can't accept all of this."

"My mom picked out all of this. She had me up at the crack of dawn. She must have debated each piece a dozen times, asking if I thought you'd like it."

Pavia didn't have a response. How could she say no, hearing the love in his voice when Alex talked about his mother?

"The two of you have a special relationship. You have a closeness… a special bond."

A shadow passed over his face. "When you've been through a traumatic experience with someone, you share a bond that's"—his voice grew gruff—"hard to explain."

He was talking about Enzo, he must be. Just how bad was the abuse they'd endured? She wanted to know more, curious about what Alex's childhood was like. The little pieces she'd learned about the Contis' past challenged her belief that they were the villains in her father's story.

Pavia had lumped all the Contis in with Enzo, and that was wrong. There were more victims than just her father.

"I—every child deserves a happy childhood. I'm sorry you and Nick have to live with those memories," she said instead of asking more questions.

Alex's jaw ticked. "Just me. Nick was too young to remember. Thankfully," he muttered quietly.

"Is that why you're so protective of your brother?"

"In part." He ran his hand through his hair with a heavy sigh. "Don't all big brothers or sisters protect their younger siblings?"

Pavia nodded her head in agreement. "I guess that's true. My brother, Robert, made dating almost impossible when I was in high school," she laughed softly. "He made sure every boy my age in Blue Ridge knew they had to get through him before they could ask me out."

Alex's eyes lit up with amusement. "And were there a lot of boys your brother had to chase off?"

"No," she answered honestly. "There were a few who managed to get my father's and brother's approval that didn't really like me."

He wrinkled his forehead. "What does that mean exactly?"

"They liked the idea of me but not me." She tapped her chest with her finger. "They were curious about the mixed girl who looked different from everybody else. I'll never forget hearing a boy brag to a group of his friends that he stole a kiss from the"—she held up her hands, making air quotes—"freak girl. Some wanted me to be the Native American girl. They wanted me to be a character from *Dances with Wolves*. Others wanted me to be more Black, a Fly Girl with the hip-hop dance moves."

The moment she saw Alex draw back with a look of shock mixed with pity on his face, Pavia regretted being so honest. She wasn't even sure why she'd told him. Those were memories she didn't share with anyone other than her cousin Sophie. They were as close as sisters, even though Sophie was the third cousin from her grandfather's side, the White side of the family. She always listened and understood that Pavia didn't want pity when she shared her frustrations and disappointments with dating.

"That was a little too honest," she said with a shaky laugh.

"I'm sor—"

"Oh no." Pavia jumped up into the back of the truck, shaking her head. "Let's not do that. I didn't tell you that looking for sympathy."

Alex climbed in next to her and took her hand in his. "I don't feel sorry for you."

She'd said too much, and he was too close. Pavia drew in a deep breath to calm the butterflies that had decided that moment was a good time to take flight in her stomach. He looked down at her with his blue eyes that matched the early morning sky.

"The more I get to know you, the more I… admire who you are. I know it didn't seem like it the day… when we learned about Grandad's will, but the way you sat there keeping your composure while we lost ours? There was no way I couldn't appreciate you."

"You shouldn't," she said in a breathy whisper.

"But I do."

She wrapped her hands around the curved metal bed frame as if it would anchor her somehow and keep her from being swept away by the stormy look in Alex's eyes.

"Not now," she whispered. "I'm not ready…."

His lips grazed her temple. "Neither am I, but we both know we can't stop—I don't know how to describe it—orbiting each other."

"Stars colliding," she said with a smile.

"We're hurtling through space," he said, gently reaching out to wrap a curl that had escaped her ponytail around his finger.

"More like through time. Three generations and here we are. Maybe…." She gripped the bed frame tighter until her skin stretched over her knuckles. "Maybe too much time, too many past memories that aren't ours will make it too hard for us to…."

Alex sighed. "I don't know."

Side by side, they stood frozen, unable to move forward under the burden of the past.

"One thing at a time. Let's finish unloading the truck, and then we'll talk."

Alex wiped sweat from his forehead with his T-shirt, revealing toned abs. Pavia quickly looked away when she noticed him glancing her way.

"Is there anything else you need help with?" he asked with a knowing smile.

Damn it.

Pavia lifted her chin. "No, I can take it from here, thanks."

"We can't keep doing this."

"What are we doing?"

"Avoiding talking about the past, our families." He reached out, his fingers briefly grazing her cheek. "We need to talk about how there's something happening between…us."

She swallowed and backed away, out of the temptation of his touch. "Yes, we… we should… need to… do that, but"—she eyed George's truck coming up the driveway—"now isn't a good time."

Alex glanced over his shoulder and frowned. "No, it's not." He turned on his heel and stalked back to his truck, then exchanged a curt nod with George and Sam as he drove past them.

"I'm in so much trouble," she said under her breath, watching Alex drive away.

ANGER FLASHED in George's eyes, watching Alex leave. "Is that boy giving you trouble?"

Yes, but not the kind you're thinking of.

"It's fine, Mr. Matsui. Alex was just dropping off some furniture Mrs. Conti wanted me to have." Pavia noticed Sam's eyes light up at the mention of furniture. "Come on, let me show you what he brought."

They followed her into the cottage, and Sam immediately gravitated toward the library table with spiral carved legs. He traced the graceful curves with his fingers.

"Amazing, this is done by hand. These days someone would use a lathe," he murmured to himself.

"You can play with your furniture later. We've got work to do," George said.

She exchanged a knowing glance with Sam, then gave him a sympathetic smile. He'd mentioned more than once that his dad didn't take his ambition to start his own furniture making business seriously.

The rest of the morning sped by. With the cottage repairs finished, the three of them turned their attention to the barn, going over her ideas for how she wanted to use the space, the materials they'd need, and what permits would be required. She was eyeing her bank account with growing anxiety. Five million dollars was a lot of money, but when you're opening a winery, it would disappear quickly. She still had equipment to purchase and at least two workers to hire to help with the harvest, and that was being conservative.

With nothing left she could do to help George and Sam, Pavia headed back to the cottage. She stopped midstep, suddenly overwhelmed, fully understanding what she'd taken on for the first time.

Her phone rang. The opening notes of "Boujee Natives" by Snotty Nose Rez Kids made her laugh. Her brother put it in her phone as the ringtone for his number when she'd made the mistake of leaving it open and unattended. The first he called and she heard it, she'd laughed so hard tears were streaming down her face when she answered.

"Hey, Sis. How's it going?"

Hearing her brother's deep voice, a more youthful version of their dad's, made it difficult to answer past the lump in her throat.

"Sis?" Robert's voice softened.

"How do you always know when to call?" she asked with a shaky laugh.

"You're my little sister. I'll always know when you need me. What's going on?"

Pavia shared her worries, listing all the projects and supplies she still needed to order, careful not to mention the work the cottage had needed and other unexpected expenses from repairing the damage Nick caused.

"You've got the vineyard, but the rest is starting from scratch. You know what you need to do. Just take it one step at a time. Any sign of budbreak?"

She eyed the row of vines closest to her. The buds on the Syrah canes were swollen. If she stood very still, it seemed as if she could almost see the leaves within straining to break out and unfurl.

"Any day now."

"I know it's your favorite time of year. I figure you're sitting on those vines like a mother hen waiting for her chicks to hatch."

"I'm trying not to go out and check every hour."

"And how are things going with the Contis?" When she sighed, he said, "That bad?"

"No, it's not bad, but it's not good either. It's… complicated."

"Do they talk about Dad?"

"No, not really, but what happened? The past is like this big thing between us."

"I wondered if it felt like being surrounded by ghosts, the spirits from the past."

"That's exactly what it feels like sometimes. There's a heaviness here. There's all this grief and guilt and… I don't know how to describe it."

"You're one of the strongest people I know, Sis. I couldn't have done it. I'd be walking around angry all the time. I wouldn't want any part of it."

"There are days." She kicked the dirt at her feet.

"We all have them, Sis. You don't have to do it all on your own either. It's okay to ask for help, you know."

"Yeah, I know."

"I know you. You hate asking for help. You always want to do it all on your own. I remember your first day of kindergarten. Mom wanted to hold your hand and walk with you to the bus. You threw a fit, insisting on doing it by yourself, and made me keep at least twenty paces behind you."

She laughed softly. "I wanted to be my own independent woman."

"And you are. Knowing when to ask for help isn't a weakness. It shows you know your strengths."

He was right. Robert was one of those annoying big brothers who was always right. He had the same calm, thoughtful demeanor as their father, while she'd inherited her mother's fierce determination.

"Yeah, okay, you're right," she admitted.

"Do me a favor?"

"What do you need?"

"Call more often. Not just when you need help or advice, but just because. And not only me, but Dad too. Being independent doesn't mean you can't check in with your family once in a while."

Guilt washed over her.

"I'm sorry. I've been so wrapped up in everything going on here. I… I don't want to say anything that will hurt Dad."

"I get it, Sis, but it hurts him more when he doesn't hear from you."

She squeezed her eyes shut, fighting back a wave of tears. "I'll do better. How—" Her voice broke. "How is he? How are you? I miss you all so much."

"We're good. Dad's out in the field with a new group of viticulture students from the university."

"And what about you?"

"I'm good."

She wanted to ask more, but the pang of homesickness making her chest ache, and making her want to jump in her truck and start driving back to Blue Ridge, made her clamp her mouth shut.

"I've got to go, but I'll want more details when I call in a couple of days," she said, trying to keep her voice light.

"Love you, Sis."

"Love you too."

She hung up and went into the cottage. In her bedroom, she wrapped herself in her mother's quilt, clutched the diary to her chest, and let her tears fall. When she regained her composure, she went into the bathroom and splashed water on her face.

"No more moping," she said to her reflection in the new medicine cabinet mirror.

Pavia went back to her bedroom, where they'd set the pieces of the bed frame against the wall. She blew out a long breath, eyeing the grungy pieces of metal, before she went to the kitchen to collect cleaning supplies.

She tapped her fingers on the counter while waiting for a bucket to fill with hot water. "Antonio, what were you thinking?" She waited, hoping his ghost would appear and give her some kind of explanation.

Water sloshed and left a trail of droplets as she carried the bucket, and then she set it down with too much force, creating a mini tsunami. With a frustrated groan, she grabbed a towel and started mopping up her mess.

Pavia sat on the floor, drawing her knees up to her chest and resting her chin on them. She stared at the graceful intertwined ovals of the bed frame, then dipped a rag into the soapy water and wiped away years of dust and grime. In the center of three intertwined ovals on the headboard was a tile plaque. At first it looked like hazy watercolor splotches, but as she wiped the dirt away, she saw an image of a villa on top of a hill with rows of grapevines below and tall cypress trees off in the distance.

"Beautiful," she whispered, running her hand over the crackled porcelain. The spiderweb of cracks from age made the image even more charming in her eyes.

"New things are nice, but it's the old pieces that have stories to tell," her mother used to say when they went looking for treasures at their favorite antique shops.

"What stories do you have to share?" Pavia asked.

Before they left for the day, Sam and George, with the help of a rubber mallet, fit the pieces together. Sam was able to use spare wood and cut new slats that would support her mattress, and they lifted it onto the frame for her. She put on a pair of clean sheets and spread out her mother's quilt over the pale green duvet cover.

That night, after a long, hot shower, she climbed under the covers with a happy sigh. The dresser Alex brought over sat on the opposite wall, and she was using the little chair with the delicate carvings as a makeshift bedside table. She adjusted the pillows and opened Antonio's journal.

October 26, 1943

I am teaching Henry about wine. Even with all the fighting and destruction, wine still flows here. I have discovered that Henry has an excellent palate. I think when we return home, he could work as a waiter.

I read what I wrote and feel ashamed. Henry wants more for himself, and I should want more for him. It's so easy to fall into the trap of what they taught us to believe what some people are allowed to be.

More than the taste and smell, I'm teaching him how the wine is made. Today, I explained about the terroir. Light, soil, and water, all the parts that man must work with in harmony to create a vineyard. The other men in our unit think we are crazy when Henry and I stop to pick up handfuls of soil, smelling the rich earth. I've described the minerals we are looking for and the distinct qualities each one adds to the soil. I explain what I would plant, where, and why. Henry asks many thoughtful questions, and I enjoy passing on what my father taught me.

Many of our conversations are about how the vines must struggle. Through adversity, the vines will bear the best fruit.

The other men keep asking me how it feels to be home. They are teasing me, I know, and yet I feel guilty. My father would be disappointed that I have no genuine connection to this place. I am an American, California is my home, and I long to return to what is familiar. I asked Henry if he looks forward to going home, and the sadness in his eyes spoke of a story yet to be told. Now I feel guilty for wanting something that causes my friend so much sadness. No matter where we end up, I can't help feeling now that it won't be home without Henry by my side. I have never had these feelings before, and as much as I hate this war, I am frightened for when it is over.

Pavia closed the journal and hugged it to her chest. She wanted to help Alex with his sadness the same way Antonio wanted to help Henry with his. Heartache and grief connected three generations of their family.

She replayed in her mind the words she had just read. *Through adversity, the vines will bear the best fruit.*

Did Antonio want her to understand that it wasn't just the vines that needed to struggle? She never thought of herself as having lived a privileged life, but had she ever really had to struggle? No, not really. There were tough times that would come. Was she ready? What would happen if she failed? Could she go back to Blue Ridge? She imagined her grandfather Henry. How could he bear to go back to Mississippi after seeing the world, even if it was during a war? He didn't. Henry came here, built this cottage, married, had a son. This was his home, and now it was her home. Not every harvest would bear perfect fruit, but that didn't mean you let the vines wither and die.

"WELL, HOW did it go?" Sarah asked when he walked into his office.

Alex drew up short. She said she was going to help, but he didn't expect to find her at Grandad's desk, her forehead wrinkled, looking over a spreadsheet.

"I had no idea we were paying so much for foils," she muttered.

"The price is only going to keep going up," he said, dropping into the chair across from her.

She started to get up. "Here, you can have your seat."

He waved her back down. "I still think of it as Grandad's."

They exchanged a brief pained look. Would the heartbreak of Antonio's loss ever ease?

"So?" She looked at him expectantly.

A smile tugged at his lips. "The furniture is all moved in."

"Good, I was worried Pavia wouldn't take it."

"I'm going to ask her out," he blurted.

She blinked at him for a minute. "Okay. Can I ask why?"

"Why?" he parroted back to her, taken aback by the question.

"Yes, why? What is about Pavia that makes her special? Why her?"

Alex considered her question. "I… she talks to me. No, that's not… when we talk, I feel like she's really listening. Growing up around here, being a Conti, people don't challenge me if I say something they don't agree with. No one pushes back but Pavia...."

Sarah listened to him stumble through his explanation with a slight smile. "Good," she said.

"Now it's my turn. Why do you want to know?"

"Because I didn't want you to go out with Pavia if your attraction was nothing more than physical."

Her blunt assessment made him shift uncomfortably in his seat.

"You don't need my permission, Alex. You're a grown man. I'm not going to give you any sage wisdom or words of advice. I don't think I have any, anyway. But I am going to tell you to take the day off." She spread her hands over the mess of papers on the desk. "I need some time to wrap my brain around all this and figure out where I fit in."

"I don't want you to feel you have some sort of obligation to—"

"I know, and I don't. I want to do this. It's going to be up to the two of us to carry on Antonio's legacy. That's something I haven't wanted to admit for a long time, but after last night… any hope I still had that Nick might get his act together...." Her lips trembled.

"Maybe he'll come around."

"Maybe. But when he does, working in the winery might not be what he wants to do."

Alex never considered Nick wanting a different career. He'd never considered doing anything other than continuing his family's legacy. Not that he wanted to. He embraced every aspect of working in the vineyard and the winery. The vineyard was where his heart lived. Watching the leaves slowly unfurl in the spring, and the bright green orbs tinged purple in the late summer, working in the fields filled his soul. He'd never thought of what he would do if he couldn't work at the vineyard.

"I never considered that."

Sarah gave him a sympathetic look and waved her hand toward the door. "Go, do something that makes you happy."

He left the office and stood in the hallway, frozen with opportunity. He hadn't taken a day off since Antonio died, and even before that. It wasn't quite noon, leaving him the rest of the day to do what he wanted. Feeling lighter than he had for a long time, Alex left the house, going toward the fields, and walked. Row after row, he reconnected with his roots. He eyed the vines for any sign of disease or rot and noted any that were struggling. One of the field managers waited for him at the end of a row on one of the farm's ATVs.

"Hey Mr. Conti, I haven't seen you out here in a while. Everything okay?"

"All good, Andy."

That Andy noticed how long it had been since he'd been out in the field reinforced his decision to spend more time outside of the office.

"Glad I caught you. I was going to call you about the new fence."

Alex frowned. "What new fence?"

"Your brother called me this morning saying he wants all access between your property and the Brothers Block cut off—fences, gates, whatever it takes—and he wants it done quick."

Andy shifted uncomfortably.

"Is there something else?"

"I don't want to cause any trouble, but Mr. Conti, the other Mr. Conti that is, well… he's been goin' around telling folks that if they do business with Miss Jackson, they won't get any more work from the Conti family."

His stomach knotted. Alex took a deep breath. This wasn't Andy's fault, and he didn't want his tone to reflect the anger building inside him toward his brother.

"Nick no longer works for Conti Vineyards. Any decisions will come from myself or from my mother going forward." The words came out without consideration.

Andy's eyes widened. "Yes, sir."

Alex pinched the bridge of his nose. His grandfather ran a tight ship and insisted on certain formalities.

"Let's stop with the *Mr. Conti* and *sir*. Call me Alex, okay? I'll send out a memo about my brother to the rest of the staff this afternoon."

"Yes, si—okay, Alex. I won't say anything to anyone else until the memo goes out."

"Thank you, I would appreciate that."

He spent a few more minutes talking to Andy about his observations from his walk and set up a standing appointment to walk the fields with the four field managers for the vineyard three days a week.

With heavy steps, Alex made his way back to the main house. His mom was still in the office, and as soon as he walked in, her face fell.

"What's wrong?"

He sat down in the seat he'd occupied before and steepled his hands. "We have a decision to make. No, that's wrong." He blew out a shaky breath. "I just made a decision, and I hope I have your support."

He explained what he'd just learned from Andy, and what he'd decided.

"I have half of the business. You and your brother each have a quarter. You and I have majority control." She clasped her hands tightly and looked Alex in the eye. "I support your decision."

They sat in silence. The weight of their decision made the air in the room heavy. After a few moments, his mom got up and gestured to her vacated seat behind the desk.

"Let's draft the memo."

Alex nodded. It was the right decision, but his gut filled with bile as they drafted the announcement. While Nick kept his ownership stake in the business, he would no longer be involved in its day-to-day operations. Not that he ever had been before, but the memo made it clear that he was no longer in a position to give the staff directives. The next announcement would be a bigger bombshell. Sarah insisted on giving Alex half her shares, making him the majority owner. While he wrote the memo, she called her lawyer and had the paperwork expedited.

They read over the final draft again.

"Are you sure about this?" he asked.

"Absolutely." Sarah's voice held a slight tremor. "I told Antonio this is what I planned to do when you were ready. I wanted to give you a few years to ease into your additional responsibilities and make sure this is what you really wanted before I transferred my shares." She put her hand on his shoulder. "We have to do this now to protect what we have. We can't risk Nick damaging our business, our reputation, or Pavia."

Alex looked up at his mother with a frown at her last statement. "Is what happened with the Jacksons really that bad?"

"What happened with the Jacksons hurt your grandfather more than sending his own son away and changed my life—" Her voice broke, and she pressed the back of her hand against her mouth.

Alex reached up and patted her hand on his shoulder. "Okay, Mom."

He turned back to his computer, cc'd his brother, and hit Send.

"It's done," he said in a flat, emotionless tone, bowing his head.

Sarah moved toward the windows, her arms wrapped around herself.

"There's nothing left to do. Go on with the rest of your day off, Alex."

He hesitated. "I'll go, but until we hear from Nick, I can't relax."

"Try," she said with a tense smile.

He passed Melinda in the hallway. She took one look at him and asked, "What happened?"

He told her about the decision they had made about Nick.

"It's been a long time coming," she said when he finished.

Alex cocked his head. "You aren't surprised?"

Melinda pressed her lips together and shook her head. "One way or another, things were going to come to a head. You were always going to be the person who ran the business, Alex. I know you wanted to work with your brother, but that just wasn't meant to be. I'm sorry, I know this is hard for you. It's going to be hard on Sarah too."

After filling Melinda in on what happened, Alex went to his room. Over the years, the house had been updated, so they each had their own suite. He walked into his, with southwest-facing windows that flooded the room with light. The same wood floors in the rest of the house continued into his sitting room and bedroom. Warm white walls and a Persian rug in a deep rust red anchored the sitting room space. An oversized camel-colored L-shaped sofa in front of the windows was his favorite place to end his days with a good spy thriller. The same color scheme was used in the bedroom, with another rug in the same red tones and dark cream bedding on the modern black metal bed frame. He'd splurged on his bathroom, installing an enormous steam shower and using marble with veins of cream and gold throughout the space.

Alex had created an oasis for himself where he could hide away. He knew his childhood was part of the reason. The therapist he'd seen for a few years when he first moved back home after college and was having nightmares encouraged him to create a space where he felt safe. There was nothing here that reminded him of his early childhood. Everything was designed to make him feel secure. The sight lines were clear. There were no shadowy corners or blind spots, nothing that reminded him of having to hide.

Alex let the hot water beat down on him. He rolled his shoulders, trying to ease some of the tension.

He'd started the day with high hopes. Now, he was so distracted and weighed down by what he'd been forced to do. After dressing in a pair of dark jeans with a gray sweater, he laced up a pair of Timberlands. He didn't really have a destination in mind or a plan for what he wanted to do, but he grabbed his keys and headed into town. He'd check in at the tasting room and then spend some time at The Vyne with Brandon.

Some of his worry eased when he saw his mom and Melinda sitting by the pool, laughing and talking. Melinda waved with a nod, a silent reassurance that she would stay and keep his mom company. She did it out of friendship, but also in case Nick came home tonight. So far, there hadn't been a response to the memo, and his silence was just as troubling as any rage Alex was sure his brother was feeling.

THE VYNE buzzed with laughing customers enjoying Brandon's culinary efforts. Alex kept his head down, ignoring the stares and whispers as he walked through the main dining room toward the kitchen. Seneca was a small community, and word traveled fast.

Brandon's head jerked up from the plate he was adding a microgreen garnish to. With a grim expression, he nodded toward his office. A few minutes after Alex entered, Brandon walked in, closing the door behind him.

He folded his arms in front of him and leaned against his desk. "I hear you had an interesting day."

"Is that what we're calling it, interesting? Because I'd say it was more of a...." Alex ran his fingers through his hair. "I don't know what I'd call it. I may have just blown up my relationship with my brother."

"You did the right thing," Brandon said quietly.

"That doesn't mean I feel good about it."

"Of course you don't," he shot back. "I know you. You didn't come to this decision lightly."

"No, but I came to it—suddenly. Nick was going after Pavia. He's been going around threatening workers and our contractors not to work with her."

Brandon muttered a string of oaths under his breath.

"Yeah, that's exactly what I thought," Alex deadpanned.

"How bad was the fallout?"

"So far, nothing. We haven't heard from Nick."

"That's not good."

Alex's jaw ticked. "No, it's not. There's nothing worse than waiting for the other shoe to drop."

There was a knock on the door, and someone called out a tentative "Chef?"

Brandon put a hand on his shoulder and gave it a squeeze on his way out the door. "I'm here for you, brother."

Alex left the kitchen. He'd barely taken a seat at the bar when a woman he'd gone out on a date with approached him.

She leaned against the bar with a flirty smile. "Hey there, stranger."

Alex waved off the bartender who'd approached. "Sorry, I can't stay." He ignored her angry gasp and muttered "Rude" when he walked away.

Alex took a deep breath when he emerged from the restaurant. Any relief disappeared when he found his brother leaning against his car.

"Nick."

"You're a traitor," he seethed.

"No, I'm your brother, and I don't want to see you let anger rule your life."

"How could you take away the business from me?"

"It's not like you ever wanted it," Alex snapped. "When have you ever done any of the work? Have you ever spent any time in Grandad's office other than coming in to ask for more money?" He took a steadying breath. "You're my brother, and I love you, but I'm tired of your bullshit. You don't get to take all the benefits without doing any of the work."

Nick glared at him. "That's because you and Grandad—"

"Stop. Stop blaming everyone else. Grandad and I never kept you out of the business. After you turned down every offer we made and every attempt to include you, we stopped asking. When you're ready to be a part of Conti Vineyards, Mom and I will welcome you back with open arms. But as long as you act like a bully, act like Enzo, then I won't allow you to jeopardize our reputation in this industry."

"You can't even call him Dad!" Nick shouted.

"He stopped being my dad the first time he hit me," Alex said quietly, looking him in the eye.

His brother stepped back, wide-eyed. "That's a lie."

"No." He shook his head with a heavy sigh. "Mom and I hid it from you. We thought we were protecting you. You were young enough, you don't remember."

Nick's jaw ticked. The anger in his eyes made Alex's heart ache.

"Why can't you believe me—us? It hurts, Nick. It hurts both of us. Don't lie and say you don't see the look in Mom's eyes every time you pick Enzo—Dad—over her."

"I'm not trying to hurt anyone. Why can't you see how much it hurts me when you talk about Dad like he's the devil? You had something I never got. At least you knew our dad. I never had the chance. Grandad took that away from me when he forced Dad to leave."

"If he stayed, we could have been killed!" Alex shouted.

"You didn't even try to help him get better," Nick shot back.

"Nick, I—"

When Alex tried to reach out for his brother, Nick backed away, his shoulders hunched. Hands in his pockets, he walked away.

Therapy? Anger management? Maybe they would have helped, but what would Alex and his family have done while they waited to find out? No, in his heart, he knew that his grandfather had made the right choice sending his son away.

With a heavy heart, Alex went home. Nick's car wasn't in the garage when he arrived.

The next couple of days went by in a blur. There was damage control that needed to happen, making sure the word got out that there would be no repercussions for working with Pavia. He spent hours working with his mom, defining their roles and forging a new path forward. Nick returned to their condo in San Francisco, and neither of them had any contact with him. Alex didn't cross paths with Pavia until the end of the week.

"So, what do you think? Would you like to work as our assistant?" he asked.

Tourists were scattered around the tasting room, making their selections before the bus waiting outside took them to their next destination. The young woman he'd posed the question to stared at him, her dark eyes widened in surprise.

"Are you sure?" she asked.

"Divit, you've been working here for two years now, and you've been an exemplary employee. My mother and I need an assistant, and you were recommended for the job."

When Alex approached the tasting room manager, asking if he had any recommendations for the role, he'd pointed out the young Indian woman. According to the manager, she was great with customers and eager to learn everything she could about the wine industry. Alex had slipped into the tasting room and observed her interactions with the customers and other staff. Divit had an excellent rapport with everyone she interacted with, so he pulled her aside to ask about her future aspirations and quickly knew she'd be a great asset.

She held her hand out with a smile. "I accept."

He shook her hand. "Come on up to the main house on Monday, and we'll get you sorted."

"Thank you, Mr. Conti."

His tasting room manager was disappointed to lose an employee but happy for Divit. Just as he was about to head back up to the main house, Alex noticed Pavia slip in with the next busload of tourists.

She stood toward the back of the Conti tasting room, watching the crowd. When she noticed his eye on her, she gave a little wave with a hint of color in her cheeks.

He walked over and mimicked her position, standing against the wall with his hands behind his back. "Is there any particular reason you're skulking around my tasting room?" he asked, watching the influx of customers with her.

"I'm not skulking. I'm… comparing. It's so different from our tasting room. This is six times the size of our tasting room."

Alex looked around the space, trying to see it through Pavia's eyes. Fake brick walls, arched ceilings, and wide plank floors were all designed to create the look of an ancient cellar. There were three private tasting rooms along one wall that could hold groups of up to twelve. Custom shelving filled another wall with a long counter in front that had people scattered in small clusters, swirling and sipping in a familiar ritual. Pub tables filled in the center of the room.

"I still can't get over that wineries require a reservation for a tasting here. It's like amusement parks for wine."

"I've never thought about it that way, but I guess you have a point. So what do you think?" he asked, sweeping his hand over the room, realizing he wanted her to like what she saw.

"It's nice," she said, her voice lacking any enthusiasm.

"You don't like it, do you?"

"It's not that I don't like it. It's just not my style." She continued in a rush, "It's just more commercial than what I want to do. You're producing over a million cases a year. I hope to bottle around twenty-five hundred. It's apples and oranges, Alex."

"I see," he said in a clipped voice.

Her expression clouded. "This was a bad idea. I should go."

"No, don't go." He snagged her hand as she started to walk away. "I didn't mean to sound harsh. I… it's hard to explain."

"Can you try?"

"Not here and not now." He grasped her hand, brushing his thumb back and forth across her knuckles. Her skin was soft and warm. "Have dinner with me tonight."

Their eyes locked. Her hazel eyes searched his, and her breath quickened. Heat built between them until a loud peal of laughter popped their bubble of intimacy, and they both jerked their heads up. Alex became aware they were in a public space and not alone.

She nodded, and her lips curled into a smile. "Yes, I'll have dinner with you tonight."

He walked her out of the tasting room and to her truck. Giving in to temptation, he dropped a quick kiss to her cheek.

"I'll pick you up at seven."

"I'll see you then."

Alex watched her drive away before making his way back to the main villa. His mom found him rummaging through the commercial-size refrigerator.

"What are you doing?" she asked, looking at the assortment of food scattered on the countertop behind him.

He popped his head out from behind the door. "I'm packing a picnic."

"For?"

Kicking the refrigerator door shut, he leaned against the counter. "I'm taking Pavia out for dinner."

"I see."

There was no mistaking the worry in his mother's tone.

"Is that a problem?"

She looked over the piles of meats and dips he'd amassed with a slight frown. "No, it's not a problem, it's just… Pavia is special. This can't be some sort of fling or a one-night stand. She's our neighbor, and our families have a history." Her voice hitched. "What happens if things don't work out? I don't think I can take it if anything bad happened again."

This was the second time she'd warned him. She wasn't trying to discourage him, but there was a fear in her worry that troubled him.

"Mom, Pavia and I aren't you and Anthony."

"Why Pavia? There are other women who've come and gone over the years. I've never seen you keyed up over a date with anyone like this before. What is it about Pavia that has you emptying the entire contents of our refrigerator?" She held her hands up. "It's not my place to ask. I just… you have to understand why I'm worried."

His mother said the last part almost as a plea. Alex struggled to find the right words to describe his attraction. How could he explain that when she walked into the room, he felt alive?

"I haven't felt a connection like this before," he confessed. "She doesn't see me as a member of one of the founding families, and she doesn't care about the Conti name or money. When she looks at me, she sees me." He poked his chest. "We've both tried to ignore our feelings, and it's not working. We both agreed we want to see where this thing between us goes."

"You both feel this way?"

"I think so."

She gave him a slight smile. "Then get the picnic basket out of the pantry, and I'll help you sort through all this so you'll have a nice dinner."

He came around the counter and gave her a quick peck on the cheek. "Thanks, Mom."

When they finished, Alex lifted the overstuffed basket with a grunt.

"Alex!" Sarah called out as he made his way toward the door. "One more thing. If you really like Pavia, if… if you think you see a future with her, then be brave. Have the courage to love her no matter what obstacles stand in your way. If you love fiercely, you can overcome anything."

He slowly set the basket down and gave her a hug. Her words were so hauntingly beautiful, he blinked back the sheen of tears he could see in his mother's eyes too. They'd cried together too many times, but this was different. There was hope in their unshed tears.

"IT'S NOT a date. It's just dinner," Pavia said to her reflection with a nod.

Alex had said dinner was casual, so she wore jeans and a silk camisole with a deep green cashmere cardigan that tied at the waist and some ballet flats. She left her hair down and her makeup simple, powder, mascara, and lip gloss that enhanced the natural rosy brown tint of her lips.

A knock on the door left no more time for self-reflection. Alex stood on her threshold with his hands in the pockets of his field coat and a warm smile on his face.

"Hey." His voice held a slight note of uncertainty that made Pavia wonder if he thought she might change her mind. "You should grab a coat."

She lifted her coat off the hook George put up for her that afternoon, similar in style and color to the one Alex wore. "We're twins." She pointed between them with a nervous laugh.

"I don't think anyone will ever get us confused. You're too beautiful."

Her body heated as his gaze raked over her. She returned his assessment, noting the way his coat stretched over his shoulders and his long legs were encased in denim. But there were also lines of stress bracketing his mouth.

"Everything okay?"

His jaw ticked. "Long day." His smile didn't quite reach his eyes. "None of that matters now. Let's go have our dinner."

Pavia gave him a curious look when she saw the quad.

"Trust me," he said with a glint in his eye.

They zipped through the vineyard on a dirt access road that took them toward a large barn-shaped building ten times the size of hers at the cottage. Painted a green-gray with black trim and a black metal roof, it sat low in a channel between two hills, disguising its true size. When they reached the building, Alex took a picnic basket out of the back seat, guided her toward a side door, and entered a code on the keypad. They went inside, and she let out a soft gasp when he pressed another series of numbers into a larger keypad and the lights turned on like a row of dominos. Racks with pallets of wine boxed and ready to ship stretched from one end of the cavernous space to the other. Pavia craned her neck, her eyes wide, lips moving. She started counting.

Alex must have noticed. "We ship about eight million cases a year, half from here and half from another storage facility on another part of the estate."

"Incredible," she said in a hushed voice.

"Just wait," he said, leading her farther into the barn toward a set of large arched wooden doors. He set the basket down and entered a code into yet another keypad. The door clicked and swung open slowly.

Pavia stepped forward and peered in. Her hand flew to her chest. "Wow."

Alex placed his hand at the small of her back, nudging her forward into the dark, cool space carved into the hillside.

"The barn was built to hide the caves during Prohibition. The warehouse replaced the barn, and the caves remained hidden away. Most people don't even know they exist, and only a handful of people have the code to get in."

He pressed a switch on the wall, illuminating the room, revealing a series of four interconnected cavernous spaces. Stone bricks covered the ceiling with arches and buttresses that reminded her of some of the older churches she'd toured when she lived in Italy. Layers of plaster smoothed over the rough rock walls.

Alex grabbed a wine thief and two glasses from a nearby table while she wandered farther into the space.

"There are over seven thousand square feet of caves here," he began. "Over time, through the gold rush, and Prohibition, people expanded what the monks started in the seventeen hundreds, and this is what we have now."

Alex took the rubber mallet lying on top of a barrel and gave the plastic plug a few taps to loosen it before twisting it with his hand to remove it. He dipped the wine thief in and dispensed the liquid he drew out between the two glasses. He held one out to her.

Pavia tipped the glass to her nose, then took a deep breath, hesitating before taking a sip and then another sip and swishing the liquid around in her mouth. She held the glass in front of her, tipping it so the wine rested at the rim, studying the garnet color of the Syrah.

"This is last year's harvest."

She held the glass to her nose again. "There are some really lovely notes of black cherry and sage here. How much longer do you think you are going to let it rest?"

"This will be our barrel select for wine club members only. The cellar master and I agreed to let it sit for another four months before we bottle it."

She nodded absently, holding the glass up to the light. It wasn't what she would do, but it wasn't her place to say.

Alex eyed her warily. "You don't agree, do you?"

"The acidity is just a little too bright. Give it some time to settle. If you bottle it too soon, the structure will fall apart as the wine opens," she explained while they sipped.

He looked from her to the glass and back again.

Pavia cleared her throat. "I didn't mean to be rude." She put her glass down on top of the barrel and stepped back. "It's not really my place to say."

"You're a supertaster, aren't you?"

She gave a slight nod. "Yup."

"I'm jealous." He put his glass down next to hers. "I envy people with more taste buds than the average person."

"It's not all it's cracked up to be. Some foods can be way too salty or sweet. And I hate Brussels sprouts, and kale is so bitter." She shuddered. "I don't know how anyone eats that stuff."

Alex chuckled. "I never thought of that."

He replaced the plug and left the thief and glasses on top of the barrel and gestured toward the shadow of a small alcove in the distance. "There's one more thing I'd like to show you."

The temperature dropped a few more degrees as they moved deeper into the earth. The calm silence of the caves enveloped them.

"I can't get over this space," she said.

"We have another smaller cave on the other side of the vineyard. The monks started the original wineries in this valley. Every generation of my family has expanded on the land that was originally purchased from the church. Generation after generation, we've cultivated the land and tended the vines."

"It's an amazing legacy to be a part of one of the founding families."

"You can say the same thing about your family. Your dad is a legend."

The light became dimmer, and the walls closed in around them until they stood shoulder to shoulder.

He gestured to a small door off to the side. "During Prohibition, my family allowed smugglers to use the caves for spirits and wine."

"This is incredible. How many casks do you have stored here?" Pavia exclaimed, looking over her shoulder at the long line of barrels that they had already passed.

"In this section, just under a thousand, give or take."

He pointed at a barrel that was set off to the side. A single light above gave it a shrine-like appearance.

"I brought you here to see this."

When she saw the stamp on the side, she stopped. A small gasp escaped her. Pavia crouched down and, with trembling fingers, reached out to trace the names.

Age had darkened the wood and the metal of the stays, and the wine stains had faded to a pale hue. He moved closer, and his arm pressed against hers in the cramped corner.

"Our grandfathers' signatures. This was the first barrel they produced together."

She pressed one palm against the oak and the other to her heart. Alex reached out and caught the teardrop clinging to her lashes before it could fall. It was one thing to know about her legacy, the people who brought her to this point in her life. Seeing Henry and Antonio's names burnished into the wood made their story real, just like Antonio's diary did.

"Pavia, I didn't mean to upset you. I thought you would like to see a piece of your family history." He wrapped his arm around her, pulling her close to his side.

"I can't help thinking about my dad. He should be here, not me. This was his home." Her voice broke with renewed heartache. "He lost everything, including his family history. I know it's not fair, that it's not your fault, but I...." She turned away, wiping her eyes.

"If we can't move forward from the past, what hope do we have for the future?"

The anguish in his voice made her wonder. What other regrets about the past did Alex have, other than just what had happened between their families?

Pavia opened her mouth and then snapped it shut, her lips pressed together in a thin line. "It's too much," she whispered, shaking her head.

"There's so much history. Can't you feel it? The spirits of Henry and Antonio are here in the room right now."

"But we're also here, living, breathing people," he said, reaching up to cup her face and wiping another tear away with his thumb. Alex brushed his lips against her temple, her cheek, and her mouth. He shivered when her curls brushed against his face.

Pavia sighed and, for just a moment, leaned in before stepping back. She glanced down at the signatures again, shaking her head.

"I'm scared," she admitted.

"So am I."

She looked up at him. The combination of fear, pain, and hope in his eyes took her breath away. Pushing her own doubts away, she cupped the back of his neck and kissed him. He groaned, reaching under her coat to wrap his arms around her waist and pull her closer. The coolness of the caves clung to her lips, and the taste of plum and black pepper lingered on her tongue from the wine. Her emotions became a joust between caution and desire. Desire won the battle when their kiss deepened. Appraising, tasting, devouring, they clung to each other, letting fear evolve into something far more frightening.

She broke away. Alex looked down at her, his pupils dilated with his lips slightly parted.

"Please tell me you don't regret that," he said in a low, husky voice.

"No." Pavia shook her head, unable to say anything to diminish what had just happened. She pressed her hand to his chest. His heavy heartbeat drummed under her fingertips when he dipped his head again. "But I need to—" *Need to what? Stop? Slow down?* "I want to take this slow. This isn't just about us, Alex. No matter how much we try to avoid or ignore it, our family history will influence this… us."

His hands fell from her waist to her hands, clasping them as his eyes locked with hers. "I understand, but there is something between us, and I'm not going to run away from it."

She dipped her head in agreement.

He looked around the room. "I was thinking we would have dinner here, but I think there are too many ghosts surrounding us. Come on, I've got another idea."

Alex led her back to the entrance to the cave. Grabbing the picnic basket, he turned off the lights, plunging the room into darkness again.

The door closed, and the soft electronic buzz signaled the lock had reengaged, keeping their shared history safe.

They got back in the quad, and Alex took off again, driving farther up the hill to a small clearing with a pergola and four picnic tables.

"What do you think? Will this work for a dinner venue?"

"It's perfect." She grinned, taking in the view. "This reminds me of home. We don't have as many workers of course so we don't have as many places like this on our property. We attached bathrooms and a small kitchen area with built-in barbecues about ten years ago so the workers could have a place to wash up and cook. It made more sense than bringing in Porta Potties every year."

Alex paused, unpacking the food. "That's a good idea."

She had expected him to question the expense. It wasn't cheap adding septic systems and additional plumbing. His nod of approval reminded her she still had a lot to learn about Alex.

"Shit." He slapped his forehead.

"What's wrong?"

"I can't believe I did this," he muttered, holding a corkscrew in his hand. He looked at her, his eyes wide in disbelief. "I forgot the wine."

Pavia blinked and then clapped her hand over her mouth, failing to cover her laugh.

"I thought we'd eat in the wine cave and I would grab a bottle from there."

"It doesn't matter," she laughed.

"Yes, it does," he groaned. "I own a fucking vineyard, and I forgot to bring wine to dinner."

She put her hand on his arm. "Alex, it doesn't matter. We don't need wine to enjoy a meal together. If wine is the only thing that we have in common, then…."—she shrugged—"then we're going to have a hard time being friends."

His frown transformed into a smile. "You're right."

"This looks delicious on its own."

And it was. They had a feast of chicken Caesar salad accompanied by a loaf of crusty french bread, plus Brie and thinly sliced pears. To end their meal, they indulged in buttery, sweet pecan bars. They proved to each other that wine wasn't the only thing that connected them, talking about books they'd recently read—Alex telling her about his favorite spy thriller, while she tried to convince him he should read every book Jane

Austen had ever written. Pavia figured they'd continue to argue over wine, what yeast strains were superior, and of course her ideas about biodynamic production, but now she knew they would have as much to talk about as to argue over.

When they packed the leftovers away, Pavia sighed and gazed up at the stars. "Do you think they're watching us?"

"Who?"

"Antonio and Henry."

Alex huffed a laugh. "Knowing my grandfather, he is, and he's laughing his ass off."

He leaned over and pressed a kiss against her temple. His lips moved to hers.

"It's late," she sighed.

"And you don't want this to go any further."

She reached up and let her fingers trail over his jawline. "For now."

He sighed. "Budbreak is going to happen any day now. We'll both be busy. You have a winery to build out, and it will get even more intense the closer we get to harvest. But I'd like it if we could carve out time to see each other."

She tilted her head, taking in the look of hope in his eyes. "I'd like that too."

ALEX DIDN'T see Pavia the next day. He did receive a curt text from his brother saying he was staying at the condo they kept in the city for a few days. Knowing his brother's wild ways, he was sure Nick was hitting the bars and drowning his anger and frustration with drinks and women. His brother preferred one-night stands to anything that resembled a girlfriend. It would have been better if Nick stayed in town. Alex hoped they could talk and finally confront the uncomfortable truth of their past. Nick had been protected for too long, and it was time to stop treating him with kid gloves.

Today, Alex woke up and knew without having to look that the moment every winemaker patiently endured winter waiting for was here. He showered and dressed quickly, donning his field boots and sweater before heading to the Brothers Block.

Pavia was there, bent over a vine, looking closely at one of the branches. She looked up when he approached, her eyes sparkling with excitement.

"Budbreak," he said.

"Budbreak," she answered.

They stood there grinning at each other, celebrating the magical moment when the sap rises from the root of the vine and the first buds that will become perfect flowers with the ability to self-pollinate appear. This was the moment the fate of the harvest rested on. From here on out, the vines would be carefully guarded and watched over. During budbreak, one heavy rain or hailstorm could do enough damage to the delicate buds to negatively impact a winemaker's production for the year.

"These are hardy vines." He struggled to get the words past the lump in his throat.

The first budbreak without his grandfather. The reality hit him with the fierceness of a punch in the gut, and for a moment, he fought to breathe.

Pavia moved closer. "Alex, are you okay?"

"I just realized this is the first budbreak without Grandad. I knew it was coming, but… I wasn't ready."

"Oh, Alex." Pavia wrapped her arms around him. He shuddered and let himself sink into the solace she offered. He would have been happy to stand there in the circle of her embrace through every season of the vineyard, but after a few moments, he reluctantly let go.

Dropping his forehead to hers, he gripped her upper arms gently and exhaled. "I wish there were more hours in the day, but I've got to go."

She reached up and threaded her fingers through the hair at the nape of his neck. "What if you let yourself stay?"

He'd never wanted to accept an invitation so badly in his life, but the cellar master was waiting for him, and he had an afternoon of meetings with distributors scheduled. Reluctantly, he stepped out of Pavia's arms.

"My schedule is full." He reached out and wound the curl that had come loose at the base of her neck around his finger. "But can I come back?"

"I'm not a great cook, but come for dinner tonight."

"I'll bring dinner if you supply the wine."

"Deal."

Alex stuck his hands in his pockets, fighting the urge to reach for Pavia again, and struggled back up the hill toward a day of responsibilities that he wasn't looking forward to.

By midafternoon, both his mother and Divit had had enough. They kicked him out of the office and told him to go work off some of his nervous energy in the barrel room. Hiring Divit was one of the best decisions they'd made since Grandad passed. The spacious office that once held a single desk now had three, and he was happy to share his space with his mom and Divit. They made a good team. It turned out Divit was great with social media and quickly developed a strong rapport with their distributors. His mom was taking an online course in accounting, and her confidence grew as she took on more responsibilities keeping track of supply orders. Every day, Alex felt like he had a little more space to breathe and didn't feel quite so overwhelmed. That also meant he had more time to realize he didn't have much of a life outside the family business. That was something he was determined to alter.

After showering and changing into a pair of dark-wash jeans and a lightweight sweater the color of the Italian cypress trees outside, he raided the freezer, taking advantage that his mom always kept it fully stocked. He carried a picnic basket fully loaded with lasagna, garlic bread, and a simple green salad out to his car, his eyes to the sun that hadn't hit the trees yet. He was early, but he didn't care, and he figured Pavia wouldn't mind either.

Pavia opened the door wearing a yellow dress that skimmed over her hips and swirled around her ankles. The short sleeves showed off her tan arms, and the neckline was just low enough to show a bit of cleavage.

"I'm early," he said.

She stepped back to let him in. "I'm glad."

"I hope lasagna is okay."

"If your mom made it, then absolutely." She took the basket from his hands and headed toward the kitchen.

Alex ran his hand over the grapevine inlay on the upper cabinets. "These are amazing."

"Sam's grandfather made them."

"I hear Sam is following in his footsteps."

Pavia nodded toward a narrow floor-to-ceiling wine rack that she'd added to the end of the run of cabinets along one side of the galley kitchen as she pulled food out of the basket. "Sam built the wine rack. Are you hungry? Do you want to eat now or wait a while?"

"If you don't mind, I'd love a tour of the house first. I've never really spent any time inside, and I'd like to see the work that you've done."

"Sure." Pavia went to the wine rack and pulled out a bottle, turning the label to face Alex. "Since we're having lasagna, how about we start with a Barbera?"

"Perfect."

"This is from one of my college instructors. He has a small winery east of Blue Ridge," she explained, handing him a glass.

He held his glass up to the light, admiring the deep ruby color. He sniffed, taking in the dark cherry plum aroma with just a hint of nutmeg and anise. Pavia paused, holding her glass to her lips as he sipped before taking one of her own.

"Well?"

"Beautiful," he murmured, his compliment meant for both the wine and the way Pavia's full lips caressed the rim of her glass.

Their eyes locked, and the air grew heavy. Desire swept over him. Instead of trying to tamp it down, he set his glass aside and moved to stand in front of Pavia, gently removing her glass from her hands and setting it next to his before he snaked his arm around her waist. Her breath hitched just as his mouth pressed against hers. She swept her tongue into his mouth with a soft moan, moving closer, pressing her body against his. Pavia tasted like summer, with blackberries and lavender on her tongue from the wine.

He tore his mouth away from hers, his breath ragged. "I don't want you to think I came here just to seduce you."

Her lips curved into a sly smile. "But that doesn't mean you didn't think about it."

"It's all I thought about since I saw you this morning." Alex cupped her cheek, brushing his thumb over the faint trail of freckles scattered over her cheekbone. "The truth is, I've thought about kissing you, making love to you, since the first day I saw you. I tried not to, but you've crept into my soul, Pavia. I've never wanted… needed someone as much as I do you."

She closed her eyes and exhaled before opening them again with nothing but desire in their depths. Pavia took his hand and tugged him out of the kitchen.

"Let's start the tour with my bedroom," she said over her shoulder as she led him down the hallway.

Alex hesitated at the threshold of her bedroom. "I need to know if you want this as much as I do," he said. "If you say no, this stops right now, but please"—he sucked in his breath—"please don't ask me to go. We can just have dinner if—"

Pavia reached for his sweater. Tugging at the hem, she whispered, "Stay."

His hand trembled as his fingers traced the neckline of her dress. He dipped his head and kissed the nape of her neck before capturing her mouth again while he unzipped her dress.

His heart seized when he saw her standing in the moonlight in her pale yellow lacy bra and panties. Alex fell to his knees and created a trail of kisses up her thighs before pressing his lips to her mound, the lace tickling his lips. She backed toward the bed, and he followed her on his knees, then crawled up beside her as she lay back against the mattress. The heat from her body melded with his, creating an inferno. Any lingering worries he had about getting entangled with Pavia, knowing the history between their families, vanished. Her fingers were light as they danced across his shoulders and down his back, dipping into the waistband of his boxer briefs.

"You smell like summer, so damn good," he murmured, slipping the strap of her bra off her shoulder.

He could feel the uptick in her pulse as he continued to whisper how the softness of her skin felt under his fingertips and mouth. She gasped, arching into him, as he drew her taut nipple into his mouth.

"You are perfect. Well-balanced, full-bodied, with long legs," he said in a playful tone, running his hand up to the juncture of her legs.

She laughed softly. "Do you describe all your dates like wine?"

Alex shook his head. "You are a perfect vintage."

Pavia clasped her hand to the back of his neck, pulling him down for another kiss. She shifted against him with a little impatient growl that tested the thin hold he had on his lust.

"Condoms?" he asked.

She flung her arm toward the nightstand, fumbling for the drawer, and he yanked it open and grabbed for the box. She sat up and moved to straddle him, taking the condom that he'd just extracted out of his hand.

"You're my guest," she said with a husky whisper, pushing his hands away.

She pulled his boxer briefs off, her face hovering over his length, her lips ghosting over the tip before she sheathed him. Instead of removing her panties, she pushed them to the side and in one swift movement sank onto his length. It was the sexiest thing he'd ever witnessed. The lace edge of her panties added friction as she lifted and dropped her hips, moving him in and out. Her hands were pressed against his chest as she bowed her head, creating a curtain of curls over her face. He reached up, brushing them back so he could see her eyes, and that was his undoing.

Moonlight streamed through Pavia's bedroom window as she curled up next to him and rested her head on his shoulder.

Alex wrapped one of her curls around his finger. Rubbing the soft, silky strands between his thumb and forefinger, he smiled. He had been dying to play with her curls since the day they first met. He'd spent so many hours imagining them splayed on his pillow, but the reality was so much better than any fantasy.

He felt Pavia's lips curve into a smile. "You always find a way to touch my hair," she sighed.

Alex turned on his side and propped himself on his elbow. "I don't know how to explain it. They're a part of you. I like you, Pavia. I like everything about you."

Her lips curled into a smile. "I like you too."

His smile fell. "What happens now?"

"We take it one day at a time." Pavia propped herself up, mirroring him. "I wasn't expecting this… us, and it's complicated. Your brother and the history between our families. I don't want to rush into anything or upset anyone."

Alex nodded in agreement, but that wasn't how he felt. Yes, a relationship with Pavia could cause difficulties with their families, but he wasn't going to hide his feelings for her.

"If we're going to start a relationship, I don't want to sneak around and hide," he said.

"I wasn't saying I wanted to do that. I just—"

Alex flopped back on the bed, blinking up at the ceiling. "Like you said, it's complicated."

Pavia leaned over him, her eyes sparkling in the moonlight. "Complicated but not impossible."

Her lips met his, and the world became full of possibilities when he took her in his arms again.

Pavia slept curled up next to him. They'd eaten dinner in bed and made love again before dessert. He should be exhausted, but he couldn't sleep. For the first time in a long time, he felt present, fully aware of everything at the moment: the silvery blue moonlight, the scent of vanilla on Pavia's skin, her soft sigh as she snuggled deeper into his arms. Alex lay in the darkness for a long time, embracing his contentment.

Still unable to sleep, he carefully extracted himself from her arms and pulled on his boxer briefs. He wandered into the living room looking for something to read on the built-in shelves on either side of the fireplace that were now filled with books and a few small knickknacks. He turned on the floor lamp next to an overstuffed chair that he could picture Pavia curled up in while she read. Smiling, he ran his hand over the spines of familiar books on wine before moving to a collection of Jane Austen novels and variations before he noticed a small leather-bound book lying on the shelf next to a picture of her father.

Intrigued by the wine stains and the faded yellow pages, he opened the book, and his heart stopped.

"What the hell?"

CHAPTER *Six*

PAVIA BOLTED upright when she heard Alex shout. Grabbing the quilt off the end of the bed, she wrapped it around her, followed the sound, and sprinted into the living room. She stopped short when she saw him holding Antonio's diary, a look of anger mixed with hurt on his face.

"What the hell is this?" he asked, shaking the journal at her. "Where did you get this?"

Pavia licked her lips, clutching the quilt around her shoulders. "Antonio left it for me."

Alex shook his head. The look of betrayal on his face broke her heart.

She pointed to the journal. "I put the paper it was wrapped in, in the back."

He flipped through the pages to the back of the book and lifted out the folded brown paper, her name clearly written on the front in his grandfather's handwriting.

"I found it when I was cleaning out the kitchen after… when I got here. It was in one of the drawers."

"And were you ever going to tell me about it?" he spat out.

"I-I wasn't sure when or how."

She moved closer, but he pulled away when she reached for him.

"Don't. How many other secrets are you keeping from me?"

"I'm not keeping secrets. I'm not responsible for what happened in the past, and neither are you."

He set the journal back on the bookshelf, his hand resting on top of it for a moment before he let it fall to his side. "I need some time," he muttered, brushing past her.

He emerged a second later, his jeans on but still unzipped, tugging his sweater over his head, with his shoes in his hand.

"Are you seriously going to leave? Can't we talk about this?" Pavia said.

Alex pressed his lips together and shook his head. "Maybe later, but not right now." He jerked the door open and walked out, slamming it behind him with enough force to make the windows rattle.

Pavia stared at the door in shock, listening to the sound of his car fade away. She eyed the journal and, with an angry grunt, swiped it off the bookcase and took it back to her bed. The scent of sex and Alex still lingered on the rumpled sheets. With another frustrated huff, she stripped the bed and put on fresh sheets before climbing back under the covers. The sky was already beginning to lighten as she fluffed her pillows and settled herself against the headboard with the journal in her lap.

She could barely contain her anger at both Alex and Antonio. She wasn't keeping the diary a secret, not exactly. And damn Antonio for putting her in this position. As she flipped through the pages of the journal, a sentence caught her eye.

Henry isn't speaking to me.

Pavia paused, staring at the sentence for a second. With a heavy sigh, she leaned back against the pillows and started at the beginning of the page.

October 18, 1943

Tonight, I am numb with defeat. We are part of the first group to make our way north toward Rome. On the 13th, Italy declared war on Germany, and the fighting has been fierce. Now we are north of Naples to rest and resupply. The British are going to attack at the Sangro River. We all pray they are successful. We all want to celebrate the German defeat in Rome.

There has been so much death and destruction in the last few weeks. Progress is much slower than we hoped. I am thankful that Henry and I are still alive. With every round of gunfire, I find myself fearing for Henry's life more than my own. It's made me even more selfish for the time we've had together. As thankful as I am, I feel so guilty for every moment I have with Henry, when so many are dying around us. I want everyone to understand what it means to love someone regardless of what they look like. If people could just sit down and talk to each other, we wouldn't be in this terrible war.

October 20, 1943

I lost my temper again today, kicking at the rocks in our path, grumbling at anyone and everyone. Henry and I fought last night, and now Henry isn't speaking to me. Maybe I am not speaking to him. I don't know.

The sergeant was giving Henry a hard time again, calling him foul names, blaming him for everything. I got so mad I cussed the sergeant out. I shouldn't have done it. He threatened to court-martial me. That's not why Henry is angry. He's upset because he found out I could have transferred to another unit working communications, a safer assignment, but I refused. I told my superiors I wanted to stay and fight alongside my brothers in arms. That was a lie. I couldn't leave Henry.

He said I should have told him. That it wasn't fair for me to make the decision without him. I was trying to—I didn't want him to feel guilty. Every day we follow orders, the rules of the army, and the rules of decorum, but what are the rules for us, for Henry and I?

Pavia's heart thundered in her chest. She stared at the words on the page, wondering. What she suspected made her decision about sharing the diary even more difficult.

There weren't enough cups of coffee to face the day. Pavia sat on her doorstep staring at the vines, willing them to bloom faster. She inhaled the fragrant steam from the oversized mug in her hands, her gaze flickering toward the villa. Should she try to call Alex?

She pulled out her phone, and her finger hovered over the screen for a moment before she pressed send. Moments later, her dad's voice washed over her.

"Pavia? It's early. Is everything okay?" he asked.

She struggled to speak past the sudden lump that formed in her throat. "Are you out on your morning walk?" she asked, picturing her father and brother walking through the fields. "I miss you, Dad." The words tumbled out of her as her gaze drifted over the hills. "I don't know if I can do this." The urge to jump into her truck and drive home just for a hug and her dad's calm reassurance that everything was going to be okay swept through her.

"What's going on, sweetie?"

"Homesick, I guess," she said in a shaky voice. "It's hard with the Contis. Harder than I thought it would be. I didn't expect to like some of them as much as I do."

"Oh?" he replied.

"Sarah's lovely, Dad. I didn't want to like her, but I can't help it, and I feel awful."

"Pavia, sweetheart, don't feel bad. Sarah is a generous and loving woman." She didn't miss the slight tremor in his voice. "No matter what happened in the past, that hasn't changed. I am glad you like her. I... I hoped you would. I don't want you to feel like you can't talk about the Contis. I didn't handle the news about Antonio's will very well, but the past is past."

Despite his disapproval of her decision to come to Seneca, her dad was her rock, anchoring her through any storm.

"Remember how I told you about how Nick, the younger brother, seemed nice when we met at the lawyer's office? Well," she snorted, "he's not, not even close. It's Alex...." She drifted off, unsure how to continue.

"What about Alex, sweetheart?"

Pavia wasn't ready to talk about her conflicted feelings toward Alex. Besides, they were too jumbled of a mess for her to make sense out of, let alone explain to someone else.

"He's—" She paused, trying to gather her thoughts. "He's just different from what I expected."

"There's nothing wrong with that."

The calmness in her father's voice set her teeth on edge. She didn't want calm. She wanted her dad to be outraged and tell her she should stay away from him.

"What made you decide to keep what happened here a secret? I mean, why didn't you tell Robert and me before?"

Her dad was silent for several moments. "I didn't think of it as keeping it a secret, but more of a memory that was too painful to share."

Her dad's logic made sense. Pavia took a deep breath.

"Do you... do you think Henry had any secrets?"

"What do you mean?"

"I don't know. I was just... I've been thinking about Henry and Antonio's friendship, wondering what would have happened if Henry hadn't died so young. If he had been alive when you and Sarah were in love, would things have turned out differently?"

"I can't let myself think about what-if. Those are the kind of thoughts that can tear you apart if you let it."

"Did your dad ever talk about his time with Antonio during the war?"

"No, he never did. The only person he ever talked about his time in the service with was Antonio. I'd see them sometimes sitting together and talking. I could always tell when they were sharing stories from their time in the service. There was this… intensity between them."

She had so many questions. What were Henry and Antonio's relationships with their wives? That thought led her to another.

Pavia sucked in a breath. "Dad, did you love Mom the way you loved Sarah?"

Her dad let out a pained sound that was almost a whimper, making her instantly regret asking the question.

"Pavia, I loved your mother. Rebecca was a wonderful woman. I didn't think I could love anyone after Sarah. When I met your mom, I was so broken. We were honest with each other from the very beginning. I told her I didn't think I could give my heart to another woman, but she was patient with me, more patient than I deserved, and over time, I grew to love her.

"It wasn't the same love that Sarah and I shared. It was different, more mature. We shared a companionship, a friendship that was deeper in some ways than the love of my youth." He sighed. "I'm not going to lie. There was never any grand passion between us, but I loved her."

"*Papà*, you can't go back, but you can move forward just like you're telling me to."

Pavia wanted her father to be happy, to have a happiness Henry and Antonio may have never had and one she thought she might experience with Alex.

"It's been too many years. I'm not the man I was back then. Hell, I wasn't even a man, just a boy. I can't go back, sweetheart."

"When you're ready, I'd really like you to come for a visit." She held her breath, waiting, hopeful that he would say yes.

There was a tremor in his voice when he finally replied. "This isn't about me, it's about you. Follow your heart, sweetheart. I'll be proud of you no matter what happens."

He didn't say no outright, and the glimmer of hope peeked like the first glimpse of sunlight through the clouds, a sliver of light against her disappointment.

"Thanks, *Papà*, I didn't mean to dump all this on you when I called." She closed her eyes and wiped the tears away.

"That's what dads are for, and, sweetheart… I miss you."

"I miss you so much. I miss Robert and my cousins too. I miss our morning walks. I miss being a family, and home," she choked out.

"We're still a family. We can be a hundred miles away or on the other side of the world—we will always be family. I'm here for you whenever you need me. Blue Ridge isn't that far away, and we'll always support you no matter what."

"*Ti amo, Papà.*" She took a deep breath and hung up.

The last of her coffee was cold in her cup, and her heart was still heavy. She wasn't going to ask Alex to forgive her for something she didn't do wrong. Antonio left the diary with her. Remembering what her dad said, she looked at her own situation. She wasn't keeping secrets. Maybe she was protecting the past, or at least keeping the past from causing any more harm. Either way, Antonio had given her a gift and left her with a burden.

"No offense, but my mom would have a heart attack if she saw you shoving those zinnias into the ground like you were shoving your foot into a boot."

Pavia wiped her gloved hand over her forehead, sat back on her heels, and shot Sam an angry glare.

He held his hands up and backed up a step. "Whatever it is, I didn't do it."

She stood up with a heavy sigh. "Sorry, I'm just… frustrated."

"Do I want to know why?"

"Probably not."

Sam set his toolbox down and rested his hands on his hips. "If the Contis—"

Pavia held her hand up. "No reason to get all overprotective. Not that I don't appreciate it. It's… complicated."

"The Contis have always been a mystery to me," a soft voice announced.

A young woman approached the front of the cottage, where Pavia had been trying to rehab the neglected landscaping. Her dark brownish-black hair was pulled into a low ponytail. Large brown eyes that matched Sam's looked at Pavia from a petite oval face with curiosity.

"Hi I'm Sam's sister, Lilly Matsui. I've been dying to meet you. I don't have any patients until this afternoon, so I used bringing coffee as an excuse to be nosy," she said, holding up a thermos.

"My little sister is a therapist and a nosy pest." Sam wrapped his arm around his sister's neck, which reminded Pavia of the way her brother would that do to her.

"I've been wanting to meet you since you got here. I've been slammed at work and haven't had the time before now," Lilly said, shaking Pavia's hand.

"It's nice to meet you." She smiled, instantly liking Sam's sister's warm, friendly manner.

"Sam's been telling me about the work he and Dad have been doing here, and I wanted to come and see it. I hope you don't mind. I've always been curious about this place."

"Would you like a tour?" Pavia offered.

Lilly's smile widened. "I'd love one."

"Come on in." She waved Lilly inside.

"It's just as charming on the inside as the outside," she said, peeking into the second bedroom.

Pavia folded her arms. "It's come a long way since when I first got here. I couldn't have done any of it without your dad and brother."

"Are you kidding? They love it. Most folks want everything new. They've been so happy working on restoring what's here instead of tearing it all out." Lilly ran her hand along the dining room tabletop. "I thought all the furniture had been destroyed. This is a beautiful vintage piece."

Pavia grimaced. "Mrs. Conti, Sarah, insisted on replacing it with pieces they had in storage."

Lilly cocked her head, looking at her thoughtfully. "And you don't like accepting the help."

"Maybe, partially. I don't know."

"I heard things have been a bit… rough with the Contis."

"That's one way to describe it."

Sam approached and threw his arm around his sister's neck again. "Lilly and I are going to Hudson's tonight after work. Why don't you join us?"

"Yes, you should come." Lilly nodded enthusiastically. "Chloe Garza is in town. You'll love her."

"Chloe is Melinda's daughter," Sam explained at Pavia's quizzical expression. "Come on, you've done all you can do around here for now. Come out with us and have some fun."

A slow smile spread over her face. "Sure, why not? I need to get out more and make some new friends other than—" Pavia clamped her mouth shut. She hadn't heard or seen Alex since he left and didn't consider him much of a friend, or anything else, at the moment.

Sam gave her a sympathetic smile, while Lilly's gaze was filled with curiosity.

Pavia arranged to meet them later that evening, and Lilly left for work, leaving her at loose ends. She planted the last of her flowers with more care than she'd started with and then wandered through her vineyard. The tiny leaves unfurling sparked joy that tempered some of the anger she felt toward Alex. The idea of spending a night out with new friends also helped. She had never been a big social butterfly back home, but here she'd been much more aware of her loneliness and how isolating it was moving to a new town with no friends or family. Work was an unfit companion and didn't make for a happy life.

Her thoughts drew her gaze back toward the Conti villa. It didn't seem like Alex had much of a social life either. His work and family consumed him, and now it affected hers. How long would it take for him to apologize for storming out? She kicked at the dirt. What if he didn't? With a heavy sigh, she faced the reality that Sam was right. There wasn't anything else she could do but wait for her vines to grow and for Alex to decide how long he was going to behave like an ass.

That evening, she pulled up in front of Hudson's. The location showed this wasn't a place for the tourists. Off the main drag, the bar sat nestled in a row of storefronts between a used bookstore and a tiny shoe repair shop. She gave herself one last glance in the rearview mirror. Pavia got lucky with a last-minute hair appointment at a salon a few towns over that cut curly hair, and now her golden brown locks rested on her shoulders in perfect spirals that shone from a deep-conditioning treatment. She'd chosen a dark blue silk peasant blouse paired with jeans and brown suede ankle boots. She touched up her lip gloss and fingered her favorite pair of gold hoops. They were her going-out hoops that she wore on dates.

Her gaze flicked toward the bar, watching the people mingling inside. As much as she was looking forward to going out, the idea of flirting with some random guy in a bar held no interest. Having someone try to pick her up filled her with a sense of… what? Dread? Discomfort? Or disloyalty? She and Alex weren't a couple, but she had feelings for him. Strong feelings that had led to a night of passion that obviously meant more to her than it did to Alex. She got out of her truck and slammed the door with renewed anger. No calls, no messages, nothing since he walked away. Pavia straightened her shoulders and, with her head held high, walked into the bar. She wasn't going to be one of those women who sat around pining. She wasn't going to put her life on hold waiting for Alex Conti to pull his head out of his ass. But that didn't stop her from scanning the crowd, looking for his face.

Alex wasn't there, but Sam and Lilly were, waving at her from a high-top table in the corner. Another woman Pavia guessed to be around her age sat with them. Her heart-shaped face and dark brown eyes matched her mother Melinda's.

"We ordered a pitcher. I hope that's okay," Lilly said, pouring a glass for Pavia when she sat down.

"It's an IPA from a brewery up the road," Sam added. "Pavia, this is Chloe, Melinda's daughter."

"I figured." Pavia shook her hand. "You look just like your mom."

"It's nice to meet you. My mom has told me so much about you. She's thrilled we finally have a chance to connect."

"Your mom says you're a chef."

Chloe nodded. "Pastry chef."

"The most amazing pastry chef on the planet. You should try her lemon quince tart with lavender." Lilly groaned. "It's incredible."

"You know, it's at least a year away, but I've been thinking about having a few food offerings when I have a tasting room open. Could I hire you to consult with me on something like that?"

Chloe's eyes widened, her expression becoming more animated. "I'd love to work with you."

"I approve. Chloe works at a fancy five-star restaurant in San Francisco where they don't appreciate how talented she is," Lilly said with a hint of anger in her voice. "She could do so much better, and I, for one, would like to have my friend back in in Seneca."

Chloe dipped her head with an embarrassed smile.

"There's enough Riesling fruit I should be able to get at least a hundred cases or so. Maybe you could come up with a dessert and we could have a special kickoff tasting. Once I have the winery fully open, we could create a menu with small plates."

"I love that idea," Chloe said.

They spent the next few minutes brainstorming ideas, with Sam and Lilly offering their input. Just when Pavia started to relax and enjoy herself, Chloe stiffened, her mouth flattening into a straight line.

"Oh great." Lilly rolled her eyes.

Pavia glanced over her shoulder to see Nick sitting at the bar. A lithe brunette woman with overinflated lips was pressed against his side with her arm draped around his neck like a python.

Lilly reached across the table and covered Chloe's hand with hers. Pavia looked at the three of them, zeroing in on the pained expression on Chloe's face.

"I have a feeling I'm missing part of the story here," she said.

"I grew up with Alex and Nick. My mom started working for the Contis when I was five." Chloe's expression grew wistful. "Nick and I used to be thick as thieves. Alex was always nice to me, but he was that much older. Nick and I are only eighteen months apart, and we just…." She shrugged. "He was my best friend until we started high school, and then he started to change."

Pavia guessed Chloe had a crush on Nick at some point, and based on the way her gaze kept straying in his direction, clearly a part of her heart still pined for him.

Chloe's expression clouded with anger as she turned to Pavia. "I can't believe what he did to the cottage and the way he's been treating you." She drew in a shaky breath. "I'm so sorry. I keep thinking he will remember and go back to being the boy who was my best friend."

"You don't have anything to be sorry for. Nick is a grown man, just like his brother," Pavia sighed.

Nick leaned over and whispered something in the woman's ear, and with an angry glance in their direction, he got up and led her out of the bar.

Chloe took a sip of her beer and set the glass down with a thump. "Well, I guess that's done."

"At least we only have to deal with one of the Conti brothers tonight."

Lilly's eyebrows raised. "Uh-oh. That sounds like you've got a story of your own to tell."

"It's complicated. And I—" She thought about the journal, her dad and Sarah's history, and her relationship with Alex. As much as she liked the three people sitting at the table with her, she wasn't sure how much of the story she should share or had the right to tell. She wouldn't talk about her dad and Sarah. It wasn't her story to tell. Alex knew about the journal. There was no secret to keep, and it had been left to her without any direction on keeping it private. Still, she chose her words carefully. "Alex found out that Antonio left me his journal from World War II."

"Wow, that's amazing," Sam said.

"I don't mean to sound insensitive, but why you? Why not Alex or Nick?" Chloe asked.

"I wish I knew." Pavia went on to explain how she'd found the journal.

"What's in it?" Lilly asked.

"It's a diary of his time in the war, and his friendship with my grandpa."

"I have to admit, I can see why Alex would be upset. Antonio gives you the Brothers Block, which he's wanted for a while, and then you receive his grandfather's memories. It's a bit of a gut punch," Chloe said.

"I knew he wanted the Brothers Block, but I don't think I really understood how much it meant to him. *Does* it mean that much to him?"

Chloe answered with a solemn nod. "As long as I can remember, he's talked about taking over the Brothers Block. He even talked about starting his own winery and calling it Brothers Block."

Pavia took in the information with a sick feeling in her stomach. The land and now the journal. He must feel so betrayed. Every time he heard her talk about her plans, watched her work on the land he'd wanted, it must have hurt him. She pressed her hand to her heart, trying to ease the pang of sympathy that had settled there. First thing in the morning, she'd try to talk to Alex.

Someone cleared their throat behind her. She looked over her shoulder, her eyes growing wide when she saw Alex.

"Pavia, can we talk?"

"HEY." ALEX lifted his hand in a half wave to the group at the table with Pavia.

"Do you want to join us?" Sam offered.

"No, that's okay." He glanced at Pavia. "I was just walking by, and I saw Pavia and just… I wondered if I could talk to you for a minute."

Pavia nodded. "Yeah, sure, okay."

She got down off her stool, and he gestured to the front of the bar. Opening the door, they stepped out to the sidewalk lit in a yellow glow from the vintage streetlamps that lined the street.

Pavia's gaze darted up and down the sidewalk. "You just missed Nick."

Alex grasped her shoulders. "Did he cause any trouble?"

"No. He left with his date pretty quickly when he saw we were there."

Alex exhaled, both relieved and angry. Relieved to hear his brother didn't cause a scene and angry that he was relieved.

He let go and shoved his hands into the pockets of his jeans. He should have called, sent a text, or done something before now, but he'd been so angry and hurt. When he woke up this morning, he knew he needed to reach out to Pavia, and he'd spent the day trying to work up the courage to face her. He ended up in Brandon's office at The Vyne, where he confessed to him what had happened. After his friend ripped him a new one for walking out on Pavia, he was making his way back to his car when he saw her through the window of Hudson's. He didn't stop and think. He just went in. Now he stood on the sidewalk trying to figure out where to begin, how to explain how he felt.

"Pavia, I—"

"Alex, I—"

There was a beat where they shared a smile.

"Pavia, I shouldn't have walked out. I was hurt and angry, not with you, but with Antonio. I was upset with my grandfather. I've been angry at him since he died… for dying. But I shouldn't have let my bitterness ruin our night." He reached for her hands, gently brushing his fingers against hers. "A beautiful night that meant a lot to me, that… I didn't want to end."

Pavia took a breath. "I'll be honest, I was mad." Her lips curled into a wry smile. "Really mad. But"—she put her hand on his chest when he started to speak—"I also realize how upset you must have been. Apology accepted. I was never going to keep the journal from you. If you're willing, we can read it together."

"I'd like that," he said, his voice gruff with relief.

Pavia glanced toward the bar. "I should probably get back."

"Yeah, of course."

She clasped his hand. "Come and join us."

Alex didn't expect for his evening to end with Pavia and hanging out with Sam, Lilly, and Chloe. He wasn't part of their group in high school. He wanted to be, but there seemed to be an invisible barrier that consisted of race, class, and economics that he'd never managed to breach. Those barriers were gone now, and any awkwardness he'd expected to feel quickly dissipated. The tabletop was small, and he was close enough to Pavia their arms would brush occasionally. She smiled at him with a gleam in her eye that implied she wanted to be alone with him just as much as he wanted Pavia all to himself.

After a couple of rounds and a platter of wings they all shared, Lilly announced, "I've got an early morning, so I'm going to have to head out."

"I'm her ride, so I guess that's me too." Sam paused and looked at Alex. "This was fun. I hope you'll come and hang out with us again."

"It's been nice to catch up, Alex. I've missed you," Chloe added.

A lump suddenly formed in his throat at the signs of friendship Sam and Chloe were obviously offering. "I'd like that."

And then it was just the two of them.

"Are you ready to head home?" Pavia asked.

There was an unspoken understanding between them that home was Pavia's cottage. He followed her truck, watching her headlights bounce off the rows of vines on the dark road. They were far enough away from town that the stars scattered the sky, creating a sparkling blanket over them. When he pulled in next to her at the cottage, Alex was momentarily taken off guard by how right it felt, as if they were finishing their respective days at the same time and arriving home.

As soon as he made it over the threshold, he pulled Pavia into his embrace and crushed his mouth against hers. Just in case his kiss wasn't enough to convey it, he whispered another apology against her lips. He continued to apologize with his mouth and tongue until she writhed under him.

Pavia's soft sigh of contentment as she pillowed her head against his shoulder brought a smile to his face. After a few minutes, she pulled herself up and slipped out of bed, heading to the bathroom. When she emerged wrapped in a deep plum-colored silk robe, she went over to the dresser. She glanced at him with a hint of worry in her eyes before she opened the top drawer and pulled out Antonio's journal.

He pulled himself up against the headboard as she got back into bed. She settled herself against his side and handed it to him.

"I thought we could read it together."

Alex held the worn leather book and fought back a wave of emotion. He turned it over in his hands and then brought it to his nose.

"I did the same thing the first time I held it," Pavia said.

"Have you read all of it?"

"No. But Alex…." Her brow creased with worry. "I think… I think our grandfathers were more than friends."

It took a second for Pavia's statement to register. "I—how?" He swallowed. "Does it say that in here?" He held the journal up.

"Not exactly. It's just the way your grandfather talks about Henry…." She sighed. "Start at the beginning, and then you can tell me what you think."

Alex opened the journal and began to read. Pavia drew her knees up to her chin, watching and waiting.

When he reached the entry for October 20, Pavia said, "That was the last entry I read."

He let the book rest in his lap and looked at her. "I see what you mean now. It does seem like there was something deeper between them than friendship, doesn't it?"

She nodded. "Should we read the next entry?"

He started to hand the journal back to her, but she pushed it away. "You read it."

Alex cleared his throat and began.

November 4, 1943

We heard that Major General James H. Doolittle will have a headquarters on the Adriatic coast. What Henry is excited about is the rumor that the Tuskegee Airmen will be one of the fighter groups stationed there. I keep catching him eyeing the sky, even though it may be weeks or even months before they arrive.

I feel guilty. I want Henry to have friends that are his own kind. I understand he might miss being with other Negroes. It also scares me. When we couldn't be overheard, I asked him if he'd rather have a Negro friend. I'm ashamed now. There was anger in his voice when he told me that skin color doesn't guarantee friendship. It's what's in your heart. The look in his eyes—I don't have the right words to say how I feel, and I can't write them either. I can only hope someday....

November 5, 1943
We lost a friend today. Corporal Riley was killed by a sniper. He was a good man. It's cold and wet today. The weather matches our gloomy mood. Each death makes me treasure my family and friends even more. I feel guilty. There are times when I don't want the war to end. As terrible as it is, I think having to say goodbye to my best friend at the end will be even worse.

Alex let the pages fall closed. With a heavy sigh, he rested his head against the headboard, taking in what he'd just read.

"I think you're right," he admitted, "about Antonio and Henry. My grandmother left Antonio after your dad left. Mom told me they were never happy together. My mom said the truth, maybe without knowing it. She said my grandmother always wanted Antonio to be different from who he was." He shook his head with a frown. "I always thought it meant she wanted Antonio to be more social. Mom said my grandmother loved getting dressed up and going to parties. It was a big deal for her to belong to the right country club and have a fancy car. Now I wonder if she knew."

"What happened to her?"

"She ran away with a banker she met on a trip to San Francisco. My grandma divorced Grandad and moved to Florida, and we never heard from her again. She died over ten years ago now."

"You never heard from her again?"

"She sent cards on our birthday for a while… until Antonio kicked my father out. We never heard from her after that."

Pavia covered his hand that rested on the journal with hers. "I think she knew. It couldn't have been easy knowing your husband was in love with another man."

"Do you think your dad knew?"

"I don't know. He rarely talked about his time here."

"Secrets," Alex murmured, linking her fingers with his. "Generations of secrets. I'm scared when they all come to light, they'll do more harm than good."

"What do you mean?"

"I'm thinking about my brother. Nick refuses to believe his dad was abusive. And now this, I don't know how he will react hearing that his grandfather may have been in a relationship with your grandfather."

Pavia rested her head on his shoulder. "Now do you understand why I was waiting to share this with you? It isn't easy to rewrite a story you thought you knew. When I came here, I was so sure I would never like your family after hearing my dad's story." She pressed their entwined hands to her heart. "And now here we are, and I know there's so much of the story I still don't know and a lot of my story—our story—that is still unwritten."

"Is it okay for me to still be hurt that Grandad chose you to share his story with and not me?"

Pavia let go of his hand and moved the journal to the bedside table before straddling his waist and framing his face with her hands. She kissed him and then again.

"As long as you don't shut me out, Alex. You have every right to feel whatever you feel, but this"—she pressed her hand to her heart and then his—"will only work if we don't hide what we're feeling from each other."

He looked into her eyes shadowed by the moonlight. What she was asking no one had ever asked him before. As a child, he hid his feelings as a way to survive his father's abuse. As he grew older, he wanted to show that he wasn't like Enzo, that he could control his feelings. Grandad always took pride, calling him his "level-headed" grandson. He'd taken on the role of peacekeeper in his family without ever thinking about what the personal cost was to himself. Pavia had brought desire and passion into his life, and the intensity of his feelings scared him.

Alex pulled her toward him, burying his face in the crook of her neck. "I'll try. I want to, but I've lived with keeping my feelings to myself for a long time."

Pavia reached down and gently grasped his thigh, recentering herself so that her core aligned with his stiffening member. "Then I'll just have to remind you," she said in a husky whisper. When their bodies connected, Alex didn't hide any part of himself.

NICK STOOD on the veranda, staring at the cottage, his hands fisted at his sides.

"You have to let it go, Nick," Alex warned, coming to stand beside him.

Nick glared at him. "Why, because you've decided you want to fuck Pavia?"

"Don't," he growled.

The tension was thick between them. They stood almost toe-to-toe, and yet there had never been so much distance between them.

"I haven't seen you in a while. Don't you think it's time we talked?"

"Why bother? You've proclaimed yourself king around here."

"Jesus, Nick, you're so goddamn dramatic. We're not royalty." Alex thumped his chest. "I'm trying to run a business, and you're determined to make my job more difficult instead of being the partner I wanted you to be. You didn't leave me with a choice. Your shitty attitude and recklessness damage our reputation." He ran his hand through his hair, exhaling with a huff. "I'm so goddamn tired of cleaning up your messes and being your protector."

Nick's jaw ticked. "None of this would have happened if she hadn't come here."

"Pavia is not the enemy."

Nick snorted. "When you first found out about Grandad's will, you thought she was. You were just as angry as I was about her coming here."

Alex angled his head in acknowledgment. His brother was right, they did start out with the same goal, but his point of view had dramatically changed, and now the last thing he wanted to do was to get rid of Pavia.

"That was before I met her," he said. "She's a good vintner, and she'll take good care of the land."

"It's our land, our family legacy, and she has no right to it," Nick seethed.

His heart seized, and his stomach twisted. The look in his brother's eyes brought back dark memories Alex worked hard to keep buried.

"You remind me of Dad when you talk like this," he said, forcing himself to stay calm. Only the slight tremor betrayed his body's response to his childhood trauma.

"And why is that a bad thing? Explain it to me, Alex. Why is it you can barely stand to say his name?"

Alex shook his head. "I don't understand why you insist on clinging to this idea that Dad was this great person?"

"Because someone has to. All you and Mom do is put him down. It's no wonder he left!"

Alex put his hand on his brother's shoulder, looking him in the eye. "Dad drank too much. It got so bad Grandad couldn't leave us alone with him. You were too young to remember how bad it was."

Nick's eyes grew wide for a second before his mouth turned down and he shook his head.

"You were young too. Maybe it wasn't as bad as you remember."

"I'm not going to argue this with you anymore. Enzo was a horrible husband and father. I'm glad he's gone."

Nick shook his head and stepped back, crossing his arms over his chest. "I can't—I don't believe he was who you say he was. I would have remembered. Either way, I can't believe you're going to choose her over loyalty to your own family."

Alex searched for a middle ground that he knew didn't exist. There was no good side to their father. Nick may be a pain in the ass, but their family was so small now, it was just the three of them left, and he didn't want to lose his brother. But did that mean that Nick's happiness was worth sacrificing his own for?

"I don't know what to say, Nick. You're demanding my loyalty, but you refuse to give me any respect."

Nick's eyes flashed with renewed anger. "I am the loyal one, and I have enough respect for our family legacy to keep looking for a way to get our land back."

"There's nothing to do. She's here now. Let it go, Nick."

"No. You let her go." Nick turned and stalked away.

A few minutes later, a door slamming followed by the roar of an engine rattled the silence. Alex shaded his eyes, following Nick's car as it sped down the driveway and peeled out onto the road, sending rocks flying.

It was almost two weeks before Nick strolled into his office with a big smile on his face. Alex hated to admit he'd been relieved not to have to deal with his brother. He'd lost a lot of sleep worrying about Nick's stubborn refusal to move on.

"You're in a good mood," Alex observed. He closed his laptop and pushed it away. Buried under quarterly reports all morning, he still had to meet with the cellar master. He took one look at his brother's cocky grin and suppressed a groan. That look meant nothing but trouble.

"I am in a good mood. I've finally figured out a solution to our problem." Nick jerked his head toward Pavia's cottage.

Alex narrowed his eyes. "What are you talking about?"

"You'll find out soon enough. You're always telling me how I don't take any responsibility for anything. Well, I've decided that it's time to prove you wrong."

"I don't like the sound of this, Nick. Leave Pavia alone."

His cocky grin faded to a scowl. "She has a piece of *our* property. I can't stand seeing how she has you and Mom wrapped around her little finger."

"Why does it matter so much to you? You barely spend any time doing any work here. All you do is take the winery for granted, getting all the benefits and doing none of the work."

Nick paced. "You and Mom are constantly telling me everything I do is wrong, so why should I bother? Grandad was the same. None of you ever wanted my help with the family business."

The hurt expression that flashed across Nick's face caught Alex off guard. It never occurred to him that Nick didn't feel like he was wanted. He was always closer to Grandad, but that didn't mean they left Nick out. Or did it? Whenever they tried to include him, he usually came up with an excuse for why he couldn't do the work. Alex always felt like his brother should work with him to manage the family business, not be someone who spent most of his time acting like a spoiled, petulant child. He'd welcome Nick's assistance if he thought his brother was actually capable of doing the work instead of creating chaos.

Alex decided to call his bluff. "Okay, what part of the business do you want to take over?"

Nick barked out a laugh. "I don't have to take over, and you and Mom have made it clear you don't want me. All I want is to take back what Grandad never should have given away, and that's what I'm going to do." With his head held high and his shoulders back, he walked out of the room like a soldier on a mission, leaving Alex to worry about what his plans were.

He went through his day distracted, worried about what Nick had said and the confident smirk on his face when he said it.

Finished with his last meeting of the day with the cellar master, Alex followed his nose through the house and found his mom in the kitchen, pulling a roast chicken out of the oven. He opened a bottle of wine and started to set three places on the large island when his mother interrupted him.

"I'm afraid it's just the two of us tonight. Nick is…." Sarah shrugged. "I called and tried to convince him to come home for dinner. I hoped we could talk, but he…." She shook her head. "He's so stubborn."

Alex leaned against the counter and took a sip of the estate Chardonnay he'd poured. He didn't have the heart to tell her he didn't think there was any reason to talk to Nick. What was the point?

"I thought about asking Pavia to join us, but I wasn't sure if that was a good idea," Sarah continued with a worried look in his direction.

"Why would that be a bad idea?"

"I don't want to seem like I'm matchmaking."

"But you wouldn't mind, would you?"

Sarah poured herself a glass and took a sip. She swirled the liquid with a pensive expression. "I'm not sure."

"She reminds you of her father, doesn't she?"

"So much," she said, her voice trembling.

"I wish I understood. You insist on trying to be close to her, but it causes you pain."

"I've loved getting to know Anthony's daughter. You and your brother are the light of my life, but I always wished I had a daughter."

"That wouldn't have fixed anything," he said quietly.

"No." She shook her head sadly. She reached over and patted his hand, her eyes cloudy with memories. "When it's your turn, I want you to be able to respect and trust the person you end up with."

"What about Nick? Do you want the same thing for him?"

"Of course," she sighed. "I wish I had more hope for Nick coming to his senses, but…." She shrugged. "I'm afraid it's just you and me running the business for now. Hopefully I won't botch too much."

Alex gently pushed her onto the barstool at the island, went to the stove, and started dishing up two plates of chicken with rice and some of the root vegetables she'd cooked. He set the plates down and sat next to her.

"You're doing a great job, Mom, and I like working with you. I don't want that to end, even if Nick comes to his senses."

"Thank you, sweetheart. I'm still feeling overwhelmed at times, but I enjoy feeling like I'm contributing after all this time."

Their conversation turned to business while they ate, but his mind was on Pavia.

"Mom, you don't mind—it doesn't bother you that Pavia is Black, does it? If we dated, I mean."

She pulled back, looking at him with wide eyes. "Is it that serious between the two of you?"

"We've been seeing each other, and I have feelings. Feelings I've never had before," he admitted.

"I wouldn't mind because of that, of course not. But, Alex"—she grabbed his arm—"I'm not sure Pavia's father would approve."

"Why not?"

"After everything that happened, I just don't know if it would be right."

"What happened isn't my fault. Why do I have to pay the price?"

"Alex, please." She gave him a weak smile. "You're a grown man, and I can't tell you what to do. But please, be careful with Pavia. If things end badly—"

"We've barely—it's new and barely begun, so I'd rather not talk about things ending badly. I just… I want her to see me as more than just Enzo's son. It makes me sick that she might think I'm anything like him. And when Nick…." He took a deep breath. "When Nick says things that sound just like Dad, I worry. What if he becomes—what if Nick—" He drew in a shaky breath, unable to say it out loud.

A sheen of tears clouded her expression. "I know," she whispered.

"Nick's up to something. I don't know what it is, but I'm worried." He shook his head. "No, worried doesn't begin to describe it."

"You don't have any idea what's going on?"

"He's being really tight-lipped, but he's even more cocky than he usually is. I have an uneasy feeling he's about to pull something."

His mother's face was grim when she nodded in an agreement. "I'll try to keep an eye on him."

"It's not your job, and it's not mine either. Nick's a grown man. He's responsible for his actions. The only thing we can do is hope that there isn't too much collateral damage."

Sarah closed her eyes with a shudder. "I'm not going to let the past repeat itself."

His mother was in love with Pavia's father once. Whatever happened, she never allowed herself to love again. Regret stole her happiness. Alex didn't want to spend the rest of his life wondering what if. It was time to stop playing it safe.

He fixed his gaze on the cottage at the bottom of the hill and asked, "At what point do we let go of the past and start living in the present? When do we start looking forward to the future?"

FOR THE hundredth time, Pavia stopped her work in the field to squint toward the Conti cellar in the distance. She spread her hands out, looking down at the dirt under her nails. She hadn't been expecting to work in the field, but she ended up weeding around the base of each rosebush, making sure nothing was choking them. There wasn't anything else to do in the vineyard for now except let the sun and time do their work.

The cottage felt more like home every day. The Matsuis had moved on to making improvements to the barn. For now, they were doing just enough so that she could use the space for production and storage after the harvest. She was afraid to invest any more. They made sure the structure of the loft was sound and rebuilt the staircase, bringing everything up to code. It would serve as her office and lab, and boxes with new equipment were waiting to be moved into it. Eventually, George and Sam would come back and build out a small tasting room in one corner of the barn. A large concrete pad out front they'd poured the other day cured in the afternoon sun. The additional space would hold the plastic bins to be filled with fruit during the harvest. Excitement bubbled inside her. She still had a long way to go, but right now her plans felt like they were falling into place.

Standing around watching her vines grow wasn't going to make time pass any faster, though, so Pavia showered away the dirt from the field, changed into a pale blue T-shirt dress paired with brown suede ankle boots, and grabbed her notebook on her way out the door. She still had to come up with a name for her winery. A brainstorming session at a coffee shop in town would also allow her to do a little people watching.

After parking her truck under the leafy canopy of the tree-lined main street, she made the nail salon her first stop, treating herself to a manicure that wouldn't last long with field work, but a girl needed to pamper herself sometimes.

A smile played over her lips as she made her way down the sidewalk, taking her time, peeking into tasting rooms and shop windows along the way. Blue Ridge had transformed over the years, becoming a tourist destination for wine enthusiasts just like Seneca, but it still had a small-town community charm. Seneca felt like Blue Ridge on steroids. Pavia shook her head in disbelief at some of the price tags she saw in the shop windows, and while most wineries back home charged a small tasting fee of ten to fifteen dollars that applied to a purchase, some of the tasting rooms here charged fifty! That was cheap compared to many others, and most only waived the fee if you purchased at least a case of their product.

She fought the urge to laugh out loud at some of the over-the-top decor and pretentious attitudes she observed. A minibus pulled up to the curb, and a large group of women got off, heading into the Conti tasting room just a few doors away. This tasting room was a smaller version of the one at the vineyard. The decor was the same, and customers stood clustered around small pub tables while employees circulated through the room, handing out order sheets. The well-organized and rehearsed presentation took away all the spontaneity and fun they had back home. Located in the main cellar, the tasting room at Brothers in Arms showcased the wine and nothing else. Barrels were used as tabletops for tasting. A large raw-edge plank of walnut rested on metal legs and served as the bar. While they weren't open for tastings often, they held special events and tastings for their wine club members.

Other than the group in the Conti tasting room, the streets were fairly quiet this early in the week. The lack of crowds gave Pavia a chance to take her time and explore more of the town at her leisure. She wandered a few more blocks, when a beautiful scarf caught her eye. Peering closer in the shop window, she almost choked when she saw the price of the fine wool floral scarf in swirling shades of green, blue, and purple. She could spend the money, but she didn't really need something so fancy. Farm work was dirty, and she had a hard time justifying buying anything other than work clothes. But the beautiful pattern of colors tempted her. She chewed on her lip, debating want versus need, when a voice behind her interrupted her thoughts.

"You should buy it. It would look good with your outfit."

Her eyes flew up to find Alex's reflection in the shop window.

"Hello." He lifted his hand in greeting. "What brings you into town?"

"I decided I needed a break." She held up her notebook. "I thought I'd find a coffee shop and do some brainstorming."

"What are you brainstorming?"

"I have to come up with a name for my winery."

"Ah, that's a big decision. Do you have any ideas?"

Pavia hesitated. "Well, before I came here, I was thinking Vindication. But that was before, and I was… I know you now, and I don't think that name fits," she said in a rush when Alex frowned.

"I'm glad you changed your mind," he said with a wry smile. "How about brainstorming over lunch?"

Her stomach growled in approval. "I guess you have your answer," she laughed.

Alex guided her toward a charming brick building with bistro tables on a patio in the front and bright green shutters on the windows. A discreet sign in elegant vintage script said *The Vyne* surrounded by grapevines.

The hostess led them to a small table by a window on the back side of the restaurant that overlooked a kitchen garden and another smaller brick building.

"What a cool building," Pavia remarked as they sat down.

"It was an old carriage house when we bought it."

"We?"

A large, burly man came out of the kitchen, making a beeline for their table, before Alex could answer. He grinned at Pavia before glancing at Alex with a mischievous glint in green eyes that reminded her of the mossy rainforests in her home state.

"Who is this beautiful woman you've brought me?"

"She's not yours," Alex growled.

The man held out his hand and looked at Alex expectantly.

Alex scowled. "Pavia, this is Brandon McCall, the creative genius behind The Vyne. And my soon-to-be ex-business partner if he keeps flirting with you."

Brandon shook Pavia's hand. "It's nice to finally meet the new owner of the Brothers Block."

"It's nice to meet you too."

He covered her hand with both of his. "What can I make for you today?"

"Let go of her hand, Brandon," Alex said in a clipped voice.

Brandon laughed. "What can I get my treasure today?"

"Treasure?" Pavia said, wrinkling her nose.

"Any woman who can bring a spark of passion to my friend's eyes is definitely a treasure. Now, what would you like for lunch? I'll make you anything you desire."

Alex put his hand over his face and groaned. "Please stop."

He was answered with another hearty laugh from his friend. She liked this giant of a man with wild auburn hair, whose eyes held a hint of pain behind his exuberant laugh and smile.

Pavia glanced at Alex. "What sounds good to you?"

"Do you have that pasta with the asparagus and lemon zest?"

He looked at her for approval, and she nodded in agreement. "That sounds delicious."

Brandon grinned and made a little bow in Pavia's direction. "You have excellent taste."

"It was my suggestion," Alex said.

"Maybe, but she's prettier," Brandon replied, giving Pavia a saucy wink before he went back to the kitchen.

The way Alex muttered under his breath, scowling at Brandon as he walked away, made her laugh. She'd never been a fan of men who acted overly possessive, but his annoyance at Brandon's flirting came across as more endearing than macho.

A server came over with a bottle of wine. "Chef suggested this to have with your lunch."

Alex took the bottle and turned the label in her direction.

"Oh, I definitely approve." She nodded at the Washington Sauvignon Blanc.

With their glasses poured, Alex lifted his. She mirrored him with a curious smile. "What are we toasting?"

"To unexpected lunch dates and winery names."

Their glasses met. She took a sip, her eyes meeting Alex's over the rim of her glass. She was falling for him. This was more than an attraction. Their connection was becoming deeper and more complicated each and every day. Could they have a future where they weren't always haunted by the actions of past generations?

The lunch crowd swelled and then thinned out while they enjoyed their meal, comparing their tasting notes for the wine as they drank. They talked about pruning techniques and the pros and cons of using acacia wood for barrels.

"We haven't discussed the one thing we came here for," Alex said when Brandon sent out an incredible pear tart on puff pastry with a Riesling caramel sauce.

Pavia sat back, relaxed and full from Brandon's culinary talents. "I need to decide on names for the winery and the wines so I can apply for the certificate of label approval. I know I have time, years," she said with a note of impatience, "but once I know what I'm going to call the winery, I can start marketing."

"Getting the COLA is an important step. Do you have any ideas? A theme?"

"I was thinking about Antonio's journal, maybe. I was thinking about something with a journal theme."

Alex twisted the stem of his glass with a pensive look.

"You don't like that idea?" she asked, noting his slight frown.

"I'm thinking."

"What were you going to call your winery?"

Alex sighed. "I don't know. I was thinking Brothers Block, but that was all based on a pipe dream."

Pavia reached across the table and covered his hand with hers. "Don't say that. Your goals are just as valid as mine, Alex."

He turned his hand, linking his fingers with hers, giving her hand a squeeze. "Thank you for saying that."

His hand was warm and firm in hers, and Pavia felt a deeper sense of connection between them. They shared the same dream with the same hopes. If she'd known, it would have made her decision to come to Seneca much more challenging than it already was. Guilt mingled with something she could only describe as loss swept over her.

"I have an idea. Our grandfathers, their lives, their legacies—it makes me think of the Chinese proverb 'A journey of a thousand miles begins with a single step.' What if you called your winery A Thousand Steps? There are a thousand little steps to make a great wine."

Pavia nodded, excitement bubbling inside of her. "It's perfect, Alex. It honors Henry and Antonio, and both the past and the future."

He lifted his glass again. "Should we make it official?"

"To A Thousand Steps Winery." She grinned, clinking her glass against his.

"What are we celebrating?" Brandon walked up to their table, eyeing the two of them with curiosity.

"Pavia's decided on a name for her winery."

She smiled at Alex. "Based on your excellent suggestion."

He dipped his head in acknowledgment.

Brandon turned his mouth down into an exaggerated frown. "And here I thought you were toasting my superb culinary accomplishments."

Pavia patted his arm. "Lunch was wonderful, thank you."

"So what's the name?"

"A Thousand Steps."

Brandon stroked his beard, looking thoughtful before he nodded. "I like it." He glanced at Alex. "I assume we'll be adding A Thousand Steps to our wine menu when the time comes."

Alex gave her a lopsided smile. "If the winemaker takes after her father, she may not have enough to spare."

Brandon noted the heat she could feel spreading over her cheeks with a raised eyebrow before backing away from the table. "I'll just let you, uh"—he scratched his beard—"finish. I'll put it on your tab, partner," he called out over his shoulder.

Pavia looked around. The restaurant was empty except for the two of them. In a couple of hours, the room would fill again with dinner patrons.

"I suppose I should get back home."

"I'll walk you to your car."

He put his hand to the small of her back, guiding her down the sidewalk. When they reached her truck, she hesitated, not wanting the afternoon to end.

Alex made it clear he wanted the same thing when he leaned close and bracketed her against the wood of her truck. His eyes searched hers.

"I want to see you again. I want to keep seeing you as often as I can."

Her body tingled with anticipation. "I think I'd like that."

His lips curled into a smile before they grazed her temple, brushed against the shell of her ear, and then met hers in a searing kiss. When they broke apart, his lips were still parted, his body trembling.

"Will you come to me tonight?" she asked, her voice low and husky.

He nodded and kissed her again, a low groan vibrating his throat. She tasted the pears and wine on his tongue and started to devour him, wanting more.

He stroked his thumb over her bottom lip. "I'll bring the wine."

She nodded and fumbled for the door handle behind her, unable to turn away. With a half laugh, he opened the door and gently pushed her into the driver's seat. Reaching across to buckle her in, he pressed a quick kiss to her forehead before he straightened.

"What time?" he asked.

Her body screamed *now*.

"Eight?"

"I'll see you then."

Pavia eyed the first man who'd ever made her feel powerful as a woman in her rearview mirror and smiled as she drove away.

CHAPTER *Seven*

PAVIA STUDIED her reflection. She'd eagerly accepted when Lilly suggested they were due for a girls' night out. She and Alex had been inseparable for the last week, spending their nights together reading Antonio's diary and making love.

Twisting and turning in front of the mirror, she gave her outfit one more critique before heading out. The deep V neckline of the black silk blouse showed just the right amount of cleavage, and she added a little sparkle with a delicate gold necklace. She switched out everyday jeans for skinny jeans in a dark wash, and her work boots for black-and-gold peep-toe pumps. Pavia pulled her hair up into a loose knot on top of her head and pulled out a few curls to frame her face. Simple gold hoops provided the finishing touch.

She reached up, fingering the curl at her cheek, her thoughts turning to Alex once again. She closed her eyes, remembering the warmth of his fingers against her skin. Turning to the side, she looked over her shoulder. Field work kept her in good shape, and it showed in every curve encased in the midnight blue denim.

A half an hour later, her heels clicked on the sidewalk leading down the alley toward The Vyne. On a Friday night, customers mingled outside, waiting for a table. The courtyard buzzed with conversation, while the jazzy, soulful sounds of Nate James drew her inside. Pavia made her way past the line of diners at the hostess station, heading toward the bar. Weaving through the heavy crowd, she kept an eye out for Lilly and Chloe, when two large hands fell on her shoulders.

"My treasure is here." Brandon smiled down at her. "Hello, Treasure."

"Hi, Brandon." She stood on her tiptoes, giving the giant man a kiss on the cheek.

"What brings you out tonight? Are you meeting Alex?" he asked with a knowing smile.

Pavia shook her head. "Not tonight, I'm meeting friends," she said, nodding to where Lilly and Chloe were sitting at a small high-top table.

Brandon's smile disappeared and was replaced with a scowl.

"Do you know Lilly and Chloe?" she asked, surprised by his reaction.

"I do," he answered through clenched teeth. "Chloe is welcome in my kitchen anytime, but that one"—he jerked his head toward Lilly—"needs to learn how to mind her own business."

Lilly jumped off her stool and walked toward them, acting oblivious to the tension radiating from Brandon. "Hi, Brandon," she said with a bright smile.

Brandon glared down at her, his mouth set into a thin line. He crossed his arms and remained silent. Pavia gave him a sharp elbow to the ribs when he didn't respond.

"Ow!" He frowned at her, and she looked up at him with a raised eyebrow. He shook his head before storming back into the kitchen.

Pavia stared at Brandon's retreating back with her mouth open. "What in the world is that about?" she asked, turning to Lilly.

Lilly's shoulders drooped. Looking over at the swinging doors Brandon just went through, she replied, "I'm afraid I didn't make the best first impression, and he's never forgiven me for it."

They moved back over to the small table Lilly had claimed for them. "What happened?"

Lilly crossed her arms, leaning her elbows on the table. "He came into the clinic one time. I tried to help him out." She sighed. "I may have pushed too hard. It was right when I first started, and maybe I was a little too eager. I'm afraid it's a hazard of the job. When we first start out, we believe we can save everybody." She looked longingly toward the kitchen. "I shouldn't be talking about this. We have very strict patient confidentiality rules."

Hunching her shoulders, Lilly frowned down at the table. Her long, dark brown hair fell in a curtain, hiding her face, but Pavia didn't miss the tremble of her chin. Her heart went out to her. She already knew Lilly well enough to know she would never do anything to intentionally hurt someone. Lilly lifted her head, her concerned gaze going toward the kitchen.

"Alex told me about Brandon's PTSD," Pavia offered, following Lilly's gaze.

"He came in for help, and I chased him away and then—" Her cheeks tinged pink.

"You didn't do it on purpose," Chloe said.

"There's something else?" Pavia asked.

Lilly carefully straightened her place setting. "He doesn't like how I order my food."

Pavia was going to say something snarky, but her laughter died in her throat when she saw the look of anguish on her friend's face. She reached across the table and gave Lilly's hand a comforting squeeze.

"You don't have to talk about it if you don't want to."

"Sam and I both have OCD," Lilly said. "He's able to use his to his advantage. Being meticulous and obsessed with details helps him make beautiful furniture. Mine just makes people think I'm weird." She hunched her shoulders, and leaning forward, she continued in a hushed voice. "I have a hard time with food. It's not anorexia. Sometimes I wonder if that would be easier to explain. I… I have rules about food. Some of them don't make sense, and I know that, but I can't help it."

Pavia didn't know what to say, so she decided listening was the best support she could offer. Chloe scooted closer to Lilly and put her arm around her.

"I work with a nutritionist and a therapist." Lilly shook her head with a slight smile. "Therapist, heal thyself. Brandon, being a chef, just… well, let's just say we're never going to be friends."

"Be patient. Maybe someday he'll give you another chance," Chloe offered.

Lilly stood up. "I'll go get the first round of drinks," she said, heading toward the bar.

"Lilly wants to fix everyone and everything," Chloe said. "She has such a good heart. I wish Brandon would pull his head out of his ass."

"I hope so too."

Pavia scanned the crowd while Lilly wove her way to the bar. Tourists mingled with locals, and the flirting was heavy.

"What about you? How long are you back for?" Pavia asked Chloe.

"Just the weekend. I needed a break, and I wanted to visit with my mom. There'll be hell to pay for taking the time off," she said with a grimace.

Pavia continued scanning the crowd, looking for one face in particular.

"Anyone you're looking for?" Chloe asked with a raised eyebrow.

She felt the heat rise in her cheeks. When Lilly returned to the table, carefully balancing three glasses of wine in her hands, Pavia grabbed one and hid her blush behind it while taking a large sip.

"I hope you saved any good gossip for my return."

"I was just commenting that Pavia seems distracted, like she might be looking for someone."

"I think we both know who that is," Lilly laughed, and then her face fell. "I have no business giving you a hard time when I find a way to piss off the one man…." She bit her lip, swirling her glass.

"Lilly, I'm sure—" Chloe started.

Just then, the kitchen doors burst open. Brandon stalked toward their table with a grim expression and set three plates down. He stood over them with his feet set wide and his arms crossed.

"I didn't mean to be rude before," he muttered. He waved toward the plates. "Here." With that, he turned on his heel and stalked back into the kitchen.

Lilly's eyes grew wide. "What was that?" she asked, looking from her plate to the kitchen and back again.

Chloe smiled. "That was a first step."

Lilly stared at her plate. She picked up her fork and began to carefully separate the ingredients into individual sections before taking a bite of a portobello mushroom.

"I know he doesn't believe I think so, but he is an amazing cook," she said, taking another bite.

Pavia laughed and speared a piece of portobello. Just as the fork reached her mouth, she froze, narrowing her eyes as the wrong brother headed her way.

"What's wrong?" Lilly asked. She followed her gaze across the room while reaching for her drink. "Uh-oh."

Nick staggered toward their table. Pavia didn't take her eyes off of him, tracking his movements. Glassy-eyed, he dragged his feet, stumbling every few steps. He clearly had been at the bar for quite some time already.

He reached the table, rattling the dishes as he leaned his weight against it. "Well, look what we have here."

"Nick." Chloe's voice trembled.

He turned his glassy stare toward her, and his expression softened for just a moment. "Hey, Clover," he slurred.

"It looks like you've been here for a while," Lilly said, gesturing toward the glass in his hand.

Nick flung his arm in a wide arc that made Pavia duck so she didn't get hit. "This is my place," he said loudly, "and tonight, I'm celebrating."

Chloe sucked in her breath. Lilly stood up, placing her chair between Nick and herself. Pavia leaned back in hers, trying to keep a safe distance from him.

"You don't own The Vyne. Alex is Brandon's partner," she said quietly, never taking her eyes off of him. Drinking had dulled his senses and exposed his envy for his brother's success.

"Everything here belongs to me!" he shouted, leaning forward into her face. The smell of alcohol on his breath turned her stomach. "Nothing here belongs to you."

Pavia turned her face, leaning away from the stench. Nick's hand snaked out and grabbed her arm, digging his fingers in and making her wince. She jumped up, and her chair fell to the floor with a loud thud.

"Take your hands off me," she said through clenched teeth. She glared at him, balled her hands, and braced herself. For a moment, she imagined her father in the same position with Nick's father, Enzo. Her heart pounded in her chest loudly, drowning out all the other sounds in the room. Everything faded away as she focused on Nick, her body tense.

Nick tightened his grasp and tried to pull her toward him. His eyes glittered with an unnatural brightness that too much alcohol can provide. Taking a deep breath, Pavia remembered what her father had taught her. In the next moment, howls echoed throughout the room. Nick rolled at her feet, clutching his balls with one hand and his nose with another.

"I told you to take your hands off me."

Brandon appeared at her side with a very nervous Lilly behind him. Chloe grasped her arm, looking down at Nick with eyes filled with unshed tears. Brandon glared at him for a moment and then barked a loud laugh.

"I'm glad to know your daddy taught you how to defend yourself, honey," he said, clapping her on the shoulder.

Nick struggled to get to his feet. A line of blood trickled from his nose. With his hands balled into fists, he advanced toward her, shaking, his face contorted into a mask of rage. Pavia took a step back and dropped into a fighting stance with her fists held up in front of her, ready for whatever he was dumb enough to try next.

Before he could make another move, Brandon grabbed the back of his shirt. "Nick," he warned, "count your losses, and be thankful you only took one hit. If you still had a hand on that girl when I got here, a knee in the nuts and a bloody nose would be the least of your problems."

Lilly reached up and put her hand on Brandon's arm. He glanced down at her.

"I'm fine," he bit out, and she quickly snatched her hand away.

"Brandon, I didn't mean to make a scene," Pavia started to apologize, looking around at the crowd that had gathered, whispering and pointing. She cringed when she noticed a few cell phones had been pulled out and people were obviously filming.

Brandon's expression softened. "It's okay, Treasure." He gave Nick another shake. "It's not your fault." He pointed his finger at Lilly. "You're always trying to take care of someone. Take care of your friends."

Pavia reached for the table with a shaky hand, trying to steady herself as the rush of endorphins began to fade away. Lilly put her arm around her, guiding her into a chair.

"Let me get you some water," she said.

Chloe continued to stare at the door to the kitchen, which Brandon had hauled Nick off through, her face pale.

"Chloe, sit down," Lilly gently ordered, pushing her back into her seat.

One of the bartenders came over with a tray of ice waters and a glass of whiskey. "The boss says you're supposed to drink this"—he shifted, swallowing before he continued—"and don't argue," he said, handing Pavia the glass.

"I think we'll need two more, please," Pavia said with a worried glance at Chloe. She pushed her glass toward her. "I think you need this more than I do."

Chloe's chin began to tremble, and a tear rolled down her cheek. "What happened to him? That's not the boy I… we…." She buried her face in her hands.

Lilly rushed to her side and put her arm around her. Pavia wanted to punch Nick again for not realizing how much his actions hurt the people around him.

Pavia gave Lilly a weak smile. "Not the best girls' night out, I'm afraid."

Lilly looked at her while she rubbed Chloe's back, trying to comfort her friend. "Pavia, you need to be really careful around him. I'm glad my dad wasn't here to see that. He would have skinned him alive," she said with a worried glance toward the kitchen.

"Let's not tell him, okay?" Pavia wrinkled her nose. The waiter returned with two more glasses of whiskey. It wasn't her favorite spirit, but she took a sip. Disobeying Brandon wouldn't be a very good idea when he was in full protective mode. She shuddered thinking about the thunderous expression on his face as he'd hauled Nick out of the room.

Pavia swallowed the rest of the contents in her glass, letting the fiery liquid burn a trail down to her stomach. Nick's behavior scared her, but wondering what Alex's reaction would be when he found out troubled her more. She looked into the empty glass in her hand, wishing there were tea leaves swirling around in the bottom that would somehow magically give her the answers to figure out this mess.

The bartender returned, looking even more nervous than before. He set three plates of pasta in front of them, replacing the plates of food that had been swept away during the altercation, with the same instructions.

"The boss says eat this and don't argue."

The three of them all looked toward the kitchen, where Brandon glowered in the doorway with his arms crossed. Pavia watched Lilly blush to the tips of her ears when she and Brandon locked eyes for a moment.

They each took turns trying to make small talk and failed, leaving the three of them to pick at their food in silence. Pavia pushed her food around on the plate. Like everything Brandon made, it was delicious, but every bite sat like lead in her stomach. She set her fork down and pushed her plate away with a sigh.

"I was really looking forward to this. I'm sorry."

"Don't you dare blame yourself." Chloe narrowed her eyes, the sadness in them replaced with a flash of anger.

"Chloe's right. You didn't do anything. This was all Nick's fault." Lilly gave her a worried look. "Are you sure you're going to be okay?"

Pavia straightened up and gave her friends a reassuring nod. "Of course." She forced a bright smile. "We'll look back on this and laugh about it one day."

Lilly shook her head sadly. "No, I don't think we will."

"I hate to say this, but this girls' night sucks. We're going to have to up our game next time," Chloe tried to joke with a shaky laugh.

They navigated out of the bar, ignoring the curious stares from the other patrons. Collectively, they took a deep breath of the late spring air when they stepped outside. They said their goodbyes, agreeing to a do-over the next time Chloe was in town. Pavia gave Chloe one more hug and reassured Lilly that she was okay before heading to her car.

ALEX HAD been focused on adding his own notes alongside the cellar master's, tracking release dates in the spreadsheet, when he saw Brandon's name on the caller ID. He frowned. If Brandon was calling on a busy Friday night, something must be wrong.

"Everything all right?" he answered.

"You're not going to be happy with what I'm going to tell you." Something in Brandon's voice sent a chill down his spine.

"You need to keep Nick there," Alex spat when Brandon finished. "If I see him, I *will* kill him."

"Not a problem. He's out cold and will stay here tonight. You make sure she keeps her doors locked good and tight from now on."

His frustrated shout echoed in the valley when he hung up with Brandon. Alex didn't know how long he would have to wait on Pavia's doorstep, but it didn't matter. He wasn't going anywhere until he could see for himself that she was okay.

When she pulled up, he jumped to his feet and stalked toward her car. Alex yanked the door open and pulled her into his arms, and Pavia resisted for a moment before she sighed and sank into him. He took her face in his hands, looking for any sign that Nick had hurt her, even though Brandon had reassured him that Pavia more than held her own against his brother.

"Are you all right?" he asked, running his hands over her arms and back, continuing to check for any sign of harm. His heart wouldn't stop racing until he checked for himself.

Pavia reached up and grasped his wrists. "Alex, it's been a long night. I suppose you're here because Brandon called, but I'm fine, and there's nothing you can do."

He ran his hands across her shoulders and down her arms, still looking for any sign of damage. "Maybe not, but I'm not leaving you."

She looked him in the eye. "He didn't hurt me."

Maybe not physically, but Alex could see the hint of stress in her eyes, and his heart stilled in his chest. Nick could go to hell.

He held her. "I just need to know you're okay."

She shuddered and sank into his arms.

"What can I do?"

She lifted her head and gave him a weak smile, brushing back a stray curl with a shaking hand. "You can try to teach your brother some manners."

"He's an ass." He tightened his hold on her. "If he hurt you—"

"I'm okay!" Pavia shouted, wrenching herself out of his arms. "I can take care of myself! If one more person asks me if I'm okay—" She sighed. "I'm embarrassed, okay? Everyone at the restaurant saw what happened, the entire valley will be talking about it. I don't want our relationship to be something everyone is gossiping about." She barked a laugh. "That's probably too late, but it would have been nice."

"I'm not embarrassed by us. I don't care if the entire state knows how I feel about you."

"I didn't say I was embarrassed about us. I just don't want—" She wrapped her arms around his waist and rested her head on his chest. "I wish we'd been able to meet and get to know each other without all this stuff from our past."

"Maybe we needed the past to bring us together. I was so mad at Grandad for giving you the Brothers Block." He kissed the top of her head. "Now I'm thankful." He reached for her hand, laced their fingers together, and pressed them to his heart. "Let me take care of you. Let's go inside, and I'll fill the tub for you. Wouldn't it feel nice to relax in the tub for a while?"

She reached up and wrapped her free hand around the back of his head and drew him down until his forehead rested against hers. "It would, but it would be even better if I had some company."

He kissed her forehead, her nose, and then brushed his lips over hers. She sighed and lifted her face to his, one small tear escaping and rolling down her cheek. He followed its trail with kisses before capturing her lips again.

Arm in arm, Alex guided her into the cottage. He insisted on making her a cup of tea and that she take some aspirin. While she sat up on her bed with her mother's quilt around her shoulders, he filled the tub and gathered candles from the living room. When he brought her into the bathroom, candles were lit in the corners of the tub and on the vanity. He undressed her, checking every inch of her body, reassuring himself again that his brother hadn't caused any physical harm.

She stepped into the hot water with a sigh and then reached for his hand. "Stay with me."

He undressed and climbed in behind her. Her skin looked like golden brown satin in the candlelight. She hummed with satisfaction as he ran the soap down the valley of her breasts.

"Better?" he asked after he'd made sure that he soaped and stroked every inch of her body, until she shuddered with release.

"Much better," she sighed. "Can we just stay like this forever?"

He lifted her fingers from the water, where the pads had wrinkled. "I'm afraid not."

Pavia stood up. The water sluicing down her body, damp curls caressing her shoulders, she appeared like the daughter of Poseidon. She held a water-slicked hand out to him. He grasped it, pulled himself out of the water, and after they stepped out of the tub, he lifted her up and she wrapped her legs around him as he stumbled toward her bedroom. He laid her down on the bed, then propped himself up on his elbows, looking down at her flushed face.

"If we couldn't stay in the bath, can we stay here for the rest of our lives?" she asked.

"Pavia, we can't hide. Morning will come, and we'll—"

She cut him off with a kiss. "Wake up in bed together."

Alex couldn't have left her even if he wanted to. If he did, he'd be leaving his heart behind.

THE NEXT morning, Alex slowly made his way up to the villa, trying to decide what made him more miserable, leaving Pavia's bed or having to tell his mother about Nick. His hands clenched into tight fists thinking about what happened the night before. Nick's out-of-control attitude toward Pavia had just crossed dangerous a line.

He found his mother in her favorite spot, out in the garden, kneeling by a bed of lettuce. A basket sat next to her, already filled with spring peas.

"Good morning, sweetheart." She gestured toward the rows of vegetables. "I have so much here I thought I would see if Pavia might like some." Her smile faltered when she saw the frown on his face.

"Have you seen Nick this morning?" he gritted out.

"No, why? What's going on?" She looked at him, her eyes full of concern.

Alex flinched and knelt down next to her. There was no way to tell her what had happened without hurting her. He took a deep breath.

"There was an ugly scene between Nick and Pavia at The Vyne last night."

"What are you talking about?" She jumped up, knocking over the basket at her feet. "What happened?"

"He was drunk."

He didn't need to say anything else. With one look, he communicated everything his mother needed to know.

She wrapped her arms around herself. "Oh God," she whispered.

Alex put his arms around her. "I hate having to tell you this."

"Is Pavia okay?" she asked, her voice shaking.

"She's fine," he said, leaving out how he'd spent the night reassuring himself.

"We have to put a stop to this," Sarah said.

"How? We've already removed him from the family business. What now?"

"I don't know."

"I'm supposed to be giving a talk at the Mondavi Institute tomorrow." He scoffed. "They want to talk about the next generation at Conti. What am I supposed to say? I have no idea what the future holds when my brother—what do I say when they ask me about Nick? That between the two of us, he's most like our father and I don't want to work with him?"

"There are no easy answers, Alex."

He swallowed the lump that suddenly formed in his throat. No, there weren't any easy answers, especially when he didn't know the full story. He wasn't going to be able to deal with Nick and find a future with Pavia without knowing everything that had happened. He had to stop being afraid that whatever secret his mom had been keeping would destroy what he had with Pavia. He'd been fighting the past his whole life, and he didn't want to do it anymore.

"I need to know what happened between you and Anthony, Mom. I need to hear it from you. I can't keep walking around not knowing the full story."

Sarah's expression shuttered before she nodded. "Pavia's father was forced to leave here because of me. Anthony and I were in love, but my parents and Enzo's mother were determined that Enzo was the man I was supposed to marry. I-I didn't have a choice." She took a deep breath, swiping at her eyes with the back of her hand. "Enzo caught us together. He beat Anthony and… and took me away. He told my parents Anthony assaulted me. Anthony had to leave, or he would have been put in jail. It was the sixties. They would have—" Her voice shook. "He could have been killed."

"You didn't love Enzo. Why did you marry him?"

"I was raised in a traditional household. Daughters were supposed to obey their parents. My parents sold me for a business deal with the Contis." She pointed to the western part of their land. "The Contis got the land they wanted, and my parents got to claim an association with one of the most prominent families in the valley. What I wanted didn't matter."

It was hard to comprehend. Alex considered his growing feelings for Pavia. If he were in the same position, he would have fought. Why didn't his mother fight for the man she loved?

"We need to confront Nick. I refuse to let him cause any more problems for this family."

Alex thought about what his mother had shared as they walked back into the house. Now that he knew the story, some of his worry had eased. He and Pavia could manage the past. Together they could put what happened behind them and move forward. The expression "love conquers all" came to mind, bringing a slight smile to his face. A smile that quickly fell when Nick stumbled into the kitchen, his eyes shooting daggers at Alex as he poured himself a cup of coffee.

Nick slumped into one of the barstools at the kitchen island, dark circles under his eyes and his clothes a rumpled mess. "I suppose you heard about last night? I can't believe that bitch attacked me," he said in a sullen voice.

"Nicholas Lorenzo Conti, you will not call any woman a bitch in this house." Sarah jabbed her finger at him. Nick slumped further in his seat, avoiding eye contact.

"From what I heard, it sounds like she had every reason to defend herself," Alex said with a deadly calm.

"It wasn't my fault," Nick muttered.

"It never is, is it? You always have an excuse for not being responsible for your actions. Why does everyone have to live by the rules but you?"

Nick glared at them with a sullen expression.

"Nick, you need to stop behaving like this… like your father," their mom said.

Alex closed his eyes, dreading the denial he knew was coming.

Nick sat up and put his hands on the counter, leaning forward. "Good, I want to be like Dad. I wish he were here. He would understand what I'm trying to do."

"What in the world do you think you're doing?" Alex shouted.

"Fighting for what's ours."

"Your father never fought for anyone or anything but himself. Nick, I know you think you know better, but believe me, you would not be better off if your father was here." Sarah reached for him, but Nick pulled away. "You were too young to remember, and we did everything we could to shield you from the man your father really was. I'm glad you don't remember any of the bad things, but you have to believe us, Enzo wasn't a good father or the best husband."

Nick's jaw ticked, and he shook his head in denial.

Alex didn't know what else he could do for him, for all of them. "Nick," he said, trying to keep his voice calm, "we all did you a disservice letting you think Dad was a different kind of man than what he really was. We didn't want you to have the kind of childhood memories that I have. Mom, Grandad, and I, we all tried to shield you. I see now that was a mistake we made. You idolize something that never existed."

Nick pointed a shaking finger at him. "You never liked him, never showed him any respect."

"Before I knew what he was, I wanted to be just like him," Alex confessed. He saw his mother wince out of the corner of his eye. "At first, even when he hit Mom, I didn't know what he was doing was wrong. I was too young to understand the things he yelled at her. I didn't understand what"—he swallowed, the words he was about to say choking his throat—"what a… I can't say it." He took a deep breath. The language Enzo used made sense now that he knew what had happened.

Enzo's hatred of one man became hate for an entire people. "Dad used a lot of ugly words to describe Black people. As I got older, I began to understand more. Mom did the best she could to shield us, and Grandad tried to protect us from his rage. It got harder and harder to hear the hateful things he said to her."

Alex took a deep breath before continuing.

"One day, Grandad wasn't home, and I tried to help...." He shrugged, grasping for the right words to describe their father's rage. "Mom was in the hospital for three days with three broken ribs and a severe concussion. The bruising was awful." He shook his head, trying to erase the vision. "I only had a broken arm and some bruises."

"I don't believe you. I'd remember something like that," Nick said in a shaky voice. He pushed away from the counter, glaring at them.

"You were with Grandad when it happened. Do you remember when Melinda's husband took you on that fishing trip?" Sarah asked.

Nick grimaced, nodding.

"I didn't want you to see, so I asked him to take you. When you came back, my bruises were faded enough that I could cover them with makeup."

"You told me you broke your arm climbing one of the olive trees," Nick said in a hushed voice.

Alex swallowed, blinking back tears. "That's when Dad left. Grandad told him he was no longer his son."

"I thought Dad died," Nick said, confusion clouding his face.

"When Grandad came home and found Dad standing over me, Grandad was so angry Mom was afraid he was going to kill Dad. Grandad kicked him out of the house and ordered him to leave. Dad tried to come back, but Grandad wouldn't let him anywhere near us. We never saw him again after that. He died in a bar fight years later. Either his drinking or his temper was going to get the better of him. It was only a matter of time. For the rest of his life, Grandad felt guilty for what his son did to us. I used to be thankful you were too young to remember. I can see now we were wrong. We should have told you. But now you know, and if you still continue this way, I can't have you in my life."

"Even if Dad—Enzo—was a terrible man, that doesn't make the Jacksons any better."

"You can't compare, Nick. Now that Pavia's been here for a while, I see that Grandad did the right thing. The Brothers Block is in good hands. The right hands."

"You would choose her over me, wouldn't you?" Nick replied in a hollow voice.

"I love her." Alex drew in a sharp breath, surprised at his own admission.

Nick jumped up and stormed out of the kitchen.

"He can't keep running away," Sarah said.

"No, he can't, but he'll avoid facing the truth for as long as he can."

PAVIA GLANCED toward the villa. She was worried about Sarah's reaction when Alex told her what had happened with Nick the previous night. Maybe she should have gone with him. He left promising to return as soon as possible, but that was a few hours ago, and she worried he had crossed paths with Nick.

When Alex pulled into the driveway a few hours later, Pavia ran up and wrapped her arms around him as soon as she saw the lines of stress around his mouth and eyes.

"Is your mom okay?"

He sighed and tightened his hold on her. "Yeah, she's okay." He inhaled, nuzzling her neck. "I remembered before I came down here that I'm scheduled to give a talk at the Mondavi Institute tomorrow." He chuckled. "They asked me to talk about the economics of large-scale production and what's ahead for the next generation. I'm afraid I'm going to burst a lot of bubbles with the harsh realities of running a winery."

"I'm sure you'll also have some of them even more inspired than ever."

Alex dropped his head to her forehead. "Thank you."

"For what?"

"For believing in me, for thinking I'm inspiring." His lips curled into a smile. "For inviting me to stay again tomorrow night when I get back."

Pavia threw her head back and laughed. "Oh, is that what I'm going to do?"

It wasn't really up for debate. Alex had been spending most of his nights at her place, and Pavia was happy to fall asleep in his arms and wake up the same way.

"Here, let me try to convince you," he said, pulling her closer and into a deep kiss.

She moaned, opening her mouth, welcoming his warmth as his tongue danced with hers.

"I don't want to leave you, but I have to go," he whispered against her mouth. "When I come back, let's sneak away to San Francisco or LA for the weekend before we get any closer to harvest."

"I'd like that."

He stepped back, but his hands lingered at her waist. "I have to make sure my presentation is ready, and I'll be up and out early in the morning."

"That's okay. Come back when you can, and we'll have dinner," she offered.

"That sounds good. It will be even better if I can have you for dessert," he said, his voice dropping low, making her whole body tingle with anticipation.

"I suppose that can be arranged," she said breathlessly.

After a long, lingering kiss, Alex went home, and Pavia spent the afternoon going over her accounts, making sure she was still on track and not overspending before she hired a small crew to help with the crush in the fall. Reassuring herself she would be okay, she headed into the vine rows, grinning at the first small clusters of fruit that were beginning to form.

When Lilly called to see if she wanted to meet up for a late lunch, she happily accepted. They met at a small café near Lilly's office and spent an hour catching up. Afterward, she stopped at the grocery store and picked up the makings for a simple chicken dinner to prepare for Alex. That wouldn't tax her basic cooking skills.

Biting down on her lip, one worry still lingered. What would her dad think? She knew he loved her unconditionally, but she still wondered if he would be hurt that she had fallen in love with a Conti. In love. Her heart stuttered. Yes, she'd fallen in love with Alex. The realization caught her off guard. A relationship and love weren't something she'd been looking for at this stage in her life, but with Alex she'd found a partner, someone who would support her dreams as much as she supported his.

They could build something special together and forge a new path, leaving past hurts behind.

Maybe that's what Antonio wanted her to learn from his journal. He and Henry had tried to make a life and home for themselves here, but the time wasn't right. Society and their families kept them from living the way they wanted to. Then, it happened again to her dad and Sarah. Maybe this was the time. Maybe this time she and Alex could live and love the way they wanted to. She wanted to tell him how she felt. She'd asked him to be honest with his feelings, and she needed to do the same.

Pavia was caught up in her daydream about the evening ahead when she noticed the man on the tractor as she turned down the road to her cottage. At first she thought he was on the Conti land alongside hers. No! She let out a scream and slammed on the brakes. Her truck skidded violently before it came to a stop, and she jumped out, leaving the engine still running.

Running toward the tractor, her heart pounded in her ears, her shouts sounding far away. "No! Stop!"

Nick just sneered down at her with a vile, evil grin on his face as her vines were turned under. The trellis wires twisted and curled as they broke apart, and the wood posts splintered with an ominous crack.

She pounded her fists against the side of the tractor. Trying to climb on, she fell into the dirt when her foot slipped, a piece of wire piercing her palm. Footsteps. Someone was running toward her. Alex flew past with a farmhand on his heels. They attacked the tractor, pulling Nick away from the controls. Alex wrestled him off the machine while the farmhand brought it to a stop. Now the sounds of punching filled the air as Alex and Nick wrestled on the ground.

Sarah appeared at her side, her face streaked with dirt, panting. She cradled Pavia's bleeding palm for a second before she yanked at her shirt, trying to tear it. "We need to get the bleeding stopped."

Pavia didn't respond, staring at the destruction Nick had caused. Only one row of the Brothers Block remained. The rest were ripped out of the ground, crushed under the tractor's wheels and scraper blade, leaving nothing but broken roots visible.

"What the fuck is wrong with you, Nick?" Alex shouted, landing another punch to his brother's stomach.

Nick managed to squirm out of his grasp and stand up. Swaying slightly, he wiped the blood trickling from his swelling lip.

"You." He pointed a shaking finger in Pavia's direction. "You think you're so much better than we are, but I know the truth. I've been trying to find a way to get rid of you since you came here." He tried to lift his swollen mouth into a smile, but only succeeded in a bloody sneer. "I hired my own lawyer, and you"—he turned his attention to Alex—"overlooked one important detail. Grandad's will stipulates she inherits the land, but that doesn't mean she gets our vines. She can start from scratch if she can afford it."

The sound of Alex's fist connecting with his brother's nose filled the air.

"Nick, no!" Sarah whispered at the same time, looking at her son with disbelief.

Nick staggered but stayed upright, while Alex stood with his chest heaving, his fists clenched at his sides.

"You're always lecturing me on how I need to take more responsibility. You couldn't stop thinking with your dick long enough to take care of the problem." Nick jerked his head in her direction. "So I did. All I did was take what she wasn't entitled to."

"You bastard!" Alex growled.

"I'm doing what's best for our family."

"Get that out of here!" Alex called out to the farmhand. "Tell Andy I want a locksmith out here now and the locks changed on every building, including the main house."

The farmhand started the engine and nodded, darting his eyes between the two brothers with a worried expression.

"What are you going to do? Turn me out the way Grandad did to our dad?"

"Yes."

Nick flinched. "You can't run me off so easily."

Pavia stood speechless, staring at Nick. Anger began to morph into shock, and her body began to shake uncontrollably, making it difficult to get the words out. "You won't run me off like your father did to my father."

Nick sneered at her. "And you won't try to steal a member of my family like your father did to my mother. I know everything. I have the letter Mom wrote about how your father tried to rape her."

Sarah gasped, shaking her head as the blood drained from her face. "Nick, no, that's not what happened."

"You don't have to lie, Mom. I saw the letter. I was going through the trunks in the attic looking for anything I could use to fight the will, and I found it." He moved toward her. "It's okay, Mom. You don't have to hide the secret anymore. We all know what that monster did to you."

Sarah grasped Pavia's arm and backed them both away. "No, you don't understand. Anthony was trying to save me. Enzo is the one who raped me."

Alex gaped at his mother. "Why didn't you tell me?"

Sarah's face filled with horror. "Please don't make me say it," she sobbed.

Nick stopped. Confusion clouded his expression. "But the letter—"

"The letter was a lie. My parents and Enzo forced me to write it."

"No." Nick shook his head. "Anthony did this to you."

"Liar, you are a goddamn liar!" Pavia yelled.

"Nick, you're wrong!" Sarah said.

"Why are you standing up for him after what he did to you?" Nick turned on his mother.

The blood drained from Sarah's face, and she began to shake. She wrapped her arms around herself and bent forward. "Nick, your father and my parents forced me to write that letter. Nothing in it is true. Anthony and I were in love. I wanted to marry him, but my parents were determined that I marry Enzo.

"Enzo found us together. He almost beat Anthony to death, and then he—" A sob broke from her. When she continued, her voice was less than a whisper. "After he—" She drew in a breath and spoke louder. "After he took me back to my parents and told them he found us together, there was blood, so they believed him. I tried to refuse, but they were yelling and saying so many terrible things. I was scared and hurt, and I-I don't have an excuse for being too weak to fight harder." Her face twisted. "Enzo said he would marry me to save my reputation, and my parents were so"—her voice broke—"grateful."

Nick shook his head, his lips pressed into a thin line. "I don't believe you. You're always making Dad the bad guy."

In one swift movement, Sarah was in front of Nick, and her hand connected with his cheek with a loud echo. "I'm sick and tired of not being listened to. My father, Enzo, even Antonio and you!" she screamed.

"The only person who ever listened to me, who ever saw me as more than just a prize or a pawn, was Anthony. They ripped him away from me, and now you're going to tear your brother and Pavia apart." She pounded Nick's chest with each word.

Nick stood stone still, staring at his mother with a look of shock.

The anguish in her voice brought Pavia rushing to her side. She wrapped her arms around Sarah's waist and forced her back a step, whispering, "Don't. Don't do this, Sarah."

The confident expression Nick wore earlier had faded. Uncertainty was clear in his voice when he asked, "How could you have married him if Dad was so terrible?"

Sarah stiffened in Pavia's arms. The color drained from her face until her skin took on a sick, chalky hue. "Because I had to," she sobbed. "I prayed, I prayed so hard, but it didn't do any good. I was pregnant."

Pavia's gaze flew to Alex as Sarah collapsed against her. The impact of her confession registered with him first. He stumbled back as if he'd been shot. He opened his mouth, but nothing came out as tears began to streak down his cheeks. Nick looked back and forth between his mother and Alex, the truth of what had happened beginning to settle in. Pavia tightly held on to Sarah, feeling furious with Nick for making his mother confess that she had been assaulted. She was afraid Sarah would fall to the floor if she let go, but watching Alex silently fall apart, she wanted to go to him.

"Are you happy now, Nick?" Pavia snapped. "You wanted to hurt me, and look at what you've done."

Nick pressed his lips together. His head shook slightly.

"I was born nine months after you were married," Alex said in a flat voice.

Nick stared at his brother. "I-I didn't think that... I didn't know," he stammered.

"No!" Sarah wrenched herself out of Pavia's arms. "You didn't listen." She lunged toward him, but Pavia grabbed her, pulling her away.

"Don't," she whispered in her ear. "It won't undo what's been done."

A low keening sound filled the air, and Nick's eyes grew wide as Sarah sank to the ground. Pavia gathered her in her arms, holding her as she sobbed. Nick slowly backed away until he tripped on a broken post and fell to his knees. He bowed his head in his hands. Pavia continued to hold Sarah, rocking her back and forth, comforting her as she wept, feeling helpless as she watched Alex struggle to come to terms with what he'd just learned.

Eventually, Sarah's sobs grew quieter, and she pulled herself up and looked around. "Where is Alex?"

Pavia shook her head. "I… I don't know."

Panicked, her eyes darted around the fields surrounding them. At some point when she'd been trying to comfort his mother, Alex slipped away.

Nick cleared his throat. "I'll go look for him." He looked at Pavia. "I… I'm sorry."

Pavia closed her eyes. "Don't ask me to forgive you. Don't you dare. I will plant new vines, but what you destroyed here will never grow again."

Now it was Sarah offering comfort as she put her arms around her. It was a useless battle against the sting of tears she felt. Pavia refused to allow herself to break down, afraid that if she fell apart, she would never be able to put the pieces back together again. She had to stay strong for her father, for Sarah, for Alex. She silently cursed Antonio for thinking she had the strength to endure this much pain.

"Your father doesn't know," Sarah said once Nick left.

"Please don't ask me to keep any more secrets."

"Oh, honey." Sarah cupped her cheek. "No more. You"—she took a deep breath—"we have all suffered enough. We're going to find Alex, and we're going to make everything right."

Pavia shuddered. "I'm not sure that's possible anymore."

"Sweetheart, please, don't give up hope."

She wanted to be strong. She wanted to believe that everything would be okay, but how could they move forward? The look on Alex's face when he realized he was conceived from a violent act haunted her.

"I'm going to look for my son," Sarah said, grasping Pavia's arms. "Don't give up. Don't give up on the one you love. Don't repeat my mistake." She gave her a little shake as she spoke.

Pavia nodded numbly, wincing slightly when Sarah's hand clasped hers tightly. "I'm sorry." Her voice broke as a tear rolled down her cheek.

Sarah stopped in her tracks. "You have nothing to be sorry for."

"If I didn't come here, you would have been able to keep your secret."

"No." Sarah shook her head. "Secrets don't stay secrets forever. Even when we think we're hiding something, we're telling the story in little ways."

"Did you know about Henry and Antonio? Did you know their secret?" Pavia blurted out.

Sarah gasped. "I wondered. How did you know?"

"I don't. Antonio left me his diary from the war, and I think… I don't know. Alex and I talked about it. We both think their love was deeper, something more than just being brothers in arms. How do we recover from generations of secrets and lies?" Pavia asked.

She looked up at the stars partially obscured by wispy clouds. The early evening light cast shadows over the destruction, creating eerie, grotesque lumps of dirt, vines, wood, and wire. In the distance, Nick called out to Alex, his voice sounding more and more desperate as it moved away.

"I've been trying to make sense of why Antonio gave me the Brothers Block, why he wanted me here. Right now, I'm angry at him for doing this to you, to us."

Sarah grabbed her hand, her expression almost wild. "Don't leave, Pavia. Don't give up."

"You should call Brandon. Maybe Alex went to him." Her eyes scanned the shadowy fields. "I don't know if I can stay here without him."

"I'm the one that needs to go."

Sarah and Pavia spun around. Alex stood in front of them, his shoulders slumped with his fists clenched at his sides as if he were holding himself together.

"Alex." Sarah rushed forward and wrapped her arms around him. She held his face in her hands. "Remember what I said that day in the kitchen when we packed the picnic dinner for your first date with Pavia? Now is the time to be brave. This is the moment when love overcomes everything."

He remained stiff in his mother's arms while she pleaded with him. Pavia took a step toward Alex, and he wrenched himself away.

"Don't touch me," he said, his gaze locked on Pavia. "I can't— please don't try to tell me it will be all right."

"Alex, I don't want to console you. What you learned tonight"— she shook her head—"I don't know what words I could offer." She took another step toward him. "What I can do is love you. You may not want me to comfort you right now, but," she continued, her voice quavering, "I lost my vineyard. I can't lose you too."

Pavia could see it in his eyes. A crushing sense of defeat crashed over her. Her love wasn't enough to bring Alex back from the painful place his mother's revelation had sent him.

Sarah put her hand on Pavia's arm. "Let me talk to him," she said in a firm, motherly voice.

They exchanged a silent look of understanding. She noted that Alex winced when she stepped away, but his expression remained shuttered and distant. She turned and saw Nick standing off to one side watching the scene, looking lost. His eyes flicked toward hers, and she shook her head.

She held up her hand. "Don't. There's nothing you can say right now, Nick."

He shoved his hands into his pockets and dropped his head.

Numb, Pavia stumbled to her truck and somehow managed to make her way back to her cottage, not knowing where else to go or what to do. Who knows how long she sat in her truck crying. Her body and her heart aching, she slumped onto her front step. Drawing her knees up to her chest, she put her head in her arms. How could she tell her dad what had happened? He would never forgive Nick for what he'd done. She loved Alex, but what kind of future could they have with nothing but abuse, hate, and shame from the generations before them?

Her phone rang, and in a panicked voice, Sarah told her that Alex had left. Pavia was empty. She had no words of comfort to give Sarah and none for herself. She stumbled into the cottage and crawled under her mother's quilt with Antonio's diary clutched in her hand, her tears mingling with the dirt and wine stains on the edge of the pages. Mourning replaced sleep. When the light outside her window showed that her dad and brother would be walking the fields, she called home.

CHAPTER *Eight*

I'm the child of a monster. Numb, Alex stumbled away from the vineyard, his mother, and his heart. He wouldn't dare ask Pavia to love him now that he had uncovered the truth about himself. He spun on his heel and took off, running blindly until he dropped to his knees, hiding his face in his palms. His past, present, and future intertwined, bringing him to a place of darkness where time held no meaning. He had no clue how much time had passed when his mom eventually discovered him, and she fell to her knees right beside him.

"It's not your fault," she said, pulling his hands away from his face.

"Every time you look at me, you must see him. How can you love me?" Alex asked in a harsh whisper.

"You're a part of him, but you're also a part of me. How could I not love you? Alex, you made my life worth living."

His mom remained out in the field, begging him to believe that everything could eventually be okay. When she shivered with cold, he put on a mask of acceptance and agreed to follow her back to the house. He held back when they arrived at the garage.

"I just need to get something out of my car," he said.

Sarah furrowed her brow as she looked at him with worry.

"It's okay, Mom. I'll be only a minute."

"Okay, honey. I'm sure Pavia's waiting for us. We love you, and we'll make this right for Pavia and for you."

He gave her a reassuring smile and watched her until she was back in the house. His brother didn't disappoint him, leaving the car keys in the ignition. Alex kicked the engine into gear and closed his eyes as he waited. As soon as the garage door had opened fully, he slammed the accelerator, leaving the driveway quickly and ignoring his mother and Nick running out of the house, calling for him. Veiled by rage and sorrow, he left, unable to confront reality.

The yellow lines on the freeway passed in a steady rhythm. He had no idea how many miles he had gone until he realized he was traveling north. Alex drove, and the mileposts passed, and he kept going, watching the sky growing lighter as the miles went by. The need for fuel and his growling stomach made him stop at a small diner. Slowly he got out of the car, extending his tense limbs, looking around to orient himself. He realized he was somewhere on the Oregon border. He ventured into the diner and settled in at the counter next to an elderly man wearing jeans and a cowboy hat. Alex pulled his phone out to check the GPS and find out where he was. He took one glimpse at the phone with all the text messages and then put it away, turning to the man beside him.

"Excuse me, sir." He cleared his throat. His voice was raspy from lack of food and sleep. "Could you tell me which town we're in?"

The older man squinted at him, rubbing his chin. "You're in the Dalles, on the Oregon border. You go that way"—he jerked his thumb to the left—"you'll end up in Portland. The other way will take you east, Walla Walla, Spokane, all the way to New York City if you keep goin'.""

Alex muttered his thanks and drank a hefty swallow from the cup of coffee the server had poured. The rich brown liquid filled his stomach, and he realized he had no recollection of when he'd last eaten. He grabbed a menu, staring at it, unable to see anything clearly. He placed it on the counter and rubbed his eyes.

"Pancakes are always good." The old man threw a few bills down and got up to leave. The server approached. "Pancakes are on me, Nadine," he called out to her as he made his way out the door.

Before Alex could process what was happening, the man had vanished, and a stack of fluffy pancakes appeared in front of him. That moment of kindness was enough to make Alex feel some of the pressure lift, and he could take a breath. After his plate was empty and his second cup of coffee finished, he realized he wasn't just aimlessly driving. His brain may have been in the dark, but his heart held the answer. He grabbed a sandwich to go, got back in his car, and drove northeast.

It took him five hours to get to his destination. The afternoon sunlight filtered over the wheat fields, surrounding the abundant valley with a warm glow that looked like a sea of gold. As he drove up the winding gravel road, a modern structure of concrete and glass emerged atop a bluff. He stopped in his tracks when he saw the two men standing by the entrance of the tasting room. He recognized them instantly. Alex faced Pavia's father and brother for the first time.

Anthony Jackson advanced toward him with a menacing look. "I promised my baby girl that nothing bad would happen," he said, while Pavia's brother stood next to him with clenched fists.

"You know," Alex said, realizing as soon as the words left his mouth how stupid he sounded.

"Of course, I heard," Anthony snapped. "And it's a good thing you're standing here and not your brother." He poked him in the chest. "I pride myself on being slow to anger and a forgiving soul, but your family has a way of testing me, and this time I might just fail."

Alex lowered his head. "I'm sorry, sir," he choked out. Spots of moisture appeared on the concrete floor. He didn't know what else to say. His sorrow and remorse were too intense to be put into words.

He heard Anthony heave a deep sigh, and suddenly, a heavy hand fell on Alex's shoulder.

"Come on, let's get you inside the house," Anthony said, his voice low and tight.

He nodded his head, but stayed where he was. Pavia's father gave him a gentle shove, and he made himself move forward one step at a time.

Anthony called over his shoulder, "Robert, we'll start on the cuttings early tomorrow. I want to be on the road as soon as possible."

Alex trailed in Pavia's father's footsteps as they entered the main house, a Prairie-style home with tall windows that framed the vineyard. Anthony brought him to the great room that featured an enormous stone fireplace and a wood beam ceiling. Alex admired the clean lines of the modern furniture in warm brown and green tones. The room was far more relaxed than the formality of the Conti villa. The walls were adorned with large black-and-white photographs showing the people and their lives in the valley. He noticed one in particular of Pavia as a little girl with a smile on her face that matched the woman's she was standing next to. Pavia embraced her mother's thigh, while her mother tenderly touched her curls and held a basket of grapes in her other hand. The photograph was in black and white, yet it was vibrant with life, happiness, and love. They progressed along a lengthy corridor with several bedrooms until they reached a guest room with a connected bathroom at the end.

"Did you bring a change of clothes?" Anthony asked.

"No, sir, I drove straight through." He ran his hands over the stubble on his face, avoiding Anthony's gaze. "I… I just left. I didn't realize I was coming here until I had driven halfway."

"I'll get you some of Robert's things. There's a new toothbrush and toothpaste in the medicine cabinet and clean towels on the counter. When you're showered and changed, come out to the kitchen, and we'll talk."

"It's my fault. I should have protected Pavia, and I failed." Alex shook his head. "I couldn't keep my mother safe from my father, and I couldn't keep Nick from hurting your daughter. I don't think I will ever be able to forgive myself."

Anthony's mouth turned down. "It wasn't you. You're trying to take on a burden that was never yours to begin with. Stop being so hard on yourself, son. You need a shower and a rest. We'll talk more when you have a clear head." He gave him a soft nudge in the bathroom's direction before leaving down the hallway.

Alex could not wash away the shame and regret no matter how long he stayed under the shower. But a half an hour later, dressed in a pair of Robert's old sweats, he felt human again. He reversed his steps to the main room, guided by the quiet voices that took him to the kitchen. Anthony left the kitchen table and went to the stove when Alex came into the room. After taking a bowl from the shelves above, he ladled a thick, nourishing stew into it and gave it to him without uttering a single word. Alex's gaze dropped to the bowl, tears obscuring its contents. Anthony kept showing more kindness than he deserved.

He sat down at the table with Anthony on one side and his son, Robert, on the other. His judge and jury.

Alex took a deep breath, ready to plead his case. "My brother destroyed the Brothers Block, and I need you to come home and help Pavia rebuild."

"Why did you run away? You should have stayed and helped," Robert asked, looking at him with disgust.

"I can't help her. But you can," he said, wincing at how he couldn't even find the right words to explain. "I'll only cause more pain." He hated everything he was in that moment, a monster and a failure.

Robert stood up from the table abruptly. "I need to take a walk." He shot Alex a hostile look before leaving the room.

Anthony had settled back in his chair, not making a sound, his lips held in a thin line as Alex spoke. Alex waited for the judge to give his sentence, expecting Pavia's father to tell him he wanted him to stay away from his daughter.

"Alex, I want you to listen to me." He leaned forward. "You don't have to take responsibility for your father's or your brother's actions. You're not your father. I'm not going to lie. Angry doesn't begin to describe how I feel about what happened, but my anger is for all of us." He clenched his hands together on the table and took a few deep breaths. "We all played a part in this mess."

Alex started to object, but Anthony held up his hand, stopping him.

"You came here to make things right. That says a lot about your character. You and your brother…." Anthony's eyes flashed with anger. "If I had known what kind of husband and father Enzo was, I would have come."

"You had your own family. What would you have done, abandoned your wife and children for us?" Alex shook his head sadly. "There's nothing you could have done."

Anthony squeezed his eyes shut for a moment. "I never should have left."

"My father would have figured out a way to kill you, or have you killed, if you hadn't. And I never would have met Pavia, and she's… everything." Alex took a deep breath. "If I could bring back some of your Zinfandel cuttings, we could graft them onto the Conti rootstock. I'm hoping we could use some of the Italian clones. The yield might not be great, but it would be something." He cleared his throat. "I also thought that if I brought you back with me, it would show my mom that I am not the monster my father was."

Anthony stared at him for a moment, and then he bowed his head, pressing his fingers on the bridge of his nose. Alex held his breath, waiting for an answer.

Eventually he said, "Robert and I are already planning to take cuttings in the morning. We'll still need to get approval from the Department of Food and Agriculture to use them."

"I'll make some phone calls. I've never used my family influence for anything," Alex said, "but I'll do whatever it takes to get the permits we need. Since your rootstock comes from Conti cuttings to begin with, I think we'll be okay."

It was true. He never used his family's influence to get ahead. His grandad had made sure Alex understood that being a founding family, abiding by the rules was even more important for them. But he would move heaven and earth to repair the breach generations of his family had caused.

Anthony stood from the table. "You look dead on your feet. When was the last time you slept?"

"I don't know, sir."

"Does anyone know you're here?" Anthony cocked his head, narrowing his eyes at him.

Alex avoided making eye contact with the older man. "No, sir." He wasn't in a position to ask for any favors, but he did anyway. "I'd appreciate it if you didn't say anything. I'm… not ready to talk to anyone yet."

Anthony crossed his arms and frowned down at him. "They must be worried sick by now."

"It doesn't matter," he replied.

"Yes, it does," Anthony said in an insistent voice.

"I don't know how she's been able to stand—how can she look at me every day knowing the reason I exist is that Enzo raped her?" he snapped. Alex pressed his hand to his stomach. "I'm sick every time I think about it."

Anthony looked at him for a long time before he spoke. "How you came into being doesn't define who you are. Your mother loves you because you're also a part of her. Jesus"—he choked back a sob—"you have her eyes, Alex."

An anguished cry tore from Alex as he sank to his knees. A second later, Anthony had his arms around him.

"I'm sorry, son. No one should have to live with a burden like this." He helped Alex to his feet and grasped his arms, looking him in the eye. "You're a grown man, I can't make you call, but you're wrong. Your mother's love for you is unconditional," he said, giving him a little shake. Then he sighed. "Get some sleep, and we'll get ourselves organized in the morning."

Alex nodded, grateful that Anthony didn't argue with him about calling home. Hearing his mother's voice would shatter him, and his heart told him Pavia would call to him in his dreams that night. He stumbled toward the guest room, and sleep claimed him the minute he pulled the blankets over himself. Just as he knew she would, Pavia called to him in his dreams through the night.

He felt a little more human when he walked into the kitchen the next morning. Anthony silently handed him a cup of coffee and gestured to the kitchen table. Alex sat down and ran his hands over the smooth oak surface. He pictured Pavia sitting at the table with her father and brother, discussing the day's events, and rubbed his chest, trying to ease the pain of missing her. This was a happy home compared to his.

Later in the day, Alex stood on the small bluff overlooking one of the oldest AVAs in Washington, founded by the man standing next to him. Spread out around him were fields of the best vineyards in the state, created from the exile and sadness his father had caused. His eyes took in the sight of a seemingly endless expanse of lush vines.

Anthony's hand swept over the vineyard. "When I arrived, this was all alfalfa and hay. The other farmers in the valley thought I was foolish to plow everything to plant fruit. Around an hour to the east of here, another farmer planted vines along the Columbia River. He heard about me and asked if I'd be interested in planting Syrah. I don't know why for one second I thought I could get wine out of my blood. My father and your grandfather…." He chuckled softly. "Now you and Pavia. It's in our DNA."

Alex shook his head in wonder at what Pavia's father had created.

With a low, gruff voice, Anthony said, "There are a few Conti vines left down there, and they don't yield much fruit, but I can't seem to let them go. They're the original Zinfandel vines I brought from California. Robert is taking cuttings, and we'll bring Syrah with us too."

The field morphed into a watercolor blur. Alex didn't try to bring it back into focus, letting the shades of green, gold, and brown blend, creating a new vision. He closed his eyes, and taking a deep breath, he let scents that were both strange and familiar fill his senses.

"It's funny, isn't it?" Anthony said.

Alex wiped his eyes. "What is, sir?"

"History."

Alex shook his head. "I don't understand."

"Almost forty years ago, I came here with the rootstock from your vineyard. I kept them alive in pots while I bounced around from place to place looking for a place to call home. I knew the minute I set foot on this land this is where they were meant to take root. Now, I'm bringing them back to your home."

The wind picked up, turning the hills above the valley into a green and gold sea. Waves of wheat rolled across the land, and suddenly, his soul felt calm and clean.

"I'm not a monster."

"Of course you're not."

Alex jerked his head toward Anthony. He didn't realize he had spoken out loud.

He pulled himself up. "I need to talk to you about my mom."

Anthony's stance grew rigid. "Now you're asking for more than I can give." He shook his head.

Anthony had already given so much Alex didn't have the heart to push him for more. Instead, he stood side by side with him, letting the silence speak for both of them.

He spent the rest of the afternoon on the phone with the Department of Food and Agriculture, pushing through the permits needed to graft Brothers in Arms fruit onto Conti vines, while Anthony and Robert loaded the truck. It wasn't the best time of year to graft or plant, but he didn't want to wait. He needed Pavia to see new vines in the Brothers Block. It would help her heal, help both of them heal.

The vineyard and production facility left him in awe of what Anthony had built with Brothers in Arms. He viewed the acres of fruit, imagining what it must have been like to come here as a young man and do something no one had ever tried before. The care and attention Anthony put into his craft showed in every facet of his business. Alex hoped he could come back someday and spend more time here. *Hopefully with Pavia and our children.*

It felt good working alongside Anthony and Robert. It was the kind of relationship he'd had with his grandfather, and a fresh wave of grief washed over him. He thought about home. He had been ignoring the missed calls and text notifications from both Pavia and his mother, but he just needed a bit more time to come to grips with everything that had occurred.

Chapter *Nine*

The fog slowly cleared from the valley as the sun rose, showing the destruction that secrets and lies had created. Pavia hugged herself and gazed at the barren field, attempting to find the strength to begin anew. She had no clue where to start or if she would even want to. Her heart had broken so many times over the last twenty-four hours there was nothing left but dust.

The sound of a horn made her jump, and when she spun around, she saw the Matsui Construction logo on the first car in a line of vehicles coming up the driveway. With arms outstretched, Lilly flew from her father's truck, running to Pavia and giving her a hug. Brandon walked over and pulled her out of Lilly's arms and into his own embrace.

"It's going to be okay, Treasure. We're gonna fix it."

He kissed the top of her head, just like her brother would have done, and Pavia buried her face in his chest, breaking down all over again. Brandon tensed up, then gave her a pat on the back.

"Standing here all day hugging won't get anything done," Brandon said gruffly. He pulled his work gloves from his back pocket. "I'm gonna get the tractor ready and begin plowing. Get the tools out of the truck." Those who didn't know him well would assume he was unmoved, but Pavia saw the tears in his eyes before he left.

"We brought supplies, but I wish we had more help," Lilly said with a frown, glancing toward the empty field.

Brandon's hug had started a flood of tears. Sinking down onto the front step, Pavia buried her head on her knees and wept. Lilly waited patiently, rubbing her back and providing encouraging words until she regained her composure. Chloe eventually made her way over and, without saying anything, sat on the other side and reached for Pavia's hand.

"Alex is gone, and no one knows where he is," Pavia said, wiping her tears. "I'm more upset about that than I am this." She waved her hand toward the patch of brown earth. "If he comes back, how can I ask my father to forget everything this family has done? It's too much… I can't."

"Bullshit," Lilly replied.

Chloe opened her mouth, but Lilly silenced her with a stern look.

Pavia had just poured her heart out, and that was the response she got? "You're a terrible therapist," she muttered, wiping away her tears.

"No, that is absolute bullshit," Lilly said with a little smile. "First, Alex loves you, and he will come back. Second, loving Alex more than the vineyard is nothing to feel guilty about. Pavia, you're scared. Love can be overwhelming, but it's worth fighting for, don't you think?" She glanced quickly at the Conti villa. "How do you think we found out about what happened?"

Pavia's head jerked up. "What did you say?" Her sorrow had consumed her so much that she hadn't realized the Matsui truck was loaded with fenceposts and trellis wire. How did they know?

"Alex called all of us this morning," Chloe confirmed with a solemn nod.

Pavia's heart leapt. "Did he say where he is?"

"No." Lilly shook her head. "Only that he needed some time."

"I'm glad to hear he's okay," a voice said.

The three of them jumped up. Lilly and Chloe moved in front of Pavia, glaring at Nick, who was walking toward them.

"What the hell are you doing here?" Lilly advanced on him.

"Don't try anything, Nick." Chloe moved to Lilly's side, creating a wall between him and Pavia.

He stopped and held his hands up. His eyes flickered nervously toward her.

"I know you don't want me here. And I… I deserve to have the shit beat out of me and more. Pavia, my ego blinded me, and I… I believed a lie. You don't have any reason to forgive me. I don't know that I'll ever forgive myself. I came to offer my help because I don't know where else to start."

"So you honestly think that will redeem you?" Lilly shouted as George, Brandon, and Sam came running from the barn.

"No, I don't, but I have to start somewhere." Nick glanced toward the men advancing on him with a hint of fear in his eyes. "I don't want to be like my dad."

Numb with grief, Pavia stared at Nick. She had to decide between the present and the past. He kept shifting his feet, waiting. Lilly continued to glare at him, while a tear escaped and ran down Chloe's cheek. Pavia forced herself to move forward until she stood toe-to-toe with the man who had destroyed her future. Dark circles were visible under his eyes, and his hair was sticking up as if he had combed it with his fingers multiple times. Glancing down at his worn jeans and work boots, she sighed. He came wanting to work, and she needed the help.

Pavia motioned to a corner of the field and said in a flat, emotionless tone, "Start digging postholes as soon as the field is plowed."

Chloe wiped her face on her sleeve and took a shuddering breath. "I'll go help him."

"Are you sure that's a good idea, Treasure?" Brandon asked as Nick walked away with Chloe at his side.

"I'll keep an eye on him," George scowled.

Clearing away the remnants of trellises and vines didn't take long. The rhythmic thumping of posts being pounded into the dirt echoed in the valley for the rest of the day. Every once in a while, Pavia would sneak a glance at Nick. He worked continuously without stopping. He carried on digging postholes when the others took a lunch break, rejecting the sandwich Chloe gave him.

Brandon finally stalked over to him and shoved a bottle of water into his hands. "No one's gonna take care of you if you faint," he growled before walking away.

Nick approached her at the end of the day. "Pavia, I'd like to come back tomorrow… for as long as it takes to get you back on your feet, if that's okay."

"I appreciate your offer, Nick, but your brother also needs help. Conti Vineyards can't run itself. Even if it's just for a few days or"—her voice wavered—"however long he's gone, you need to step up and help."

Nick nodded. "You're right. I always thought… it doesn't matter what I thought. I've wasted too much time avoiding the truth and my responsibilities, and I'm not going to do that anymore, but I still want to help you."

Pavia saw Nick had a look of determination. Maybe some good would come out of this if he found his place in the world and at Conti Vineyards.

"You can come when you have time," she said.

"Thank you." He ran his hands through his hair, his face pinched with a pained expression. "Pavia, you don't have any reason to forgive me, and I don't know if I can ever forgive myself. But I get the impression we might be in-laws someday, and I want—I'll work hard to regain your trust."

His jaw was set despite his pained expression. Between her mental and emotional exhaustion and the physical toll from today's work, she was completely drained. She couldn't manage the energy to fight with Nick.

"You'll earn it one day at a time, Nick. I don't mean to be harsh, but you've run around here with a silver spoon in your mouth. What you did to me… to your family is…." She shook her head, her voice breaking. "I want to say it's unforgivable, but I can't. I hope I'll have a future with Alex, and that won't happen if I don't find some forgiveness in my heart. But there are others. You have a lot of amends to make in this community, and part of earning my forgiveness is if I see you making a genuine effort to be a better son, brother, and friend."

Nick's jaw tensed. Pavia understood her words were hard to take. They weren't easy to say, and it took a lot of effort not to unleash all the anger and hurt she felt.

Chloe emerged from the cottage. "I'm heading up to the main house to see my mom. Do you want to walk up with me?" she asked Nick.

His expression softened, and he reached out for Chloe's hand. "It's been a long time since we've taken a walk in the vineyard."

Pavia watched the two of them, and felt a little envy, as they faded away into the vines on their way to the house.

She wanted Alex to come back home.

SARAH BROUGHT dinner. Lilly made several attempts at conversation, but eventually she gave up, and a moody silence wrapped itself around the table. Pavia poked her plate of food nervously as everyone stared at her with concern.

"Do you want me to stay over tonight?" Lilly asked as they prepared to leave.

"Thanks, Lilly, but no, I just need some time alone," she said, staring down at her phone.

"How many times have you tried to call Alex?" she asked.

"Too many." Pavia fought back another bout of tears. How could he call her friends to come and help but stay away himself? It couldn't have been easy to reach out the way he did. "I don't understand how he could ask you to help me and not come himself. Where is he?"

Brandon steepled his hands. "I know what it's like to feel guilty for something you didn't have any control over. Alex will come back, but he's got to learn that his being here will not cause harm. Give him time, Pavia. He's so out of his mind with grief right now he's not thinking straight."

Lilly gave Brandon a nod of approval and pulled Pavia into a fierce hug. "It's going to be okay."

Sarah stayed behind after everyone else had left.

"He hasn't contacted you at all?" Pavia asked.

"Nothing. I hoped he would reach out to you."

"And I hoped he would call you."

"I know he'll come home."

Pavia broke down. "I can't do this without him. I don't want to rebuild without him."

Sarah wrapped her arms around her. "You won't lose him the way I—" She took a deep breath. "You're going to fight when I didn't." She pulled back and grasped Pavia's arms, squeezing so hard it almost hurt.

Pavia nodded, trying hard to believe what Sarah was saying.

"Are you sure you'll be okay by yourself?" she asked.

Pavia acknowledged her with a nod. She was grateful for everyone's worry, but wished to be alone. The only person she wanted was gone, and a piece of her heart had gone with him.

NICK HOVERED in the barn's doorway. As much as she wanted to, she couldn't ignore him. Pavia glanced at him and kept sweeping. There were so many things she should be doing right now to prepare for her first harvest. With the field destroyed, there was nothing left but to sweep out the dust in the empty storage room that would stay that way for the next few years.

Nick took another tentative step toward her. "Pavia, is there anything I can do to help in here?"

She rested her chin on the top of the broom, eyeing him. It had been three days, and Nick had shown up every day, trying to right what he had wronged.

She sighed. "Have you heard from Alex?"

He shook his head. "No, but I'm sure he's okay."

Her frustration boiled over. "Do you honestly think any of us are okay?" she shot back.

Nick's head dropped, and he shoved his hands into his pockets. "No," he answered in a shaky voice.

They stood there, paralyzed by the past and scared of the future.

"If I could go back in time and fix this, I would," he said quietly.

"Go back and fix what? How far back would you go, Nick? Back to 1943, when my grandfather met yours, back to when your father raped your mother, back to when you destroyed my field? How far back would you go, and what would you fix?"

Tears were streaming down both of their faces when she finished. Nick had his arms wrapped around himself, looking down at the floor.

"I wouldn't change one thing because it brought you here," Sarah said from the doorway.

Pavia dropped the broom and buried her face in her hands. Sarah came over and wrapped her arms around her.

"I miss him," Pavia said.

"He's okay," Nick said, moving closer. "I know it. I can't explain, but I just know he's all right."

Sarah nodded. "He'll come back."

"How, how do you know?" She sniffed.

Sarah gave her shoulders a little shake. "I'm his mother. I would know if he were truly in trouble."

Pavia wiped away her tears with the back of her hand. Nick had taken the broom away from her and started sweeping. She gave him a watery smile. She had to give him credit for his determination.

"Come on, let's have some lunch." Sarah waved him over. "Brandon has left so much food I won't have to cook for months."

He hesitated, then leaned the broom against the wall and followed them out of the barn.

"Pavia, I was thinking. You could take whatever you want from our harvest for your own production until your fruit is ready," he said, his voice quiet and hesitant.

She paused midstep, turning to look at Nick over her shoulder. His eyes were pleading. Sarah had made the same offer before, and she turned her down.

"I don't want to make any decisions without Alex."

Nick nodded. "Yeah, okay. I understand."

Forgiveness was a funny thing. Sometimes, it crept in quietly. It didn't demand but ask, waiting patiently until she was ready. Then there were days like today, when forgiveness knocked on the door before she wanted to answer.

"You're trying to help. You've been here every day, and I appreciate it. It's still going to take some time before I trust you again. You have to know that, but I see you trying, and I appreciate that."

Nick dipped his head. "That's more than I deserve. Thank you."

"Your mom made lunch. Come on, let's get something to eat."

They were quiet, sitting at the small table in the corner of her kitchen, each lost in their own thoughts and regrets as they picked at their food.

When Nick headed back out after lunch, Sarah said, "I don't think he'll ever be able to stop punishing himself for what he did."

"It seems like you have all been punishing yourselves in one way or another," Pavia replied quietly.

Sarah nodded. "We've lived this way for so long I'm not sure we know how to stop. We have no secrets left now." She shrugged. "Maybe now we can finally start to heal."

But there were still secrets. "Hold on a minute," Pavia said, getting up from the table.

In her room, she opened the top drawer of the dresser and pulled out the journal. She clutched it against her chest and took a deep breath, hoping that she was making the right decision. She went back into the kitchen and put the journal on the table, pushing it toward Sarah.

Sarah traced Pavia's name on the paper and looked at her. "He left it for you. All this time. I wonder how long he'd been planning this." Her voice was full of wonder.

"I found it in a drawer when I was cleaning out the kitchen."

Suddenly, Sarah started laughing, wiping away the tears that streamed down her cheeks. "That wily old fool. He was always a bit of a mystery to me. Now I wonder, I don't think I really knew him at all."

Pavia sat down and put her arm around her as Sarah followed the same ritual, opening the package the same way she had, lifting the worn leather journal to her nose and flipping through the pages, stopping at the ones with wine stains. Her breath hitched when she found the picture of

Henry and Antonio. Sarah let out a low moan and slumped back in her chair, holding the picture to her heart.

"They were so young," she whispered. "We all start out with so many hopes and dreams. We even carry the desires of our ancestors with us for a time. Somewhere along the way, we have to abandon those to make a life of our own. I forgot to do that."

"Forgot to do what?"

"Live a life of my own," she said with a sad smile. "After that night, that terrible night"—Sarah shuddered and wrapped her arms around herself—"I should have fought harder. I would have run away with Anthony, and that's what I wrote to him, until I found out I was pregnant with Alex. I tried not to flinch every time Enzo touched me, and he acted like a perfect doting husband at first. Even though he knew I was a virgin before, he made the most terrible threats until Alex was born, saying that if the baby came out with anything other than light skin and blue eyes, he would kill it."

Pavia couldn't stop herself from asking, "Why did you stay?"

Sarah gave her a sad smile. "Times were different. I was raised to be a dutiful daughter. My parents were old-fashioned, and they believed that nice Italian girls got married and had babies after high school. I had no skills and a baby to take care of." She dropped her head and shook it. "I'm every statistic. I stayed because I was too afraid to leave."

"I wish you had told me this before, Mom. If I'd known, I never would have—I hate I believed my father was the hero in this story," Nick said from the doorway.

Sarah clapped her hand over her mouth.

"Come and sit, Nick," Pavia said, waving him to the table.

He shuffled over and sat next to his mom, taking her hands in his. He glanced down, noticing the journal. His eyes flicked to hers and then back to his mother.

Pavia remembered that day in the lawyer's office. Nick was sitting with his mother the same way. She remembered seeing the sailboats bobbing on the waves and realized that's what they were, tiny boats being tossed by the waves without an anchor. Alex was her anchor. She knew that now. She wanted to jump up from the table and go find him, for she couldn't move forward without him by her side.

Instead, Pavia pushed the journal toward Nick. "Your grandfather left me his journal. I'd like to share it with you and Alex."

Sarah pulled out the picture of Henry and Antonio. "Nick, look at your grandfather and Henry. They were so happy amid chaos."

Nick carefully turned the pages. "Why did he leave it for you?" he asked, looking at Pavia with a pained expression.

Did he think his grandfather had betrayed him again by leaving the journal for her? Pavia was trying to figure out a way to explain something she didn't fully understand when Sarah jumped in.

She put her hand over Nick's, stilling him. "Antonio didn't do it to hurt you."

"Nick, I still don't understand why your grandfather left this for me. I'm glad he did, though. Every time I got discouraged or homesick, I would read a passage from the journal, and I don't know how to explain it, but I'd feel better."

"There was so much he tried to teach me." Nick shook his head. "I wouldn't listen. All I ever wanted was for Grandad to be proud of me the way he was with Alex. Now I understand why he was so hard on me whenever I acted arrogant. I was being just like Enzo, just like my father." He pushed away from the table and stalked toward the door.

"Wait, Nick!" Pavia called out. "Take this with you." She held out the journal.

Nick shook his head. "He left it for you."

"If it's mine, I can do what I want with it, and what I want is to give it to you to read." She took a step forward and grabbed his hand, pushing the book into it. Nick's chin trembled. She forged ahead before she lost her nerve. "Nick, I forgive you."

Pavia tossed out her anchor, refusing to be adrift on the waves anymore. Their past and future would always connect them.

Nick's head dropped, and the first tear hit the floor with a soft plop. "I… I wish you wouldn't," he replied. "I'm not ready to forgive myself yet."

"I can't help you with that," she sighed, "but I can offer my friendship." She held out her hand. "Nick, I'd like to be friends."

Nick didn't look up, but he took her hand and suddenly pulled her into a hug. "I wish Alex were here," he whispered.

Pavia looked back, thinking how naïve she'd been believing she could come here and build a winery and manage a vineyard without any help. When she'd found the journal, she wondered what Antonio wanted her to learn from it. Suddenly, she knew. It was the family you picked, the people that you chose to have in your life, that made the difference. She couldn't do it all on her own, and she wasn't supposed to. Success would come from having people she loved by her side.

Pavia pulled out of Nick's embrace and faced Sarah, who was still sitting at the table with tears streaming down her face.

"What are you going to do?" she challenged.

Sarah stared at her, wide-eyed.

"Are you going to continue letting your life live you, or are you going to live your life?" Pavia's heart thundered in her chest as she forged ahead. "I'm going to find Alex, and I'm going to make him understand that I love him. The past doesn't matter. It's the future that we build together that does." She moved toward Sarah and held her hands in hers. "And you need to do the same thing. You need to go to Blue Ridge, go to my dad."

"She's right, Mom," Nick said.

Sarah bowed her head, her hands clasped so tightly the skin over her knuckles became pale. Pavia wondered if maybe she'd pushed too hard. Just because she wanted Sarah to find her happiness didn't mean that Sarah was ready to. Pavia was just about to apologize for speaking so forcefully when Sarah lifted her head.

"I guess I have a trip to plan," she said in a shaky voice.

ALEX MADE his way back to his familiar home landscape with Pavia's father at his side. He was keenly aware that time was running out on his self-imposed exile. Time didn't care if he was ready. He was going to have to face Pavia, his past, and the future he longed for before the hand on his watch completed another circle.

Anxiety radiated from Anthony, increasing the worry Alex felt the moment they passed the first vineyard in the valley. Anthony's fingers tightened on the steering wheel, and his breathing became shallow. After a few more miles, Alex worried that he might pass out.

"Would you like me to drive, sir?" he asked.

Anthony glanced sharply at him and flexed his hands on the steering wheel. "No thank you, son," he said quietly.

Anthony lowered his chin and his jaw clenched when they passed the Conti Vineyards main gate. Despite his obvious emotional turmoil, bringing him home felt right. It felt good. Alex glanced at the main house, worrying how his mom would react to seeing Pavia's father.

Too many years had passed, and it was time to heal the wounds that still lingered from that terrible night so many years ago. Something he was working on for himself. He hoped that after the initial shock, both his mother and Pavia would be happy to see him—and that when Anthony realized Alex had deceived him and hadn't told them he was coming, Anthony would forgive him as well.

Alex sucked in his breath when they turned down the side road leading to the cottage. A heavy silence surrounded them. Both men were weighing their pasts and futures as they drove the last few feet to the house.

When they pulled up, Alex jumped out, eager to see Pavia. He took a few steps toward the cottage before he noticed Anthony wasn't moving. He walked back to the driver's side, where Anthony sat like a statue with the engine running.

Alex opened the door. "Sir?"

Anthony didn't answer.

Alex put his hand on his shoulder. "Welcome home, sir." He swallowed past the lump in his throat. "I'm happy you're here."

Anthony slowly stepped out of the truck. Gripping the doorframe tightly, he gazed at the cottage.

"Sir, Anthony, are you all right?" Alex asked, watching the play of emotions on the older man's face.

They had left Blue Ridge well before dawn, watching the sky morph from dusky purple to bright blue as the miles passed. They made their stops for gas and bathroom breaks as brief as possible, eating from a cooler of food and drinks they'd packed before leaving. Alex hung on every word as Anthony talked about the different terroir from Washington, through Oregon, and into California. It was like getting his own private master class in viticulture. Pavia's father reminded him so much of his grandfather. At some point along the journey, he remembered why— Anthony had been mentored by the same man. Some of the burden he'd been carrying lifted. Grandad's legacy as a winemaker wouldn't just live on through him, but through Anthony, Robert, and Pavia. The Jackson and Conti families would always be intertwined through history and love.

Anthony blew out a long breath, looking at the cottage. "It's the same color," he whispered.

"Pavia and the Matsuis were dedicated to keeping everything as true to the original as possible."

Anthony nodded. "They did a good job," he said in a gruff voice, brushing his hands over his eyes in a swift movement. He took a deep breath, moved away from the car, and made his way up the footpath to knock on the arched door with a fresh coat of robin's-egg blue paint.

Alex shifted, waiting with his hands clenched at his sides, wanting to see Pavia's face, and fearing what would happen when he did. "Let's go look in the barn," he suggested when there was no answer.

Just as they rounded the corner of the house, Alex stopped, frozen, as Pavia walked out of the barn with Nick. The two were in deep conversation, her face animated and her eyes shining despite the dark circles that shadowed them. Nick looked up and stopped in his tracks. His eyes grew wide. He nudged Pavia, and she looked where he pointed. In an instant, she broke into a run.

"*Papà!*" she shouted, running into his arms.

"*Mia cara ragazza,*" Anthony said, his voice breaking with emotion. *My darling girl.*

Alex turned to his brother and shoved his chest. "What the hell are you doing here?" he asked, searching Nick's face and trying to understand why he was talking to Pavia as if they were old friends.

"Where the hell have you been?" Nick shot back.

Pavia and her father were speaking in rapid Italian. Suddenly, she turned back to Alex, looking at him in wonder.

"You went to Blue Ridge?"

His mouth became dry, and his eyes darted toward Anthony, who was frowning at him.

"You lied to me, son," he said between clenched teeth.

Alex opened his mouth to apologize, when he heard his mother's voice call out.

"Pavia, Nick, I'll be ready to leave in the morn—" She came around the corner, the words dying on her lips when her eyes met Anthony's and all the color drained from her face.

"Oh shit," Alex muttered under his breath, breaking into a run when his mother swayed. Anthony passed him, reaching her first, catching her in his arms.

"Mom, are you okay?" Nick hovered nearby.

"I… I was going to come to you, after all these years." She glanced at Pavia and Nick. "Our children convinced me… I was going to come. I don't want to be afraid anymore."

Pavia, Alex, and Nick stood by, watching Anthony hold Sarah in his arms. He reached up and gently wiped away the tears streaming down her face.

Pavia grasped his hand. "You went to Blue Ridge. My dad, he's here."

As she stood there looking at him in wonder, all he could think was that he needed to buy a journal, one of his own. Alex wanted to record this moment so that other generations would learn about love and family the way he had learned from Pavia.

He turned and watched Sarah reach up to caress Anthony's face. "You're really here," she whispered.

"I'm here," he said.

"Anthony, there is so much I want to say. For so many years, since the day you left, I wanted to tell you how sor—"

Anthony shook his head. "No apologies. We've all given enough apologies for a lifetime."

Sarah straightened her shoulders. "But I should have fought harder. How could I have ever let you go?"

"I should have stayed. I could have taken you with me. I…." He shook his head. "There are too many things we could have done differently. We can't relive the past."

Pavia pressed herself to his side as they watched their parents reunite. She sniffed, and he could feel the wetness from her tears through his shirt.

"Alex, I should have told you sooner. I thought I was protecting you"—Sarah looked at Nick—"both of you, and I was so wrong."

"You did the best you could." Nick's voice broke, and he looked away, clenching his jaw.

"The important thing is that we're together now," Pavia said.

Alex pulled their joined hands to his lips, and their eyes locked. There was so much to say, but they needed to be alone when they said it.

Everyone returned to the cottage, where the space was filled with so much emotion Alex had a hard time finding room for his own. His mom and Anthony sat together on the sofa, staring at each other as if they were trying to imprint their faces to memory. *This is what a lifetime of loving someone looks like,* Alex realized, watching it reflected back to him.

Nick hovered nearby, looking between the four of them. "I'll go up to the house to get some food ready. I'm sure you guys are hungry after your trip."

He looked so lost and unsure, Pavia let go of Alex and gave him a hug. "Thank you, Nick. I appreciate how much you've tried to help these last few days. I gave you a challenge. I asked you to show me you want to change, and that's what you've been doing."

"You wouldn't have needed my help if—"

"That's the past," she said, giving him a stern look. "We're going to move forward."

His jaw ticked, and his eyes filled with tears before he turned away and headed to the main house.

"Why don't we give our parents some privacy?" Pavia said after Nick left, pulling Alex away from Sarah and Anthony, who were so lost in each other they didn't even notice that their children had drifted away. Alex agreed, understanding it wasn't privacy she wanted for their parents but for the two of them.

She took him by the hand and led him down the hall and into her bedroom. After closing the door, she turned to him and grabbed his upper arms to shake him.

"Don't ever leave like that again," she yelled at him, and then with a sob, she buried her face in his chest, wrapping her arms around him.

His fingers caressed her cheek, trailing down to lift her chin to kiss her. "I shouldn't have left," he said, pressing his forehead against hers.

She held his face, searching his eyes. "Never again."

"Pavia, I—"

She shook her head. "No, never run away again, Alex." She kissed him once more. "You don't run away from the people that you love. I'll never run from you. I love you."

His eyes grew wide. "I love you so much, Pavia."

"Whatever the future brings, we face it together."

"Together," he said, bringing his lips back to hers.

Later that night, Pavia sighed, laying her head on his chest as Alex played with her curls.

"I hope we have little girls with curls just like you someday," he murmured.

"And little boys with blue eyes just like their father," she added. Pavia propped herself up on her elbow to look him in the eye. "Alex, how do you feel about my dad and your mom, really? Now that he's here, I don't think he will be able to leave her again."

"I don't want him to. I think they deserve some happiness together, don't you think?"

"The same happiness we want?"

His lips met hers in a tender kiss. "Yes."

They spoke of love and the future, sometimes in whispers and sometimes with their bodies. He was home, surrounded by people who loved him, all of him. It was selfish to walk away, and he shouldn't have done it, but he also realized he'd had to go so that he could have a homecoming not just for himself but for his family. It wasn't Pavia who was brought to Seneca to reunite the family. It was him. He understood now that he'd had to go to Blue Ridge and bring Anthony home to heal the wounds they had all carried from the past.

Alex closed his eyes with a sigh of contentment, feeling Pavia's body against his, the rise and fall of her chest, and her heartbeat in sync with his. In the morning, they would walk out into the field and start planting new vines. Fruit that would grow and, over time, flourish just like their love would. Locking away that knowledge in his heart, he fell asleep with his future in his arms as the sky tinged lavender and pink.

Chapter *Ten*

Some kids might have felt funny watching a parent fall in love. For Pavia, every day she witnessed her father and Sarah rekindle their love felt like a gift. She leaned against one of the posts along the veranda at the main house, watching the two of them walking through the vine rows, their arms intertwined. Alex came up behind her, slipping his arms around her and resting his chin on her shoulder.

"Are you sure you're okay with this?" he asked, nodding toward their parents.

"Of course, are you?" Pavia replied, turning around to wrap her arms around his neck.

He dipped his head, pressing his lips to hers. She could feel their hearts beating in sync.

"I love you," he said against her lips.

"I love you." The words were easy to say without any doubt or uncertainty.

With joined hands, they stepped out into the garden to meet their parents.

"Alex, is your brother around? I was hoping I could talk to both of you," Anthony said. Sarah grasped his arm, leaning against him, her cheeks flushed.

"If you wanted to ask for our mother's hand in marriage, we already talked about it, and we give you our blessing," Nick announced, walking up from the field with a sheepish smile.

Nick remained a little uncertain around her dad, still trying to redeem himself for his actions, but Anthony's presence had transformed him in ways they never expected. It became apparent right after Anthony arrived that Nick wanted a father figure in his life. Nick was often at his side, taking a renewed interest in farming and viticulture.

A couple of nights ago, Pavia stood on the veranda with Sarah as the three men walked through the Conti vines together.

"My boys," Sarah whispered, watching the three of them.

To everyone's surprise, Nick had even asked about going to Blue Ridge and working at Brothers in Arms for a while. Of course, her dad made an open invitation without hesitation.

At Nick's pronouncement, Pavia's father turned to Sarah and got down on one knee, pulling a faded velvet box out of his pocket. Sarah gasped as he took her hand in his.

"Sarah, this is the ring I had with me that night so long ago. I loved you since the first moment I saw you, and I never stopped loving you. What days we have left on this earth, we should spend them together. I want to spend them with you." He opened the lid. "It's not the fanciest ring. It was all I could afford…." Her father's deep timbre shook with emotion as he slid the ring onto her finger.

Sarah pulled her father up to his feet, and he held her hand in his as she looked down at the ring. The small diamond glinted in the light, framed by two small garnets on either side, set in a band of twisted vines. She threw her arms around his neck.

"It's perfect," Sarah said, tears of joy running down her face. She turned to her. "Pavia, I'll never replace your mom, but—"

"Don't be silly. Robert and I had the same conversation Nick and Alex had. Robert is looking forward to meeting you and welcoming you into our family. As for me, *sono felice di averti per mia madre." I'm happy to have you for my mom*, she said, hugging her.

"*E sono orgoglioso di chiamarti mia figlia.*" Sarah returned the embrace.

Nick elbowed Alex. "We're going to have to work on our Italian."

"I've already started," Alex gave his brother a wink before turning to Pavia and dropping to one knee. "*Vuoi sposarmi,*" he said, pulling a ring out of his pocket and taking her hand in his. "Pavia, I love you. I want to spend the rest of my days with my best friend by my side," he said, echoing her father's words.

Pavia reached out and caressed his face. "Yes, of course I will marry you." She looked at her father and Sarah. "*Papà, Mamma, abbiamo la tua benedizione?*"

"Of course you have our blessing," her father said, giving her a hug before turning to shake Alex's hand.

Nick stood off to the side with his arms crossed, beaming at the four of them with bright eyes.

That night after dinner, Pavia led her family into the cellar and stood with Alex in front of the barrel signed by Antonio and Henry.

"I want to share something with you all," she announced. Pulling out Antonio's journal, she read the last entry.

May 2, 1945
The men in the camp are shouting with joy! Such a different sound than the constant sound of gunfire that has echoed through the forest for weeks on end. The announcement of the end of the war made battle-weary men jump for joy. We will celebrate the war's end long into the night. I picked up a bottle of wine and went to search for Henry. I found him watching other men talk about their families, wives, and girlfriends back home.

Henry is an orphan, and I know he does not want to go home to Mississippi. He told me he didn't want to be a burden to the people who took him in and raised him. The Jackson family raised him as one of their own, but Henry felt like an extra burden, another mouth to feed. He worked alongside his family in the fields, making sure to earn his keep. Henry told me he joined the army so that he wouldn't be a burden to his adopted family.

I know Henry won't be satisfied going back to working in the cotton fields. He has seen too much of the world beyond rural Mississippi to go back.

I found Henry leaning against a tree separate from the other men.

"Henry, have a drink with me. Let's celebrate," I said, offering him the bottle.

Henry smiled slightly, taking the bottle from me. "Don't you know you're not supposed to drink from the same bottle as a black man?" he said.

I pushed the bottle toward him. Just as he tipped the bottle to his lips, it was slapped out of his hands. We didn't notice the sergeant.

"Boy, that ain't for you," the sergeant said to Henry.

I've had enough of the sergeant! Henry and I have served our country with honor. I told the sergeant that wine should never be wasted over ignorance. He ignored me and stuck his finger in Henry's chest.

"Boy, it's a good thing this war is comin' to an end. You're gettin' to be too big for your britches. We need to get you back in the cotton field where you belong," the sergeant said.

Henry stood still. I could see his jaw clench, his nostrils flare in the darkness. He would not fight back.

The sergeant continued to yell at Henry, "You ain't got no family to go home to. What else are you gonna do? You ain't good for nothin' else."

I had enough. I hated this man and everything he stands for! I put my arm around Henry's shoulder, and I told him, "This is my brother. His home is in California making wine with me."

The sergeant said, "You two deserve each other," before he spat on the ground at Henry's feet, then turned and walked away.

Henry tried to tell me I shouldn't have talked back to the sergeant, but I don't care. I pulled the letter from my father out of my pocket. I told him about my plan. Henry will come back to California with me. My father has given him a small cottage on our vineyard. We are going to make wine.

Pavia reached for Alex's hand as she read the last sentence. They decided to let each family member come to their own conclusions about Antonio and Henry. For Pavia and Alex, they treasured the gift of Henry and Antonio's love because it was the beginning of their love story.

Sarah and Anthony were married a month later in a simple ceremony at the cottage. Sarah went back to Blue Ridge with her new husband, glowing with happiness.

Pavia and Alex were making their own wedding plans, leaning toward a ceremony in the town she was named after. It felt right to say their vows in the same place Henry and Antonio had fallen in love.

The crush arrived amid the whirlwind of forging new family bonds. Nick threw himself into helping with the harvest, spending each day in the field from early morning until late in the day, until the last grape was harvested. Pavia and Alex's connection deepened with each day they worked together.

With the year's harvest in barrels beginning a new journey of a thousand steps, steps that would lead to a new beginning for the Conti and Jackson families, Pavia spent the morning in the Brothers Block. It would take years before they would have a harvest again, and her heart still hurt as she walked through the rows, but the healing had begun. She was fingering one of the new rosebushes Alex had planted for her at the end of a row when someone cleared their throat behind her.

"Ms. Jackson."

Pavia looked at Antonio's lawyer with surprise. She dusted her hands on her coat and shook his hand.

"Mr. Hendricks, this is a surprise. What brings you all the way out here?"

He pulled an envelope out of the breast pocket of his suit. He tapped it in his palm, looking uncertain for a moment, before he held it out to her.

"I heard about your engagement to Mr. Conti, congratulations. I wasn't supposed to give this to you before the end of the five years stipulated in Mr. Conti's bequest, but with the announcement, I've decided that Antonio would agree that you should have it now."

Pavia gingerly took the envelope, turning it over in her hand before she clutched it against her chest. She took a deep breath. "Thank you."

Mr. Hendricks smiled. "You're very welcome." He scanned the newly planted vines. "I'm glad to see that you've replanted. I must admit I was worried that you might give up."

"My fiancée is one of the strongest people I've ever met. There was no way she was ever going to give up." Alex walked toward them giving her a tender smile.

Pavia knew he wasn't talking about the vineyard but about them.

They both stared at the envelope in Pavia's hand after Mr. Hendricks said goodbye.

"Do you want to read it first?" Alex asked.

She shook her head and wrapped her free hand around his waist. "No, we'll read it together. From now on, we do everything together. It's you and me, Alex."

He kissed her temple and whispered, "You and me."

They waited until they were in bed that night with Pavia's quilt wrapped around both of their shoulders.

Drawing in a shaky breath, she opened the envelope.

Dear Pavia,

I am an old man with many regrets. Leaving the Brothers Block in your care is my small way of trying to make amends. By now you have read my journal, and I hope you understand. I have no doubt that by now your winery is up and running and you have made it a success.

Pavia bit back a sob.

I also hope that my instincts were right and you and Alex have found your way to each other. I knew when I met you that you were the right partner for my grandson. If my hope for the future is right, the Brothers Block is exactly where it should be, in both of your hands.

Henry and I tried to love the best we could. We were selfish, wanting to have families of our own and each other. I have many regrets, but I do not regret loving Henry, even with all of the pain it caused.

I'll leave it up to you how much you want to share with your father. Henry and I did our best never to hurt anyone, and in the end, we wound up creating generations of hurt.

Pavia saw the next line and let out a small gasp. She read it in a choked voice.

Enzo knew.

I don't know if our secret is what turned him into a hateful man. I do know he overheard Henry and I talking about Anthony. Anthony is the son we would have had if such a thing were possible. So much of the world has changed since Henry and I met. In a different time, maybe we would not have been afraid to live as we wanted to.

I'm at peace now, knowing that you will have the chance Henry and I never did.

You are Henry's granddaughter. Selfishly I feel that you are my granddaughter as well. I am proud of all of my grandchildren. You will each have your own challenges in life. There is nothing you cannot overcome if you are brave enough to love without hiding in the shadows.

I'd like to believe Henry and I will be watching you. I'll be with the love of my life, and I hope you will be with yours.

Take care, my dear. Be happy, and love fiercely.

Antonio

Pavia and Alex held each other as they shed tears of remembrance and love for their grandfathers.

"I can't believe Antonio did this wanting us to end up together. What if he'd been wrong? What if—?"

Alex gently cupped her face and stopped her with a kiss. "Let's not live our lives thinking about what-if. I thought Grandad was taking away the Brothers Block, but he was giving me the greatest gift he ever could have given me. You."

The next morning, they walked hand in hand out into the field, their hearts filled with gratitude. Her fingers trailed along the support wires, her engagement ring glinting in the sunlight, bringing a smile to her face.

Alex fell in step alongside her, wrapping his arm around her shoulder before pulling her close and dropping a kiss on her temple.

This was what they both always wanted, to walk side by side. The Jackson and Conti families were joined again, and it felt good. It felt right.

Pavia smiled. Somewhere in the vineyard, she could swear she heard Henry and Antonio laughing.

Keep Reading for an Excerpt from
The Way Forward
by Eliana West

CHAPTER ONE

TIME STOOD still in Colton, Mississippi, or at least it seemed that way every time Dax Ellis came back to visit. Nothing in his hometown had changed since he left. Like many small towns in the South, Colton was a place where folks were afraid of letting go of the past and fearful of moving forward into an uncertain future. The only thing that changed over time was the worn welcome sign showing the population, which only went down.

When Dax Ellis drove across Mockingbird Bridge it went up by one.

He rolled down his window taking in the cool morning air. His gaze swept over the small patch of green with a gazebo at its center. Absolem Madden Colton Park was the centerpiece of Colton's downtown. His mouth began to water as he drove by the Catfish Café. Sometimes the fact that nothing changed was a good thing. He'd have to stop in for some of Tillie's pecan pie if she'd let him in the door. Hopefully, it tasted as good as he remembered. The barbershop pole continued its lazy twirl on one side of the town square while the neon lights for Walker's Pharmacy flickered a dull orange glow. The K blinked twice and went dark just as he drove past. Seven years since he came home for his father's funeral, and the town had faded even further into obscurity since then. He'd come back to do his best to make sure it didn't disappear altogether.

Dax nudged his charcoal-gray Ford F-150 into a parking spot next to its much older twin. A man wearing a pair of worn overalls and a huge grin stood next to the vintage truck. Dax jumped down from the cab and pulled his uncle into a bear hug.

"I didn't expect to see you this early. Welcome home," Uncle Robert said, his voice gruff.

Dax looked into a pair of dark brown eyes that matched his own, framed with a few more wrinkles from squinting into the sun. He rubbed his chest where a sudden ache formed. He'd forgotten how much his uncle and father resembled each other. They shared the same straight brown hair, only now more silver poked out from beneath Uncle Robert's baseball cap than brown. If his father had lived past sixty-five, would he have looked the same? He shuddered when he thought of where he would have ended up without his uncle's guidance.

"Once I hit the road, I couldn't wait to get here. I didn't even mind the speeding ticket I got along the way," Dax confessed.

His uncle cuffed him on the shoulder. Dax grinned. "I've missed you, Uncle Robert."

"Seven years is way too long for you to be gone."

"It is." Dax agreed, "You know it wasn't about you." He looked around the town square, his gaze zeroing in on one building he'd always admired. "It's good to be back."

"I've got the keys to the Barton Building if you want to take a look now." Robert jangled a set of keys in front of him.

Dax rubbed his hands together. "I sure do."

They walked across the park toward the building he loved since he was a boy.

"Are you positive you want to take this on? It's a big project," Uncle Robert asked.

"I'm ready for the challenge now."

"What's changed?"

"The Army has given me the skills to start my own business, and the last few consulting gigs have given me the money I'll need to fix this place up and make it my home."

Inside the sun barely penetrated through the dust and grime on the windows; the scent of age mixed with a mustiness filled his nose. Dax coughed, waving the dust particles out of his eyes. They wandered around the main floor, their voices echoing in the empty space as they discussed the repairs Dax would need to make. The building was in surprisingly solid condition, and it wouldn't take much to restore the main floor to get his cybersecurity business up and running. They climbed the creaking staircase to the second floor. Standing in the middle of a large open space with rotting floorboards and crumbling plaster, Dax rested his hands on his hips, admiring the large arched window that faced the street and flooded the space with light. Converting the cavernous space into apartments would be an enormous task, a challenge Dax was ready for.

Uncle Robert kicked at one of the rotting floorboards. "You're right. It's gonna be an expensive project, but it will be worth it."

When his uncle mentioned several months ago that the building was going up for sale, Dax jumped at the chance to buy it. Next to the courthouse, she was the tallest building in Colton, standing proudly over the rest of the single-story buildings in the town square. Built in the Beaux-Arts style, the Barton Building once served as an office for cotton traders in the early 1900s.

The main floor would serve as headquarters for Ellis Technologies, his cybersecurity consulting firm. He'd convert the top floor into an apartment for himself and the second floor into four apartments, hoping to convince a few of his friends that Colton was a town worth saving and that moving in would be a good investment. His mother would throw a fit when she found out that Dax bought the building and didn't have any intention of moving into the family home, but sometimes a man just had to follow his heart.

Robert Ellis stroked his salt-and-pepper beard. "This place has sat empty for too long, and once you're done with her, she'll be a queen."

"Does anyone know I'm the one who bought the Barton Building?"

Uncle Robert shook his head. "Nope, you asked me to keep it quiet and that's what I've done."

"Good."

The Army had kept him on the move for the last thirteen years and he'd loved every minute of it, but it was time to settle down, and with an agreement to continue as a private contractor, he had the income secured not just to invest in the Barton Building but the town as well. *It's time to rebuild this town after everything I tried to do to destroy it.*

Dax crossed over to one of the windows and looked down at the deserted street below, thankful there weren't many people around. He wasn't ready, not yet. He left with a reputation he was ashamed of now.

"You're going to need help," Uncle Robert said.

"My buddy Jacob Winters is coming down just as soon as he gets his discharge papers."

"Does your friend have the right skills to help you out here?"

"Jacob is good with a hammer and has always been able to make something from nothing."

Uncle Robert joined him at the window. "How do you feel about ending your career with the Army?"

"It was time," Dax said. "I'll be happy to have Jacob's help and I'm hoping there will be opportunity for a few other guys I served with to move here. Jacob wants to set up a contracting business. He can look for other jobs while he helps me rehab this place."

Uncle Robert studied him thoughtfully. "There's plenty of work around here for a good carpenter. I can think of one off the top of my head, the librarian could use some help with a bookstore she's trying to open."

"Since when did you start hanging out at the library?" Dax asked, picturing his uncle flirting with a gray-haired lady.

"Don't look at me like that, boy, I know how to read."

Dax laughed and nudged his shoulder, surprised to find solid muscle beneath his hand despite his uncle's age. His uncle would never admit it, but he was slowing down just a little bit. Dax wanted to be around to help him and repay him for all the kindness and guidance he'd given him when he needed it. But if there was a sweet, older librarian in the picture, he'd happily share the duty with her.

"I've got to get back home," Uncle Robert said, "but if you have time, you might want to go over and meet the librarian and tell her about your friend."

They walked back downstairs and back across the park.

"I hope the folks will give me a chance to show that I've changed."

Robert swung the truck door open and climbed inside. "Remember who you are, not who you were," he said, through the cab's open window.

Dax watched his uncle drive away, as the soulful notes of Coltrane drifted from the truck before turning to take a closer look at the little library. The colorful display in the window stood out from the papered-over abandoned storefronts on the rest of the block, piquing his curiosity. Opened in the sixties by Richard Colton, the Colton Public Library was Richard's pride and joy. Colton, Mississippi, started out as the Colton Plantation, the town growing out of the rubble of the Civil War. Two families dominated the town, both Coltons.

One Black and one White.

The descendants of the slave owners and the slaves still lived and worked on the same land as their ancestors. Dax frowned. Unfortunately, there were those who still remained segregated. Some by history, and some by choice. A descendant of one of Colonel Madden Colton's slaves, Richard Colton had been a well-known figure in town. Returning after leaving for Chicago during the great migration, he'd brought a drive and determination to bring the sleepy town back to life. He insisted that the town needed a post office, a clinic, and a library—the last of which he funded with his own money. "For the young people," he always said. He made sure all children, no matter the color of their skin, had a book in their hand when they came into town.

Downtown may have withered away over the years, but the library was the one business that never closed. Taking a closer look, Dax admired the restored brick façade on the building. Cream paint on the window had been redone, the vintage lettering proudly declaring "The Colton Public Library" outlined in gold. The windows had fresh robin's-egg-blue trim that matched a new awning and a bench out front. On one side, another storefront had papered windows and a sign announcing, "Bookstore and Coffee Shop Opening Soon." Dax's lips curved slightly. He wouldn't be alone in trying to revitalize his sleepy hometown.

He entered the air-conditioned coolness of the library. The old wood floors had been refinished and polished into a dark rich sheen. The original bookshelves were given the same treatment. A long table took up the middle of the room hugged by two long benches on either side. Two overstuffed chairs covered in a blue floral print sat in one corner with a small bookshelf and floor lamps beside each one, inviting readers to stay for a while.

The pale cream walls and schoolhouse light fixtures made the space feel warm and inviting. Dax stopped at the small counter by the door. Everything was neat and tidy. A new computer and bar-code scanner sat at one end. The old library had finally caught up with the times.

His hand hovered over the bell on the corner of the desk when he caught sight of a head of deep golden-brown curls popping through a doorway at the back of the room. Dax froze as blue-gray eyes that had haunted him since childhood stared back from a light brown face frozen in shock, her expression quickly changing to fear. The stack of books she had been carrying fell to the floor and she put a hand to her mouth.

Numbness washed over him. He wanted to leave, but his feet refused to cooperate.

She was the one to take a step back, her eyes locked onto him, wide with anxiety.

Breaking eye contact, Dax forced his fingers to wrap themselves around the warm metal of the door handle before wrenching the door open. He turned and fled.

The actions of getting in his car, of driving through town, were a blur as his heart raced from the shock of seeing her in the flesh.

Callie Colton, of all the people he'd hurt, he hurt her the most.

Rocks flew as Dax slammed on the brakes, pulling up to his uncle's house.

On the outskirts of town, Uncle Robert lived in a two-bedroom cabin surrounded by seven acres of cornstalks that already came up to Dax's waist. Clearly expecting him, his uncle sat in the same rocker on the wide shaded front porch that Dax remembered from his childhood.

"Damn it, Uncle Robert, you knew Callie Colton worked at the library!" Dax charged toward his uncle like a guided missile.

Robert continued to rock, a book open on his lap. Dax stood in front of him, his heart pounded in his ears, drowning out the dull chirp of cicadas in the heat. "How could you just let me walk in there like that?" he asked, voice low.

Robert closed the book and set it aside. "Wasn't my place to tell you."

"Bullshit, you could have given me a heads-up."

Robert jumped up, standing toe to toe with Dax. "You're a grown man, and I'm not here to hold your hand."

Each poke of Uncle Robert's finger in his chest took Dax back to the first time his uncle confronted him about his behavior on this very same porch. That confrontation led to a lot of long talks that ultimately saved him. Dax took a deep breath and let the anger drain from him. He had no right to be mad when he was the one who'd caused all the hurt. "You're right."

They remained silent for a minute giving Dax a moment to gather his thoughts.

Dax stepped back and leaned against the porch railing. "How long has she been here?"

"'Bout a year. Her grandparents were killed in a car crash, and they left her the whole block of buildings including the library. They knew how much she loved it."

He shifted his weight on the railing. Of all the things he was prepared to face moving home, he wasn't ready to face Callie Colton again.

His uncle went into the cabin and returned with a couple of beers. He grabbed the bucket of peanuts by the front door, setting it at their feet before he leaned against the railing next to him.

"I expect you're going to want to stay here tonight," Robert said, handing him a bottle.

Dax took a long swig. He dreaded going home knowing his dad wouldn't be there. Many things about Colton felt like home; his mom wasn't one of them. Their relationship had always been complicated. She loved him, but it wasn't until he left home that he realized her love was conditional.

Dax nodded and took another drink. "If you don't mind."

"Always happy to have you here, you know that," Uncle Robert said, handing Dax a handful of peanuts.

Dax cracked open the nuts and threw the papery shells out into the yard. A cardinal swooped down to peck at the remains.

"Sorry buddy, didn't mean to fool you," Dax muttered, throwing a peanut next to the shell. He glanced toward Robert. "I didn't think she would be here." He studied the pattern of squares on the peanut shell in his hand for a moment before he threw another treat to his new friend. "I wasn't ready. If I had known—"

"Would it have made a difference?" Uncle Robert cut him off. "She's here, and the two of you would've run into each other sooner or later."

"You're right, I know that, but I would have preferred later."

"You've had plenty of time to prepare for this day. If you weren't ready, why did you come back?"

"Because I realized even after all the trouble I caused, Colton is home. I want to be a part of a community and do my part to…to help the town survive. Too many small towns are dying, disappearing, only remembered as a forgotten spot on an old map."

The cardinal flew back, hopping a little closer to the porch. Dax threw another peanut, and with a flash of red, the bird caught it before it hit the ground. It never occurred to him that Callie would feel an attachment to a place she'd only visited during the summer. He squeezed his eyes shut, trying to block out another wave of memories. They weren't easy memories, either.

"Let it go, son." Robert's voice washed over him.

"What do I do? How do I…?" Dax rubbed his hands over his face, trying to get the image of stormy-gray eyes out of his head, but they were burned into him. "She has no reason to forgive me—no one in the town does—but Callie…" How could he explain the way he treated her haunted him through the years?

Dax jumped up and paced the porch. The cardinal hopped a little closer, tilting its head to look up at him, waiting, while Robert sat forward with his hands clenched. Like a baseball player standing in the outfield waiting for the pitch. Years ago, his uncle sat in the same position waiting for Dax to decide which path he was going to take in life.

"How am I going to avoid her?" he asked, turning to face his uncle.

"Colton is too small. You can't avoid her so you're going to have to figure out a way to talk to her."

"Easier said than done. You didn't see the way she looked at me."

Robert's eyebrows shot up. "No, but I can guess." He glanced at Dax, adding, "She's grown into a beautiful young woman, hasn't she?"

Dax swallowed hard "You're not helping." Beautiful was an understatement. The luminous gray eyes were still there and still looked at him with weariness, but the gangly arms and legs were gone, replaced by soft curves. Daily life in the southern sun had turned her skin a tawny brown and the curls that cascaded over her shoulders a deeper shade of golden brown. Callie Colton was a stunning woman. "I need to figure out how I'm going to approach her again and start with an apology."

"She's not going to want to talk to you at first, so start by being a part of the community and show you care."

"Any suggestions?" Dax asked.

"There's a meeting next week you might want to go to, for a start."

Dax frowned. "Meeting? What kind of meeting?"

"Book club."

"Book club? What the hell are you talking about?" Years working for the CIA had made his uncle a master manipulator, a skill that had always driven Dax crazy.

Robert went inside and returned a few moments later carrying another book in his hands, which he handed to Dax. "The next meeting is Tuesday night. You better catch up."

Dax arched a brow. "*The Barista Mysteries: M is for Macchiato?*" He held the book up. "This doesn't seem like something you'd read."

"You need to be more open-minded." Robert sat down in his rocking chair. "The book is good, but that's not important. Book club meets at Callie's house."

Dax turned the book over in his hand, reading the back cover blurb. "I've heard of this author before. She's popular."

Robert nodded. "Katherine Wentworth books are always popular with the book club."

Dax thumbed through a few pages and then flipped it over, reading the back copy. The cardinal flew back, landing at his feet. Dax held his empty hands up, "I don't have anything more for you." The bird cocked its head, as though believing that if he waited long enough, Dax might change his mind. Instead, he held up the book. "Besides, it looks like I have some reading to do."

Uncle Robert left him alone on the porch, and Dax sat down, opened the book to the first chapter and began to read. The chaos of his first day in Colton gave way to the quiet calm of the end of day. The leaves of the giant oak tree began to rustle in the evening breeze. Reading a romantic mystery on his uncle's front porch wasn't how Dax expected to spend his first night back in Colton. But this was home—the good and the bad— and he knew he was in the right place.

It was also the only place where he could make amends.

Meet Eliana West

Storyteller, adventurer, and diversity advocate.

Crafting captivating tales while making a positive impact on the world.

Recipient of the 2022 Nancy Pearl Award for genre fiction, Eliana is a dynamic and acclaimed author who captivates readers with her spellbinding narratives. She loves connecting with readers through her website.

WWW.ELIANAWEST.COM

THE WAY *Forward*

MOCKINGBIRD BRIDGE

BOOK ONE

ELIANA WEST

Mockingbird Bridge Book One

The small town he couldn't wait to leave is calling him home....

Dax Ellis returns to Colton, Mississippi, a changed man. He traveled the world, earned a fortune, and made a lifetime of memories, but now he longs to put down roots. Time hasn't been kind to his hometown, and Dax wants to help—if only he can convince everyone he's not the same petulant boy he used to be. Especially the one woman who has every reason not to trust him.

Librarian Callie Colton cherished summers with her grandparents, in the town her ancestors helped build, in spite of the boy who called her names. Now that Colton is her home, life is quiet until Dax returns… and, along with him, threatening letters on her doorstep. He may still have the power to hurt her, but she's not the same scared little girl she used to be.

But as the danger escalates, Dax will have to face his past to find a way forward for the relationship they were cheated of once before.

Scan the QR code below to order

THE WAY *Home*

MOCKINGBIRD BRIDGE

BOOK TWO

ELIANA WEST

Mockingbird Bridge Book Two

A letter from the past will transform their future…

Taylor Colton always loved the crumbling plantation house passed down through his family for generations. Now he's bringing his popular renovation reality show to the small town of Colton, Mississippi, so he can bring the plantation house known as Halcyon back to life for the cameras.

After an ugly breakup, Josephine Martin needs a new start to heal her broken heart in peace. A hidden letter reveals a family secret that leads her to Colton to protect her family's history and honor a promise made before the Civil War… and to a house she didn't know was hers.

Suddenly, Josephine must decide if she's ready for the challenge of restoring a rundown mansion and its history, and Taylor's facing a challenge he can't charm away. Together, they must untangle a tragic history, a rocky relationship, and risk everything they love. Can they overcome the past to find their way home?

Scan the QR code below to order

THE WAY *Beyond*

MOCKINGBIRD BRIDGE

BOOK THREE

ELIANA WEST

Mockingbird Bridge Book Three

When she finds out his secret, will he lose her for good?

Jacob Winters has a secret: he's come to Colton undercover as an FBI handler. He didn't plan to stay, but the small town has charmed him with a sense of community that he hasn't felt in a long time. And his attraction to the beautiful Mae Colton complicates things even more. Jacob doesn't do relationships—he won't risk making memories he might regret.

Mae Colton loves her little town of Colton, Mississippi, and doesn't want to leave. In fact, instead of moving on to bigger things—namely a political career in DC like she'd planned—she wants to run for a second term as mayor of Colton. But not everyone in town supports this choice, including the commitment-phobic Jacob Winters.

Mae is ready to make their secret relationship official and go public, but that would break Jacob's one rule. When a threat against Mae's life forces him to admit the truth of his feelings, he has to race to save the woman he loves before it's too late.

Scan the QR code below to order

A HIDDEN *Heart*

MOCKINGBIRD BRIDGE

BOOK FOUR

ELIANA WEST

Mockingbird Bridge Book Four

Rhett Colton has spent the last two years working deep undercover for the FBI. He's forsaken his friends and family to keep his community safe, but now that his mission is over, he's haunted by what he's done and is having a hard time returning to his previous life. Only two things are keeping him from becoming totally lost—his dog, Rebel, and the beautiful new town veterinarian.

Jasmine Owens is ready to start over in the charming town of Colton, Mississippi, by opening her own veterinary practice. Jasmine knows what it's like to constantly have her abilities questioned, but she's strong enough to persevere. When she agrees to board Rhett's dog while he's away in DC, they begin talking every night over the phone and she realizes Rhett isn't the man she thought he was. He's so much more and sparks quickly fly on both ends.

But when new threats surface, Jasmine and everyone in Colton's safety are threatened. Rhett will need to make a decision. He's always sacrificed everything for his job, but is he willing to risk their relationship too?

Scan the QR code below to order

ELIANA WEST

COMPASS OF THE HEART

When Steve Bernard finds his college classmate Ava Jones stranded in the rain, he takes his chance to be a knight in shining armor and offer her a ride home. Only instead of a white steed, he's driving a white Volkswagen camper van named Pearl.

State by state, Ava and Steve get to know each other on the road trip of a lifetime. When they reach the West Coast, will the compass of Ava's heart point toward a new home?

"Compass of the Heart" is a short story originally included in the *Loving Hearts* Anthology in honor of Richard and Mildred Loving.

Scan the QR code below to order

www.ingramcontent.com/pod-product-compliance
Lightning Source LLC
Chambersburg PA
CBHW060401310726
48976CB00003B/908